D0981651

McCLELLAND & STEWART

# HARMLESS

JAMES
GRAINGER

Library and Archives Canada Cataloguing in Publication
is available upon request

ISBN: 978-0-7710-3669-9
ebook ISBN: 978-0-7710-3670-5

This is a work of fiction. Names, characters, places, and incidents either are the product of the author's imagination or are used fictitiously. Any resemblance to actual persons, living or dead, events, or locales is entirely coincidental.

Typeset in Sabon by M&S, Toronto

Book design by Terri Nimmo
Cover image: © Raimund Linke/Stockbyte/Getty Images

Printed and bound in the United States of America

McClelland & Stewart,
a division of Random House of Canada Limited,
a Penguin Random House Company
www.penguinrandomhouse.ca

1 2 3 4 5 19 18 17 16 15

*For Laura, the love of my life*

CONTENTS

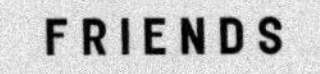
FRIENDS

They made a nice picture: Franny and Rebecca, walking through the high grass in the July sun, the forest in the background, the bright blue sky above. Franny and Rebecca, friends since they were babies, keeping to a languid, almost liquid pace, impossible for anyone but an almost-fifteen-year-old to maintain. The girls swayed and nudged each other at the shoulders as if the ground kept tipping their bodies into collision. They pointed and laughed, evoking phantom enemies with comic-strip gestures, two giggling teenagers passing secrets and outrages, confirming what they'd learned about the world since their last meeting. Franny wore the short shorts Joseph hated and the shirt with too much "V" at the front but he'd kept his mouth shut, obeying the self-imposed, seventy-two-hour no-nagging policy in effect since they'd boarded the train that morning. She was fine. No one would see her out there, among the wildflowers, oldest friend at her side, furrow-browed dad watching from the kitchen window like a hidden entity, lightning bolts at the ready.

Such parental concern: if only he had an audience.

*Fuck it*—he was here, wasn't he? Their weekend in the country, a rare Divorced Dad Promise kept. Never mind that neither of their hosts was home to greet them.

He turned away from the window, trying to push his hangover to the margins. He should have slept on the train. It wasn't like he'd pulled off his heart-to-heart with Franny, the dreaded conversation he'd rehearsed all week, committing his thoughts to mental cue cards, reminding himself what *not* to do: don't lecture her; don't try to be her friend; don't deliver the equivalent of your weekly column. Just disengage her from several text-message conversations and begin: "Franny, I spoke to your mother, and we both feel . . ." Easy enough, but when the moment came he blew it. It was as if he'd spent a week rehearsing with a stand-in, only to freeze on stage when the leading lady stepped from the wings.

"There will be time," he whispered only half-ironically, facing the big airy kitchen, which smelled like toast, scrambled eggs, and good coffee, a combination that pulled him back to the city, where he could be sharing an overpriced brunch in a faux-homey café with one of six people he knew well enough for that. The cupboards were painted a pale yellow that held the light, and he recognized a couple of Jane's favourite art-gallery prints on the creamy white walls, the decorating touches marking the kitchen as her territory. Alex must be in charge of the grounds and outbuildings then, he and Jane claiming their domains like an old farm couple.

Joseph walked over to his wheeled suitcase and launched

a quip into the empty kitchen—"It is time to don my comfy pants for the weekend!"—reminding an idealized studio audience there was no situation he couldn't joke his way out of.

A car was pulling into the yard. *Let it be Jane*, he thought. *Just Jane*. He wasn't ready to deal with Alex.

He heard the car door slam and Jane telling the barking dogs to calm the hell down. He smoothed back his thick hair and patted it on top, a vain gesture she used to tease him about, and stood waiting next to the table. What he needed was an acceptable role for the weekend—prodigal family friend, big-city magazine columnist roughing it in the sticks, Chief Mythologizer of the Good Old Days. He wasn't picky.

The front door flew open, letting two huskies into the narrow sunroom outside the kitchen, where they growled and leaped with such exaggerated abandon that he saw them for a moment as two children who'd found a pair of wolf skins to play in. Jane stomped on the front steps, sending the dogs' rollicking sight-gag back into the yard, before she pushed through the sunroom door into the kitchen, her arms weighed down by canvas grocery bags, her piercing squint reminding him he'd waited five years to visit her in the country. She shook her head, twisting the knife in a little deeper, enjoying the old game, then handed him the two heaviest bags, warning him to be careful, the idiot at the store put the egg carton at the bottom.

"Why did I buy eggs, you ask? There's a dozen chickens in the yard and I bought fucking *eggs*."

The swearing was for his sake, a nod to old times and a reminder the kids were outside.

"Chickens," she said, as if Alex's latest agricultural enthusiasm was an embarrassing secret, like the knowledge of herpes or a sexually abusive uncle.

Joseph followed her across the kitchen. She opened the fridge and pushed her face toward him, her bright hazel eyes sending him scrambling for a funny line—even at his age, he still needed to get her laughing. "Fresh eggs are good," he said, already smiling.

"So are the eggs I bought, and the carton doesn't shit all over the yard and wake you up at six a.m."

They laughed again, but her shoulders stayed locked in place as she repositioned the standing army of three-quarters-empty jars lining the fridge door, and her high forehead, which pushed her hair off her face like a scarf, was puckered. He had a thing for women with high foreheads, a fetish she'd planted in his senses when he was still a teenager.

"Liz and Mike and the kids are also staying the night," she said. "They don't want to drive home drunk. They actually live in town, but you probably know that."

Liz had filled him in on that and more on the drive from the train station. *Jane's waitressing again*, she'd told him, not hiding her anger at Alex for forcing Jane back into the profession she'd sworn off more than fifteen years ago. Alex's custom furniture store wasn't exactly raking it in, according to Liz, who couldn't disguise the hint of triumph in her voice. She'd never forgiven Alex for inadequately disguising his contempt for Mike.

"Did Liz tell you who else is coming? Julian! Can you believe it?"

"*Jewels*? I didn't know he was still alive."

"Neither did I. Liz tracked him down. You know her." Jane tapped at her head, indicating the detailed mental file cards Liz kept on their high school friends. "He's not Jewels anymore, by the way, and he's bringing his lover with him. What a *groover*, eh?" She smiled at the old-timey word. "We don't call him Jewels, and we don't say he works in a circus. And we don't bring up his drug problem, which he's over."

Joseph arched an eyebrow, and Jane stifled a laugh by slapping his arm.

"What?" he said. "I always liked him." What was *not* to like? Fearless skate punk, acid head, teenage Lothario, Julian was the blondest of the Lotus Eaters who'd gathered in the old bus bays at Eglinton station, warming up for the party with guitar noodling, spiked orange juice, and group back rubs.

"And don't call this a reunion," Jane said. "Since you finally decided to pay us a Royal Visit, I figured I'd ask Liz and Mike over—God knows she needs a drink. Then she told me Julian was working at a Renaissance fair nearby—don't you dare laugh—so I said let's make it a party."

Alex couldn't be happy about that. Bad enough that Joseph was here for the weekend, now he had to put up with Jane's old wrecking crew, grown-up Party Boys and Girls hitting the booze and dusting off war stories, many of them no doubt new to Alex.

Joseph watched Jane stuff cans into the cupboards, his attention drawn to her full hips before his eyes even registered them. He'd seen her a few times since she and Alex and the kids left the city, but the lovely shifting of weight to her hips and thighs might have happened last week. What else had he missed? Her hair was darker, the last of the blonde notes shrugged off like affectations once she hit forty.

What was he doing? Hungover in a strange house, ogling his ex-lover and dreading the arrival of her husband.

A collage of photos was stuck to the fridge door: Alex and their son, Liam, at a soccer tournament; a younger Rebecca on a pony; and, in the top-left corner, Franny and Rebecca at age eight standing on a dock, Franny holding the head and Rebecca the tail of a small pickerel, the girls pretending to strain under the weight of the fish. Behind them, Alex was offering his hand to Martha, Joseph's ex-wife, as she stepped out of an aluminum boat.

*Fucker*—as if it wasn't enough for Alex to be a model father and husband for his own family, he had to play the same role for Joseph's too. Joseph should be grateful that Alex and Jane had given Franny a few idyllic summers in the country after his and Martha's marriage came crashing down, but he felt his own absence from the photo as if he'd been cut out with a penknife.

He drifted over to the crowded kitchen table, a massive structure of varnished boards flanked by wooden benches that Alex probably built from scratch. The breakfast dishes looked hastily abandoned, as though the family had been called above decks by an iceberg sighting, and a wasp circled a bowl of milk-bloated cereal. He imagined Jane cooking eggs still warm from the hen while Alex helped the kids with homework, a lovely image of bustling informality that only sharpened his headache.

He opened a bulging folder at the table's far edge—property specs, blotchy house photos, fiercely affirmative introductory letters offering a free property appraisal, variations on a pitch to dowse the hidden equity in your home during a recession. Liz selling real estate; Jane back to waitressing; Alex making cabinets—Joseph was too exhausted to add his own lowered career and financial prospects to the list.

"Liz, eh," Jane said, her arm grazing against his as she closed the folder. "Can't be away from property specs for a day. Is she showing a house now?"

He nodded, distracted by the patch of tingling skin where Jane had touched him. "*You never know when you'll get an offer*," he said. "She actually told me that in the car." He'd nodded politely when he realized Liz wasn't building to a punchline, then listened to her rhapsodize about her and Mike's three-bedroom Victorian house, which had cost them about a third of what they would have paid in the city.

"She never goes halfway," Jane said. "She has to do the real estate seminars and read books on positive thinking."

"Remember her Zen phase?"

"And *Deep Ecology*."

"She'd bawl me out for not recycling a beer cap."

"God—we're being mean to Liz already."

Jane walked to the kitchen window, so certain he'd follow that she spoke just as he took his place beside her. "Look at them."

Franny and Rebecca were heading back to the yard, the blue sky above so bright it might have been freshly painted.

"Franny looks more like Martha every time I see her."

"I'm going to be spending more time with Franny." He hated the defensiveness in his voice.

"That would be a start. God, I'm sorry."

"No, I deserve it. I do want to get Franny out of the city more. Away from her friends." He left the comment to hang on its low branch.

"You don't have to worry about Franny—she's a good kid."

Invisible hands seized her words: *Franny's a good kid*. Just a typically confused teenager pushing her parents' boundaries.

"Rebecca's a good kid too," he said, assuming it to be true.

Jane crossed her arms. "She's pushing me, Joseph. She's quit everything. Soccer, horseback riding, writing—quit, quit, quit."

"Franny too."

"It's all too *boring*, too *haaaaard*. She just wants to hang out at the McDonald's with her townie friends."

"It must be easier for Alex to deal with her." He was groping for a happy father–daughter ending.

"Are you *kidding*?" Her indignation steamed the window. "Alex is on her about staying on the Internet half the night. He says—to *me*—that she dresses like a porn star."

"A lot of girls do. They're pressured to be hyper-sexualized." He'd written a column on the topic. The trick was to not quote himself.

"Alex is afraid for her." Her tone was softer now. "It's this bleak picture he has of the future, what the world's going to look like in twenty years."

Jane squinted into the metaphorical distance, as if seeing the apocalyptic mind-pictures everyone under fifty carried with them: the video loops of floods and droughts, fish-emptied seas and dead coral reefs, calving glaciers, and super storms ravaging the cities.

"I don't talk to the kids about that stuff," she said. "But Alex has to tell them the Truth." She spoke with fresh bitterness, as though he'd used the word in a recent argument. "A child shouldn't have to think about global warming. It's like asking a ten-year-old to do a grown man's labour."

"Yeah, what are you going to tell your kids? 'You're going to live through a catastrophe comparable to the last ice age, but your loving parents did nothing to stop it.'"

"Please—give me something I don't get every day." She let out a long breath. "You'll party with me tonight, won't you?" Her voice was husky, private—she could be speaking to him from the shadow of her high-school locker door. The sunlight revealed the fine down on her cheeks, burnishing the golden skin beneath.

"How long's it been?" he said.

She met his gaze. "We don't do a lot of drinking here in Eden. Alex doesn't always get along with Drunk Jane."

He laughed and put his hand to the window, steering his mind away from the dark shoals of erotic speculation. He formed a half-frame around Franny, then shifted it to bring Rebecca into the picture as the girls walked out of sight. When he lowered his hand, it was as if he'd peeled a sticker from the window to reveal Alex walking across the field toward the house, his body bulging and folding like a flag in the rising heat. Jane shifted, putting distance between her body and Joseph's.

"What's he done now?" she said, heading for the kitchen door. There was nothing for Joseph to do but follow her into the yard.

On the night he'd met Alex, Joseph was riding the bliss of a four-pint high that expanded to envelop every stool and table in the pub. Friends, rivals, ex-lovers, all were gathered to celebrate Jane's return from a year-long trip around Southeast Asia and Europe, where she'd met Alex, who'd moved to Finland to make a documentary on deforestation. Jane, engaged to be married—it was big news, and Joseph was happy for her, he really was. He'd been dating Martha for a few months, and he was telling friends he was "in a good place," ready for some necessary life changes. Why begrudge Jane for staking out a proper adult life with the stolidly handsome man who was moving through the crowd, shaking hands and laughing at jokes, gathering more of the room's energy to himself with each greeting? No reason to envy Alex's broad shoulders, a trait Joseph had coveted since puberty. No need for rancour, even if Alex's arrival did mark the end of Joseph's wild, seven-year affair with Jane. Joseph was even glad for the transformation Alex had worked on Jane, the ten necessary pounds gained and the doomed-waif haircut abandoned. So when Alex cut straight across the room to greet Joseph, his half-embarrassed smile advertising his noble intentions, what could Joseph do but share a few pints with the man who'd stolen Jane from him? It was as if, from their first greeting, Alex had called out to what was most magnanimous in Joseph—a dynamic that defined their more than decade-long friendship until the day Alex decided Joseph was past saving.

But that was an old story, one they'd be tiptoeing around all weekend if Joseph got his way. He followed Jane past a garden that was lush with tomatoes, carrots, salad greens, even a few rows of corn. They stopped at the edge of the field, the grass before them as bright as a lake beneath the stinging sunlight. Alex was less than a hundred feet away, his brown hair lighter and a little thinner, his shoulders wider than Joseph remembered, his body as solid as the wooden cabinets he built and sold in town. He was elevating his cupped left hand as though it protected a living thing, perhaps a caterpillar on its way to a terrarium by the store's cash register, where its transformation to a butterfly would serve as a metaphor for societal regeneration.

Alex nodded at him with exaggerated propriety before saying hello, making Joseph wonder if Jane had even told him about the visit. Would she have gone that far to make this reunion happen? Joseph tried to read her face but she was grimacing at Alex's hand. She flattened out his palm, releasing a thin stream of blood and revealing a small puncture in the fleshy wedge beside his thumb that could have been a small berry ebbing juice. Joseph looked from the wound to the dry ground, where the blood had clotted in the rough shape of an anvil, and then out to the forest, his mind alert, as it always was in Alex's presence, to the hidden connections between things. But there was nothing to see but grass and trees, thousands of them, standing in line across the field.

"It's nothing," Alex said. His face was deeply tanned and his brown hair bleached by the sun, his thick back straight and his shoulders squared, a few extra lines around his eyes the only sign that Country Life wasn't everything he'd envisioned. When he tried to lower his hand Jane held it up to catch the sun, then closed it.

"What happened?" she asked.

Alex shrugged, too casually. He had a story to tell her, but he wanted a little coaxing. He was too warm to blush but his face radiated pride and curiosity. The walk in the woods had activated the optimistic vitality that was his best feature.

"I made it about three-quarters of the way to the old commune by Smith Road," he said. "I was checking out a few abandoned mines."

"Alex has been mapping the ghost towns and abandoned mines and logging camps."

"In there?" Joseph said, pointing to the forest.

Jane nodded and rubbed Alex's shoulder, caught up in a rush of affection that Joseph interpreted as more familial than passionate, as if Alex was a younger brother who was going to do the family proud. Or so Joseph chose to read the gesture. Maybe he was being petty.

"I didn't know people still lived in communes," he said.

"Some vets and draft dodgers started a commune in the hills, decades ago," Alex said. "It kind of went to seed."

"Drugs, wife-beating, incest—real sixties stuff," Jane said. "I'm not worried about a bunch of old hippies. You know there's a grow-op out there."

"The new local economy." Alex could barely suppress his anger.

"We talked about this," she said. "Stay out of it. You'll get yourself shot."

Joseph turned away, feeling like an interloper. An itch skittered across his scalp like a line of ants escaping a magnifying glass. The sun was relentless, and the first wave of booze sweat was surfacing on his forehead like diesel oil rising from a sunken ship. He should have slept on the train. He reached into his back pocket, but he'd left his BlackBerry at home for Franny's sake, only to realize ten minutes into the trip that the last thing she wanted was his undivided attention.

"You should get into the shade," Jane said. "Alex can show you the lay of the land. I'm going to get a bandage."

The men took the hint: she wanted them to work something out before the other guests arrived. It hadn't occurred to Joseph that she was also carrying an idealized version of the weekend, or that she was an adult with a detailed life plan, though she'd been that woman far longer than the wild Jane he'd known as a young man.

They walked to a maple tree near the road and stood beneath the canopy of branches to take in a full view of the property. So this was it: an old farmhouse, a fallow field, and a bursting kitchen garden—the Great Leap Forward on two acres of land. Joseph hadn't given much thought to what he'd find here, but surely a grander set-up than this. Didn't Alex's idealism and unflagging energy demand more? Joseph studied Alex's face for the beginnings of an answer. Two deep lines stretched from his mouth to his chin, and his brows came down over his eyes like a hard ridge, giving a preview of the old man he'd be one day—biblically stern, the flat blue eyes taking in the measure of his land, separating the clean from the unclean, the fertile from the barren. Something in that expression, its total identification with the landscape, repulsed Joseph. Sure, the city was going to hell, but as he scanned the fields, wondering where the cows were but knowing the answer would only depress him, Joseph saw nothing to replace the city and all it represented—culture, progressiveness, the energy of self-invention.

Alex saw something more. *Good for him.*

Joseph finally settled his eyes on the forest across the field.

"You should see the forest," Alex said. His mouth had softened into a self-mocking grin. "Even a nature hater like you would love it."

"Are people more authentic in the country?" Joseph asked, instantly regretting his flippant tone.

"People do live closer to the land. They're not waiting for the World-Historical Individual to fix their problems."

The World-Historical Individual—who else but Alex still referenced Hegel?

Joseph nodded, his attention drawn to a little house near the garden, maybe six feet tall and surrounded by a low chain-link fence. It was a wooden replica of the brick farmhouse it faced across the yard, the colours, angles, and lines so well matched that he felt like he was staring at an allegorical painting.

"What is that?"

"It's actually a chicken coop," Alex said. "More of a carpentry project I did with Liam." He kept smiling as they walked over to the miniature farmhouse. It was a child's dream fort, with framed windows and a green-shingled, peaked roof topped with a tiny metal weather vane of a man running to nowhere on pinwheeling legs. There were even little window boxes painted beneath the windows.

"It must have been a nightmare to build," Joseph said.

Alex shrugged. He hated to let a project go unfinished. Back in the city he'd set up a communal garden in the park near their old apartment, and helped found a food co-op and a collective for independent filmmakers. He'd even spearheaded a parent-run alternative school, an idea Joseph enthusiastically supported until the other parents backed out, conceding that, despite their multiple M.A.s and Ph.D.s, they had nothing practical to teach their children. "It's too bad we didn't take the basket-weaving course of right-wing lore," Joseph had joked, scoring a laugh with everyone but Alex.

"None of the chickens will sleep in it," Alex said, stepping tentatively closer to the coop, as if he were slightly afraid of something inside it.

"Where do the chickens sleep?"

"In the bushes, the trees, everywhere but their house."

"I'd live in it. With my debts, I may have to." Joseph laughed, but the knots in his neck tightened. He stooped to look inside a tiny window, relieved that no face, human or avian, stared back. Alex's determination to finish what most men would have abandoned both shamed Joseph and made him feel slightly superior, but it did not lessen the queasy presentiment that a face, grotesquely out of proportion to the house's miniature accessories, was about to appear at the window.

He stepped away from the house, the sweat on his back over-performing its cooling duties, the rising heat from the fields setting the not-so-distant trees in motion so that his throbbing eyes saw them as a bannered army on the march. He squinted again and traced the grey-brown line of trees as it stretched west out of view and northeast along the narrow highway, the forest forming a natural boundary for the farmland, imposing itself on the ordered fields and pastures like the wall of an ancient fortress—if such places had ever existed.

"It's all Crown land now," Alex said, studying his face. "Tens of thousands of acres, then it becomes a national park."

How much land did that add up to? It must be the size of a city. He imagined ancient groves and green hilltops and lush meadows, creeks and swamps and lakes, the idea of sleeping so close to the wilderness casting a pleasant, archetypal shadow over the weekend. He wished Franny were around. The images of ancient forts and groves were right out of the adventure novels she used to read, tales of brave Byzantine slave girls, Celtic women warriors, Maori princesses.

"Do people ever get lost in there?" he asked.

"Sure. Some never find their way out."

Another line of oily sweat coiled down Joseph's back.

"Can't you tell what direction you're going by checking the tree moss? It only grows on the north side of the tree."

"That's a myth," Alex said. "Moss grows on every side."

Of course it did, and of course Alex knew that.

"People wander in circles for days, passing the same trees, driven half-crazy by the bugs. If you know how to walk north, south, or east, you'll eventually come to a road."

Joseph looked west toward the rolling pastures behind the farm. "What if you walk west?"

"You'll find out who your real friends are."

Once again Joseph waited for a punchline that didn't come.

So this was the heart of Alex's domain: a farmer's shed about twenty feet long and ten wide, an old wood stove in one corner, a work table stacked with crates of his old film equipment, and shelves lined with tools, wood solvents, DVDs, and the overflow from the family book collection, which Jane had refused to pare down before the move. Joseph recognized a few of her history textbooks stacked on top of a row of kids' books. She used to fantasize about owning a house with a library, about indulging in a rare burst of geekiness by arranging her book collection by subject on the future floor-to-ceiling shelves. He saw a crate on the table marked *Film Projects* and wondered if his script for Alex's planned documentary on homelessness was in there, the script he'd abandoned without warning when things fell apart with Martha. There was a smaller tabletop covered in old farming implements and rocks, but he saw no evidence of the "new political project" Liz had alluded to with such scorn in the car.

Joseph and Alex and Mike had entered the shed to grab an axe but were interrupted by the opening synth chords of

"The Final Countdown," Mike's favourite good–bad rock anthem, signalling a call on his iPhone. As they waited for Mike to finish, Joseph scanned the book spines on a handmade bookcase big enough to entomb a family of four while Alex scowled at Mike's persistent use of the word *dude*. He was too progressive to use the word, but when it came down to it, Alex thought Mike was a *pussy*, a man-boy forsaking proper adulthood for sleeve tattoos and Converse sneakers, a buddy to his kids instead of a father. Jane and Liz were no doubt playing caretakers to their husbands' anger in the kitchen, their decades-old friendship the neutral site for negotiations. It was a nice enough set-up for the men, but their wives wouldn't be happy travelling back in time to claim the fixed gender roles waiting there. Joseph could picture the women slicing carrots or some other hard root vegetable at the counter, but for all that he knew about them, all the times he'd seen them bingeing or drying out, infatuated or depressed, he had no idea how they spoke as one wife to another.

"How's the store working out?" Joseph asked Alex, fighting off the shed's closed-in atmosphere.

"Not bad. It took a while. The locals can buy a bookcase made in China for eighty bucks at the big-box store, and the tourists found my work too slick—they want rough wood grain, *authenticity*." He spat out the word as if it were a fly he'd inhaled.

"I told him to grow one of those neck-only Mennonite beards," Mike said, pocketing his iPhone.

Alex actually smiled. "It would go with my wool cap—my labourer of the Ellis Island period. The locals don't trust anyone whose great-grandparents weren't born here, but they're coming around. And I show the tourists my workshop behind the counter, let their kids plane a board."

He'd be hard to resist, the wood and carving tools imbuing his strong body with an aura of self-reliance, the smell of solvents and sawdust satisfying yearnings for simpler times.

"You're probably doing better than me," Joseph said. "Arts features columnist, also doing the former website copyeditor's job for free. There's a hundred writers who'd do my column for a third of the pay, which has been frozen for years."

It was Alex he'd gone to for advice when the editor of the city's glossy monthly sent Joseph a gushing email about a blog post he'd written on the post-9/11 family car's metamorphosis into a domestic army troop carrier, all wraparound bumpers and side windows narrowed to tinted slits. The editor called Joseph's work "just the thing" for the magazine's relaunched website and Joseph himself an edgy voice to anchor the content, establishing "edgy" as a marketable publishing niche and setting off several internal alarms. It was Alex, clinging to the Internet's liberating potential, who urged him to take the gig—"Think of the *good* you can do writing for such a large readership," he'd said, using that most unfashionable word. Joseph took the job, and by the time he'd adjusted to the magazine's ad-friendly mandate, he and Alex were no longer speaking.

"I'm not getting radio work either," Joseph said. "I wasn't delivering the quota of tips on awakening listeners' Inner Parisian or the best beach reads of 2010." He wanted to laugh but his mouth was dry. "You'd think they'd want to build an audience through the cultivation of reliable"—he had to be modest here—"*informed* opinion."

"Maybe they're just going young," Alex said.

*You fucking cunt*—Joseph almost said it out loud.

"My students are the same," Mike said, tossing his half-ironically feathered bangs from his forehead, his hands forming a triangle, gestures likely honed in the human communications course he taught at the local community college. "They can't follow an abstract argument or complex text. They need conflict, resolution, characters they can identify with. Forget reflection and analysis—the inner life is dead."

Mike's cultural doomsdaying was an easy dig at Alex, whose stern face was framed by the rows of art-house DVDs, literary novels, and biographies lined up like a panel of judges from a more thoughtful age.

"Maybe you should write my column," Joseph said to Mike. His editor had emailed him a reminder that morning, in a lower-case blurt, that he was expected to present three months of column topics at Tuesday's "content" meeting. He had five so far, two of which would be deemed "too political." Not that it mattered—his bosses wanted him gone. He was too cerebral, too expensive.

"I'll be your ideas man," Mike said. "Alex, show our urban friend your gun." He pointed at a shelf running above the windows, where a rifle was rested on piles of old phone books. "Have you ever held a rifle?"

"I've never even stood beside a man holding a gun."

"City Boy has seen a thousand movies about men with guns, and yet, *ironically enough*, he's never fired one.

What's it like to actually hold a gun, to fire it? There's your column."

It was a good idea. He should write it down. His memory was shaky at best, a condition his last girlfriend put down to gluten intolerance.

"You could do a series," Mike said. "*Postcards from the Country*: wry Lake Wobegon–style sketches of rural life, with Alex and I appearing as recurring characters. I want to be called 'Jerod'—Jerod the well dowser. Alex can be the local quack veterinarian. Hashtag josephintheboonies."

Alex took down the rifle and examined the barrel. It was amazing how quickly the gun gathered significance to itself, as if it were the single splash of colour in a black-and-white photograph. He cocked open the rifle and closed it, snapping the stock to his shoulder and sighting in the barrel using what had to be the minimum number of movements it would take to shoot a man. How many would that be? Four? Five? Alex would know—he'd spent two years in the army, one of the many institutions that failed to meet his standards. He aimed the gun at the window, fixing on a target in the pasture behind the farm, then he handed the rifle to Joseph and stood back to watch. It was a pump-action rifle, heavy but finely balanced, the weight falling mainly in the middle section. As Joseph nestled the stock in a convenient hollow between his shoulder and chest he hadn't known existed, he was startled by a sense of impending climax. He stared down the barrel at a pile of boulders outside. Imagine if a man was standing in front of them. Who did he want it to be? Everyone had a list of worthy targets these days—bankers, CEOs, hedge-fund managers, career politicians, religious fundamentalists, climate-change deniers. He squeezed the trigger, wanting the room to fill with sound, smoke, and broken glass. He handed the rifle back to Alex, disoriented by a sudden feeling of weightlessness. It had felt good to hold the gun in his hands.

This was more like what Joseph had in mind—hard, useful work in the sun, honest sweat, the smell of cut logs. The first guy did the chopping, the second set up a fresh log and stacked the cut pieces, while the third cooled off in the shade of Alex's shed, assessing the other men's work. Mike soon wedged the axe into a knot-riddled log and tried to pull the handle free by working it up and down like a water-pump handle, an ineffective method Alex would correct if asked. Mike swore and pounded the fused axe and log into the earth a few times before stepping away.

It was Joseph's turn. He lifted the axe and tried to pound the log free, hoping that Franny could see her father bent to outdoor labour. He hadn't seen her for at least an hour, but why should that matter? He went days without speaking to her, putting off calling her until he was less tired, less distracted, wanting only to talk to her when he was at his best. Not that his absences seemed to bother her anymore.

A rooster wandered over to the woodpile, scraping his miniature dinosaur feet through the dust, his polished black eyes fixed on the men. One good swipe would take the little fucker's head off. Joseph wiped the booze sweat from his face. *Why drink so much when you need to be your best self the next day?* His answer came in the form of several mental snapshots from last night's summer arts gala—the society matrons' faces frozen into Botoxed kabuki masks, their husbands tanned the colour of two-hundred-dollar-a-pound cured meat. Then the taxi ride home, the screen embedded into the back of the passenger seat playing clips of Caribbean family vacations he couldn't afford.

"You could do a column on the bluegrass band I formed with some local guys," Mike said.

"That didn't take long," Alex said.

"I'm trying to be helpful. We've recreated a pure thirties sound, right down to the microphones. There's a real resurgence."

Joseph was too tired to resist the bait. "Mike, your last band camped up the hillbilly stuff. You even did a bluegrass version of 'Ace of Spades.' Now you're aiming for neo-authentic. What gives?"

Mike shrugged, as if maintaining both musical positions was as easy as holding a cup of hot coffee in one hand and a glass of ice cubes in the other. "Our singer is Derek Hermann."

That was interesting. "Derek Hermann, aka *Dee Herr*," Joseph said, reciting the future band profile as he set down the axe and log. "Former front man of Hardwar, a late-eighties, alt-rockabilly band that almost hit it big before their guitarist, obeying the dictates of rock cliché, overdosed on his honeymoon. Derek briefly rebranded himself as a character actor in a few indie thrillers."

"The intervening years have been less column-worthy." Alex continued the riff in a more sarcastic key. "After a marriage to a two-decades-younger woman and relocation to the country funded by Hardwar's one hit single, he now plies his trade as mechanic and drug dealer." He stepped forward and pressed his foot on the log, pulling the axe free.

"Derek doesn't fit Alex's definition of a local businessman," Mike said.

Alex's face twisted as though a noxious gas cloud was drifting past, and his knuckles went white as he tightened his grip on the axe handle. "Some of these logs are still damp," he said, as if it was Mike's fault. He stood the log back in place, planted his feet apart, and raised the axe so that the double-sided blade hovered two feet above his head like a hawk riding the thermals. With a subtle shift of his stance, Alex transferred his body's force to his back and arms, and he split the log with a loud crack, exposing wood as stringy as chicken meat. Even Mike was impressed. Alex wiped his hands on his loose tan pants—"EU pants" Mike had dubbed them when he still cared enough to test Alex's capacity for teasing—and he watched the rooster peck at the exposed wood. The house's glass back doors slid open, loosing Liam and Liz and Mike's boys—little Sam and the older brother whose name Joseph kept forgetting—into the yard, chasing a soccer ball.

"They must have seen kids on TV playing," Alex said, his dig aimed at the extended TV session Mike had okayed after lunch.

"I'm catching Sean up on sitcoms," Mike told Joseph. "We've made our way through the American classics—*The Odd Couple*, *All in the Family*, *The Mary Tyler Moore Show*—and now we're moving on to the Brits. How can the children understand their father if they don't know his favourite shows?"

Joseph couldn't tell if Mike's deadpan delivery was deliberate or the side effect of decades of ironic detachment and pot smoking. Maybe he had the right idea. Bereft of ancestral lore, national myths, holy books, and rituals to bind the generations, Mike was initiating his sons into the world of the Cool Geek, where aggressions and aspirations were channelled into superheroes, video games, movies, TV shows, and the right pop music.

"Franny and I watch a few of the oldies together," Joseph said. "She likes how the audience laughs at the funny bits and goes *aaaaah* during the reconciliations, and how the serious conflicts are overcome in a single ratings-week 'issue' episode."

"So how's that working for you?" Alex said. "Spending your time with Franny watching TV."

Alex's tone of personal disapproval confirmed what should have been obvious: he was completely up to date with Franny's recent struggles and with Joseph's dismal parenting record, having heard about every missed dance recital, school play, and alimony payment during Martha and Franny's regular visits to the farm. What did he want, a fucking medal for his virtuous treatment of Joseph's splintered family? The men faced each other across the quartered logs, Mike watching with a boy's expectation of a good fight. A pickup truck pulled into the driveway, seemingly igniting detonation caps under several chickens and calling the dogs in from the field. Mike dropped the log he'd picked up and jogged toward the truck, and as the log rolled away Joseph imagined future archaeologists speculating on the domestic drama that had sent a single log three feet from the pile.

He watched as a man in jeans, plaid shirt, and ball cap jumped down from the blue pickup, a practised sight-gag not as funny as Mike's laugh made it out to be. Joseph took a step toward the truck but was halted when Alex ordered him to wait. A teenage girl emerged from the passenger side, her armour of boredom marking her as the driver's daughter. She was either a little older than Rebecca and Franny, or more willing to display her body, which was barely wrapped in a belly shirt and cotton shorts.

"*Ruby*," Alex said, his voice hissing like a dynamite fuse in an old cartoon as Rebecca and Franny swooped onto the driveway to greet the new arrival, Franny hanging back at the last second to pat the cell phone in her back pocket as if it were an emergency store of medicine. The girls formed a triangle and complimented each other's clothing, continuing this almost-courtly ritual as they walked back to wherever Franny and Rebecca had been hanging out.

Alex's expression seemed to slip loose as he watched the girls, leaving him slack-faced, his eyes strangely animated. He gripped Joseph's arm, the sudden intimacy like an unexpected kiss, then waved him toward the back deck with precise hand gestures. Joseph followed Alex's crouching figure as they crept past the deck, feeling caught up in a kid's war game until Alex stopped beside a withered bush at the corner of the house and crouched further down.

What the hell were they doing?

The bush gave them a clear view of a narrow, grassy corridor running between the side of the house and a chain-link fence marking the southern property line. Joseph leaned forward but couldn't see anything until Alex pointed at an old apple tree on the other side of the fence, where the three girls stood beneath the gnarled, ash-grey branches and towering blue sky like figures on an old prog-rock album cover. The sight of Franny pinching her unblemished face around a joint brought a frightening stillness to Joseph's mind, cutting off the background noise. His little girl, two weeks shy of her fifteenth birthday, smoking a joint with the casualness of an office worker on her second cup of coffee. He remembered her at age eight, filling a notebook with elaborate floor plans for castles and dungeons, street maps of medieval towns, ladies with crayon-coloured dresses, and suits of armour for the knights. Had that girl just disintegrated like a cloud with a pleasing shape when he wasn't paying attention? Was the girl under the tree any more solid?

Franny passed the joint to Rebecca, and Joseph was washed with relief when Rebecca handled it with the same proficiency. Jane and Liz came through their druggy stage intact. He had to keep perspective.

Ruby was catching the girls up on a recent triumph at a talent competition. "I *brought* it," she said. "I mean, you have to."

Rebecca nodded, clearly impressed. Franny texted highlights to distant friends, her powers of attention fully evolved for amphibious habitation of earth and digital ether.

"The nationals are *soon*, trust me," Ruby said, falling into the hypnotic rhythm of blasé cool and breathless disclosure perfected by celebrity clip-show hosts. "I'm going to the city next weekend to cut an audition tape. That's how Jeremy works."

Jeremy? Joseph guessed a casting agent or Svengali-esque producer.

"When he wants you to do something you just go. It's *such* an opportunity."

"What about your dad?" Rebecca was primed for scandal. "I *meeannn* . . ."

"He *got* me the gig. Dad knows everyone there. It's like . . . Knock knock."

Joseph felt his heart stumble as Franny mouthed the first syllable of *Who's there?* before stopping herself in time, turning her head sharply left, as if a girl beside her had said something ridiculously uncool. The bush he was hiding behind seemed to contract, stealing the air from his lungs. Alex was watching him. *Pay attention*, his eyes said. *It gets worse.*

"*Sooo*," Ruby said, nodding at Rebecca, "Dave been stalking you lately?"

Alex's breath hit a wall—he didn't know about Dave.

"You're over Dave. I can *so* tell."

Rebecca made a vague hand motion, as though refusing a second helping of vegetables. "He's lurking my Facebook page."

"I should charge my lurkers admission."

Franny rolled her eyes at this typical male behaviour. And why shouldn't she? Joseph himself had peeked at her page a few times, studying the campy glamour poses with friends and solo portraits of scantily clad introspection, the backlighting rendering the setting as anonymous as a porno shoot. In one picture he thought he saw a face at the bedroom window, the deep eye sockets too big for the head.

"So . . . *Dave* . . . you're not super excited about him," Ruby said. "You can't force these things—*trust* me."

"To be perfectly honest, I'm not excited." Rebecca closed her eyes, twin eyeliner smears taking on emblematic significance in the clear country air. Poor Alex—why was his little girl wearing makeup on a Saturday afternoon? Who was it *for*?

"Just tell him, 'I *like* you, you're a *great* guy. It's just timing. I'm not ready.'"

"He's going to freak."

"That's what guys *do*."

Alex clenched his fists. Over the past fifteen years, those same hands had forged a loving relationship with Rebecca, building it with science projects, plants and stones gathered on nature walks, fishing trips, games of catch, and digging in the garden. Was he supposed to store those hands in the closet while she went off the rails and fucked up her life?

"What about you, girl?" Ruby asked Franny. "Any boys chasing you in the city?"

"Are you kidding? I have to beat them off with a stick," Franny said, cracking a smile.

"Kinky!"

Joseph knew it was an illusion brought on by his non-blinking stare, but his mind no longer recognized Franny and her friends. The girls were gone, replaced by three strangers whose fat-free bodies made the objects of his own adolescent crushes look Rubenesque. They exuded self-denial and a sensual receptivity focused at the mouth, neck, and belly, their backs as rigid as aristocrats' wives in seventeenth-century portraiture. Time rushed forward and he saw each girl at eighteen, her body a map of tattooed Celtic knotwork, Chinese calligraphy, and Native American icons, a map for lovers, with piercings marking the erogenous zones.

Why couldn't he have had a son?

Joseph squeezed his eyes shut. Did he really just think that? A *son*? Alex was getting to him, willing him to see something worse than three girls experimenting with what passed for rebellion these days.

He nudged Alex, and the two men crept back behind the house. A response was being demanded of Joseph, and by the scowl on Alex's face, he was ready to pull out his own eyes and pop them into Joseph's sockets to get what he wanted. Had he always been such a bully?

"What is it going to take?" Alex said.

"For what?"

"Do you want me to say it?" He lurched closer, his lips flecked with spittle, his shoulders seeming to flare up like an angry cat's back.

Joseph stepped back, his nerves humming with a cold, dizzying fury. "You don't think I have my own Father's Worst Nightmares scrapbook?" Of course he did. Fifteen-year-old boys so addicted to porn they couldn't cum without pulling out and exploding in their best gal's face. The gang-bang, rape, beat-down, and drunken-fuck videos initiating kids into the global Race to the Bottom. His favourite: the "rainbow" parties, where lipsticked girls displayed their fellatio skills on the cocks of shark-eyed morons whose fantasies of self-actualization amounted to an eternal ride in a limo packed with strippers. He'd seen the girls, the way they used the full range of digital technology to police each other for microscopic status violations, and he'd seen the boys, so verbally inarticulate you expected them to greet each other with a brisk exchange of ass sniffing.

Joseph reined himself in. "Every generation sees youth culture as some monstrous Saturn trying to devour their children."

"Quoting your own column again?"

"Someone has to."

"Living the dream, eh?"

"It pays the bills. Not all of us are lucky enough to inherit enough from their grandparents to start over again in the country." He'd gone too far, but the words had leapt over the more acceptable retorts before he could slam the door.

Alex's expression was triumphant, as if he'd deliberately driven Joseph to hit him below the belt. He gestured toward where they'd been crouching. "When we used to take the girls to the playground, is this really what you saw in Franny's future?"

"I don't know what I saw." Maybe Alex remembered—he'd supplied Joseph with the necessary optimism and idealism for those first years of fatherhood. Joseph wiped the sweat from his face. He was so tired. "That Ruby looks like a wild one," he conceded.

"Not wild—*feral*. But you'd know all about that."

Alex had a point, but he always did. There was an aphorism about knowing the difference between facts and the truth, but Joseph couldn't remember the wording. He was terrible with details. Vitamin B12 was supposed to help. He'd buy some in the city.

Joseph recognized Ruby's father from a couple of Hardwar shows and a terrible cop drama he'd watched one insomniac night. It must have showed in his face, because after greeting Alex with half-mocking gravitas, Derek Hermann narrated Joseph's approach with winning stage patter: "White male, six feet tall, brown hair, and judging from the outfit, just up from the city." He laughed—a barking, consonant-heavy sound that evoked cottage weekends, the men at their drunken, cordial best. "Don't tell me your name," he said as they shook hands. "I've seen you before. You might be famous." Having been recognized, Derek knew no greater gift than to return the compliment. "And no, that's not cow shit on my hands. Grease from a yuppie's car I fixed this morning. You need a fucking IT guy to tune an engine these days."

The joke was an oldie but Joseph appreciated the effort. He was a sucker for men like Derek, born bullshitters and chancers.

"Liz scouting you a property?" A fresh sunburn gave Derek's face the uniformity of a mask. "You a New Pioneer?" He nodded at Alex, the expression's obvious source, earning a wince that might have been from the sharp sun.

"I'm an innocent bystander," Joseph said. "Here for the weekend."

"I came for the global warming." Derek winked as he leaned against the cab. The truck was almost all front end, the automotive equivalent of a pit bull, with massive grille and fenders dwarfing a distended flatbed that future models would shed like an unnecessary tail. "Warming's the best thing to happen to the local economy in decades—does wonders for the growing season." He glanced at Alex, whose eyes pushed back hard, as if he were trying to rewind the conversation and start again, but Derek didn't take offence.

Joseph, long scratched from Alex's list of confidants, couldn't read the subtext. He stepped back to take in the green fields pulsing in the sunlight, the rolling green sea broken by islands of trees and stacked rocks, the distant farmhouses as iconic as children's toys. The bright landscape seemed to rush at him in warm, obliterating waves, and in the stillness he felt what must have been that same protectiveness for the land Alex and Derek were each trying to define.

"It's beautiful here," he said. "It really is."

"I love it!" Derek took off his cap, as though Joseph had just spoken the most honest words heard in these parts since Pioneer times. "Give me a shout next time you're up. I'll show you the scenery—it's the only thing still bringing in any money, eh Alex?"

"For now," Alex conceded.

"Exactly! *For now.* We've got pristine lakes, forests, fishing, hunting, little picturesque villages and towns."

Liz had driven them through one that morning—a village with a main street lined with century-old trees and tan brick houses peaked by Victorian gables, a boxy limestone post office and library with a miniature classical portico, and a general store with a canoe out front. There were a few antique stores and discreet restaurants, and an old traveller's hotel converted into a B & B, the street culminating in a willow-draped creek where a restored mill housed a combination art gallery–café. Take away the cars and you had the setting for a tasteful period drama, but in real life the final effect was too uniformly of a bygone era to convince—ten feet past the mill Joseph expected to see a film crew planning the next shot. When he told Liz the place looked like a theme park, "Ye Olde-Time Colonial Town," she said that's what the tourists and buyers wanted—history, heritage, the willing away of the inauthentic present.

"And we've got crusty locals like you and Alex," Mike said.

"Alex is a *neo*-local," Derek said. "He understands what this place could be better than the inbreds on the town council do."

"Really?" Joseph said, heading off Alex's intervention.

"When Alex opened his shop the locals pegged him for a tree-hugger. They didn't want to hear about the economic forces that have been gutting this area for decades. Then, two years ago, he predicted the banking crash *to the month.* That got their attention."

Derek leaned a little closer toward Alex, his body presenting an alternative model of masculinity—weight-room bulk with a light slathering of beer fat. Alex caught Joseph scrutinizing them, and his broad shoulders, as if slipping past a distracted guard, made a show of solidarity by shifting in Derek's direction. An energy of attraction and repulsion, as unnerving as hearing a radio picking up two stations simultaneously, connected the two men. Joseph felt a little envious of Derek, an outdated, misdirected emotion he could not completely suppress.

"Now a bunch of us meet at Alex's store on Friday nights," Derek said, beaming pride at his ideological mentor. "Farmers, teachers, shopkeepers, tradesmen, a few of the local rainmakers—we even got a sexy librarian! We're getting on top of what's happening to this community before it gets on top of us."

Friday-night meetings? It sounded almost nineteenth-century—men running off leaflets on a clandestine printing press as Alex tied the banking crisis, rising unemployment, and climate change into a tight ideological bundle.

"No fucking government agency or real estate developer is going to help us," Derek said. "We have to act—now, *here*."

From far back in his throat, Alex grunted. "No. Not yet."

Derek wrestled a petulant snarl into a public smile. "See, this is what I'm talking about: political dialogue, the back and forth until we hit that sweet spot. None of that bullshit *irony*," he said to Mike.

"They're working on a secret handshake," Mike said, embracing the role of politically disengaged Gen-Xer.

"Fifty years ago this place was hopping," Derek said. "Mines, lumber mills, cattle farms, slaughterhouses, factories, a power plant—Christ, they even had a brewery. Never mind the fucking Hundred-Mile Diet—everything you needed you got from less than fifty miles away, from your own community. Then they shipped the jobs to China and any other Asian country where people shit in a hole in the floor, just so the rich could get richer. We don't *make* anything here anymore. What the hell do we *do* here but spread our legs for tourists and cottagers? Alex has seen the future," he continued. "We're heating the planet, killing all the fish, filling the ocean with plastic. There's not enough water and land for seven billion people, never mind when we hit ten, and our leaders are nothing but butt boys to their corporate masters."

Alex's eyes were vacant, but he remained watchful, as though he'd surrendered his attention to an older, more primitive part of his brain.

"Who's going to help us when the deserts spread and the coasts flood, forcing us to scavenge to survive?" Derek looked at them with utter solemnity. "Let's face it, boys, the West has shit the bed!"

The men all burst out laughing, lost in student-pub nihilism, as if they couldn't wait to watch the final reel of cinematic global destruction.

"The West has shit the bed!"

*The apocalypse*: hadn't they been promised it their whole lives?

"There's our local real estate agent," Derek said in his hale and hearty voice as Jane and Liz crossed the yard, both wearing green aprons emblazoned with the word *Kelly's* in flowing script.

"Running down the Cottage Crowd again, Derek?" Liz said, picking up the end of the argument like a discarded skipping rope. "You don't mind the money they bring into the area."

"A few of them do. Most visit their properties just enough to drive up land prices. Christ, I couldn't afford to buy my own place now."

"They tip better than the locals," Jane said.

"I'm not going to argue with aproned ladies," Derek said, his obsequious tone consigning the women to a post-sexual demographic.

Joseph waited for Jane to cut Derek's knees out from under him, but she seemed to accept the put-down as the natural course of things for a woman her age. She caught Joseph staring where the apron clung to her hips, and held his gaze.

"I stole the aprons from work," she said. "The regulars think I'm the town beauty because I'm over thirty and still have my own teeth."

Derek let out a cackle that was interrupted by the appearance of the three girls on the driveway. Where the hell did they come from?

"Nice apron, Mom," Rebecca said, her eyes radiating the false clarity of fresh eye drops.

Franny met Joseph's stare with rehearsed defiance as she passed. She used to be so protective of him, reminding him to wear a hat in winter and to stay out of the sun on summer days. He looked over at Jane as the girls gathered on the other side of the truck and felt a little better when she rolled her eyes.

"I gotta get Ruby home," Derek said. "Her mom's already pissed at me." He gave Joseph a cartoonish nod. "I'll remember your name by Monday."

Ruby held up her cell phone as Franny and Rebecca came back around the truck, Derek's eyes fixing on their asses like a pair of manacles, studying the details offered by Rebecca's paper-thin yoga pants and Franny's short shorts. Joseph's mouth went dry. An urge to protest, as faint as a child's voice from the bottom of a deep well, rose and died in his throat. He felt paralyzed by an impersonal sense of shame, as if he was every man who'd ever ogled a woman's body, running countless four-digit variations—legs, ass, tits, face—that never opened the constricting padlock in his chest.

Not every man. Alex was glaring at Derek with the righteous fury of virginity-protecting patriarchs down through the ages as Derek jumped into the truck and winked at them, christening his journey back to inscrutable, feminine weather zones. Joseph roused himself and ran up the short driveway to open the gate, stamping at a chicken on the way and relishing the rush of power when the bird went scurrying onto the lawn like a tumbleweed. When he reached the gate he wanted to leap over and run down the highway, but where would he go? He was already on vacation.

Twenty minutes later Joseph was still standing in the yard, taking shelter from the sun beneath an oak tree. He was ready to fall asleep where he stood, the sound of the cicadas in rhythm with the throbbing behind his eyes, to just pass out and see if he'd wake up before he hit the ground and sent the chickens fluttering. The sky was still bright, the clouds stretched to long tatters, and the fields pulsed green. A grey satellite dish the size of a backyard jungle gym lay rusting against the fence, its pride of place hijacked by a discreet metal plate mounted on the sunroom roof, the contrast sparking a column intro: *As TV screens grow ever larger, the satellite dishes that deliver their content are shrinking to the size of blah, with experts predicting that by the year blah the dishes will be small enough to fit into a blah blah*—cue the adjective *Lilliputian*, the obligatory reference to the 500-Channel Universe, and a 150-word sidebar on a crusty local who recycles satellite dishes into folk art. The sales team could pitch the column to the cable companies. Everybody wins.

He closed his eyes, trying to dissolve his thoughts into the cicada buzz, a sound he'd long mistaken for hydro-line surges until Franny set him straight. She used to be great for weaving historical and scientific facts into their long walks in the park, her little hand in his. He cupped his hand over his eyelids, dimming the light. His life was slipping away from him. He'd gone for a rare lunch with Martha a couple of weeks ago, and when he wasn't flirting to ward off painful topics she confessed that she'd broken the Cool Parent's Golden Rule and read Franny's online diary. The contents frightened her: Franny's odes to numbness in all caps—"I JUST WANT TO FEEL"—and broad hints of a drug habit and emerging eating disorder written to a receptive network of self-harm veterans. Martha also found two of her best work blouses, which Franny had deemed too low-cut for a "woman her age," slashed at the collars. Joseph listened to Martha as she laid her hand over his, her touch uncannily alien yet familiar, like he was holding hands with his ex-wife's corpse. She said she needed more from him, and when his eye dimmed into private fantasy, she clarified: "Franny needs a father."

"I know the feeling," he'd said, the punchline too perfect to resist.

Martha withdrew her hand, and the sordid history of their break-up lay on the table between them like a platter of freshly eviscerated entrails: his wavering commitment to their marriage; his refusal to "prostitute" his talents and settle for a nine-to-five job; his inability to quantify what he provided in place of financial and domestic stability. Then the final irony, when his very success as a columnist unleashed the long-suppressed Party Boy who destroyed their marriage—his fucking column, the *access* it gave him to the centres of cultural power, the invites to talk on TV and radio panels, all heady stuff for a certain type of younger, beautiful woman he couldn't resist.

What a nightmare. The confrontation after Martha found incriminating texts on his BlackBerry. Franny crying on the porch as he put his suitcase into the cab. Alex showing up at his hotel to talk man to man. *You can't just leave your wife and daughter*—Alex kept repeating the words, as if no man had ever fallen out of love with his wife or tried to spare his child the spectacle of an unhappy marriage. "They're better off without me," he'd insisted, sending

Alex into a tirade that effectively ended their friendship.

*Fucking puritan. No wonder Rebecca can't stand him.*

A mechanical hum cut through the cicadas as a car turned into the driveway, stopping inches before the gate. The driver's door opened and there was Julian, God's Own Groover, still topped by a blond lion's mane. He pushed the gate open, moving with the loping grace of a stoned teenager, and got back in the car, failing to notice when the gate caught on a rise in the ground. No bother: he gently bumpered the gate and drove through, and Joseph laughed to see the car, a rented Japanese sedan, put to the service of such good-natured impatience. He laughed again as he imagined Julian, former West Coast hustler and junkie, signing that car's rental papers.

Julian pulled in behind Jane's car and huddled against his female passenger for at least a minute before getting out and winning Joseph over with a nasally "Hey brother!"

The front door of the house opened to release Liam, Mike's oldest boy—Max?—and little Sam, the kids tumbling down the stoop to see the new arrivals. Julian coaxed the boys with a hand that glinted with chunky silver rings, and as the boys crept forward he pulled a massive cardboard suitcase from the trunk and laid it on the ground. The boys followed their straining eyes, watching Julian flip open the case and then stand up brandishing three Disney-style Arabian daggers with jewel-encrusted handles.

"Stand back!" he warned them. "These knives are sharp enough to cut rope."

He targeted a spot in the air above his head, drew a circle with his eyes, and sent the first dagger through the loop. The second dagger was in the air before the first began its descent, and then the whirling Ferris wheel of blades was in full motion—Julian at its centre, his arms languidly turning the glinting wheel as if it were his glad eternal task. He did a half-roundhouse kick through the daggers' path, and it was too much for Sam, who fell to his knees and grabbed at the air as though he could capture the magic forces unleashed by this Mysterious Stranger.

Julian glanced at the door and did a literal double take, the daggers clanking in the dirt at his feet, his face like that of a man seeing a friend risen from the dead. Joseph followed his gaze to the house, where it settled on Rebecca, who was standing with Franny and Alex on the stoop. How could Joseph have missed it, the striking resemblance between Rebecca and Jane at fifteen? Rebecca was taller than her mom, but she had Jane's light olive skin, slim nose, and wide mouth, features that must have sent Julian tumbling back through the time stream. Rebecca shuffled her feet in fascinated agitation until Jane and Liz rushed out to greet Julian.

Alex stayed where he was, watching Jane and Liz hug their old friend, a man probably known to him through Liz's captioned photo album, in which a young Joseph struck several party poses before the photos evolved to scenes of World Travel, Blissful Nature, and Rural Domesticity. This couldn't be easy for Alex. He'd made a point of not asking too many questions about Jane's past, insisting that her real history began the day they met.

Julian's "lover" finally stepped out of the car and nodded at the house and fields with great approval. Her hair was pulled into blonde cornrows, and her sharp black eyebrows might have been plucked into shape by a pair of specially trained crows—the final effect suggesting a violent tightening process beginning at the back of her scalp. She'd been strikingly beautiful once, but drugs and partying had stripped her looks of some vital binding element, leaving her features isolated on her face like pieces of jewellery. Alex smiled at her and stepped into the role of host, showing genuine interest as Julian showed him the juggling knives while Jane and Liz gave the other new arrival a tour of the farm.

Joseph watched the happy reunion, caught up in the excitement but also observing the scene like an impartial observer perched on his own shoulder. He wondered if Alex knew about Jane and Julian's high school affair. How much did Alex know about Jane and Joseph's relationship, and did he suspect the brief overlap between his first night with Jane and Joseph's last? Why should he care? Their generation was supposed to be cool about ex-lovers, their journeys into erotic excess teaching them the wisdom of limitations.

The late afternoon light slanted through the dusty, humid air, etching fine shadow lines around the windows and doors of the tall farmhouse. It was like looking at an oversized Swiss cuckoo clock, chickens rushing out from behind hidden doors to toll the hour as Alex and Jane, the farmer and his wife, were guided back into the house by invisible gears, followed by the children and happy guests.

Sitting at the kitchen table, Joseph scanned his inbox on Liz's laptop, relieved to find no emails from his editor heaping more unpaid duties onto his sixty-hour workweek. What was he going to do—complain? A carpenter ant might as well ask the queen to reduce his daily load of leaf fragments.

He broke another Divorced Dad Promise by checking his Twitter account, which an intern was covering for the long weekend. As of 3:15 that afternoon, Joseph was "gobsmacked" by a flash mob of dancing produce growers at a downtown farmers' market, the gushing endorsement already earning him fifty-three new followers.

*Passive-aggressive little fucker.* What was his name? Booker. All the new interns had culturally exotic names—Booker, Ellie, Shiloh, Truman, Scout—their parents gifting them at birth with entry into the creative class.

Jane stopped beside him on her way back from the sunroom, staring down at the computer screen as he closed the lid. "Something you don't want me to see?"

"It's more about what *I* don't want to see."

Liz was now at Jane's side. "Does he have a new girlfriend?"

"I have a new ex," he said, welcoming the teasing he knew was coming. He couldn't stop staring at Liz's thick auburn hair, sculpted into a wavy wedge that made her hypersensitive brown eyes look even wider and younger. A real adult haircut.

"It didn't work out with my lady friend."

"Too crazy?" Jane said.

He smiled.

"Too stable?"

"Maybe. Apparently security chafes my skin like a wet sweater."

"Listen to the *writer*," Jane said to Liz. "And no, Joseph, I don't read your column."

"I didn't ask."

"You've been dying to since you got here."

He let out a big laugh. She knew him so well.

"Don't take it personally: I don't have time to read anything."

"What's it like, being a famous columnist?" Liz asked, without irony.

"Oh, I know what it's like," Jane said, batting her eyelashes. "*Oh my God, you're a writer. You must be soooo smart.*" She played the bohemian groupie with burlesque exaggeration, but it still turned him on. "*Do you write books too?*"

"There's talk of collecting my best columns in book form." There *had* been talk, but he couldn't bring sustained concentration to any project for more than an afternoon.

"You were going to dedicate your first novel to Jane," Liz said. "It was so romantic."

"What would we have said if someone had called us romantics?" he said to Jane, expecting a laugh. Instead, she turned away and returned to her post at the stove. He was an idiot. Of course they'd been romantic. Even their fights had been operatic. Public screaming matches capping off extended drinking binges, the strategic use of other lovers—often mutual friends—to drive each other over the cliff of jealousy. He'd punched some poser who hit on her at a party, and she'd punched Joseph hard enough to loosen a molar for reasons they couldn't remember the next day, which made it so much funnier. But there was also the fantastic sex, the talking all night like a pair of kids at their first sleepover, the reading to each other in bed all afternoon while swapping tales of their latest exploits. Had he been happier since, so wrenched from his habitual emotions by an appetite for experience greater than his own? Maybe he wasn't supposed to be—every life had a high-water mark.

His face must have expressed a passing stab of regret, because Liz fixed on him with that faraway look she got when she was trying to stay ahead of her friends' pitfalls, so engrossed by other people's problems that she missed the catastrophes in her own path. It used to make her easy prey for manipulative men—users, big talkers, druggies, and wannabe artists. She'd told Joseph in the car that if he hadn't set her straight on a few of those men back in the day, if he hadn't educated her about the cold, hard world, she might have ended up in a cult. He tried to picture himself at twenty, guiding Liz through a rough patch, with no hope of sexual reward, because even his and Jane's theatrically transgressive love affair had had boundaries. He must have been drunk, transported by those raptures of generalized love that always nailed him near the end of a three-night bender. It was a nice thought—that his finest self had not been completely asleep during all that womanizing and glory chasing. He'd like to meet this noble man, hear his version of those mythic days, ask him who did what to whom. Someone must have been keeping score.

When Joseph looked up, Alex was standing beside Jane at the stove. He must have been in the living room, where the girls were watching TV, but Joseph couldn't shake the uncanny feeling that he'd overheard them talking in the kitchen.

*So what? Everyone flirts.*

Alex was almost pressed against Jane's body, his coiled posture suggesting exhausted defeat and energized resolve. He rested his hand on her hip as though he could transfer his grievances directly into her nervous system. Rebecca must have been giving him the silent treatment again. He was a good father, a model of engagement and natural authority, and his daughter couldn't get away from him fast enough. It must be killing him inside. Jane peeked into the living room and pulled Alex further from the doorway, and when she spoke he was gravely attentive, as if he was receiving counsel from a more experienced officer. Joseph heard her say something about backing off, that Rebecca had to make her own mistakes. Alex mouthed his assent, though his shoulders and hands had other ideas. He started to speak, but Jane's hand shot up between them—she'd heard enough.

—

"A man walks into a doctor's office and says, 'Doctor, my brother thinks he's a chicken.'"

Joseph got the desired groans from the boys at the kiddie table. Franny and Rebecca, locked together at the elbows at the far end of the big kitchen table, rolled their eyes. He was into his third beer, and the alcohol made him expansive—the trick was not to float *too* high above the crowd.

"The doctor says, 'A chicken? This is *very* serious. Have you told your brother he's *not* a chicken?'"

Franny tensed for the assault of an embarrassing punchline, and the joke went as hard as an egg in his mouth.

"'Not a chicken?' the guy says. 'Of course we haven't told him he's not a chicken: we need the eggs.'"

Franny started laughing before the punchline. The adults joined in, which made the boys laugh, and even Rebecca lowered her head to hide a smile.

"Your jokes are lame," Franny said with pride, proof he still had a few emotional credits left in her ledger. "I don't get it!"

"I don't get it either," Liz admitted, her pained expression causing more laughter.

They were all infused with good feelings—Saturday night of a long weekend, a big spread of food, and look who's here, Party Boy Julian, his rock-star face easing into its striking, folk-revival incarnation, his crooked smile complimented by a nose broken so many times the doctors must have left the cartilage to find its own shape. The positive vibes were even restoring his lover Amber after a shaky start to the meal, when she'd presented Jane with a small cheese from Quebec, explaining that the artisans who made it did not pasteurize the milk. The other adults, denied so many of their parents' luxuries—cottages, pensions, affordable city homes—appreciated this token of the Good Life.

Only Mike broke ranks. "So it costs *more* for unpasteurized cheese?" he said. "You're paying extra for something the artisans *didn't* do?"

Alex had graciously steered Mike's sarcasm away from its easy target, and now Amber's velvet stoner-bubble had expanded to include these *beautiful people*, old friends sharing a meal at the communal table, rediscovering forgotten *life rhythms*.

"What we forget," she said, "is that before electricity and TV, people gathered in the kitchen to warm themselves by the stove to *talk* about things that mattered—family, community, the land. Wisdom was passed from one generation to the next—stories and family histories." She looked to Julian for confirmation. "There's no *apprenticeship* anymore, nothing handed down."

Her words tugged something loose in Joseph, opening a vein of sympathy. *Apprenticeship*—scenes from a socialist mural rose up: heroically self-sacrificing men and women teaching the young to sole a shoe, weave a blanket, run a mill, and bring in the harvest, channelling the nervous, hopeful energy of youth into meaningful labour. He would have mocked the idea of surrendering his will to a craftsperson when he was fifteen, yet here he was, wishing that a crofter or weaver would help guide Franny through her teens.

Jane's waitress-holler announcing the next course prevented another Amber homily. Joseph pulled on his beer and took in the faces flushed with heat and alcohol, the girls lit from behind by the glowing kitchen window. Jane and Liz brought plates heaped with steaming shepherd's pie and corn to the table, and after the men outdid each other complimenting the cooks, everyone dug in—even Franny, who ate without stopping to do a mental calorie count before every forkful. Joseph washed down the shepherd's pie with another gulp of beer that almost drained the bottle, and looked up to see Jane squeezing Alex's hand, wrapped now with fresh gauze. He'd overheard them arguing again in the back office just before dinner, Jane ending her diatribe by telling Alex to "give it a fucking rest, for my sake. I *need* this weekend."

Alex had more than obeyed Jane's order—he was practically buoyant, restored to his place as the male half of the Golden Couple, now relocated to a modest country home where friends came to escape their overworked lives and share a meal at his handmade dinner table, venturing beyond the acceptable mealtime topics of real estate, careers, and cable TV shows that were inevitably described as being "as rich as novels." He asked Liz if she was having better luck this summer with her garden, and for the next half-hour he kept the conversation moving from guest to guest, flattering each of them with his full attention, teasing out their most engaging self. Even the girls were temporarily drawn out when Amber explained the significance of the tattoos lacing her arms, the left representing her "Celtic ancestors," the other her "Mohawk heritage."

No surprise really: Alex had always been a great talker, and an even better listener. Tonight it was as if he was using those gifts to bring out the best in his guests and to demonstrate, if only for a couple of hours, how an egalitarian community would function at the daily domestic level. And maybe two hours could be stretched into two days, and days into weeks, and so on, deep into the young century. It made Joseph wonder if the congenial host across the table was a domestic version of the Alex who was radicalizing the locals at his Friday-night meetings, drawing out their inchoate anger and directing it at a series of targets. If Derek was any indicator, results were mixed.

"Julian, I can't believe you're here," Liz said, letting Alex finish his dinner. "What have you been doing for the last, oh, twenty years?"

"I did a little bit of acting," Julian said. "I played some guitar, tried some things. I even worked for my dad for a year." He lingered on this early run of hope. "Then I moved out to the Coast. I got involved with the wrong people, picked up bad habits—*very* bad habits. I lost the plot. That's what addiction does—makes you forget who you are."

He snapped his head up, as if he'd remembered this wasn't a Narcotics Anonymous meeting, then brightened as Liam squeezed between him and Jane to grab the salt shaker. Julian tapped the boy on the shoulder and opened his mouth dentist-chair wide, sending a set of false upper teeth flying into his palm, the extraction shrinking his face so that he looked, not like an old man, but twenty-five years younger. And yet he'd had such beautiful teeth as a teenager, an honour guard of polished white shields massed behind his full lips.

Liam laughed and asked him what had happened to his real teeth.

"I lost them in a fight—*with myself.*" He capped the joke by fake-punching his own mouth.

The situation rescued, Jane turned to Franny. "I can't believe how much taller you've gotten since March. Your dad was the same way."

It felt good hearing this positive father–daughter connection asserted. "I remember my big growth spurt," Joseph said. "Seven inches in a year."

"Your dad was one of the shortest boys in school in Grade Nine," Jane said.

"I was a bit of a geek."

"*Was*, Daddy? You keep trying to get me to watch the *Buffy the Vampire Slayer* box set with you."

He let the laughs die down, admiring Franny's droll delivery. "I grew so fast that my body felt like a pair of shoes three sizes too big for me. I kept bumping into doorways and tripping on stairs." He took a deep drink from a fresh beer, letting the story pull him along as Jane watched from over her wine glass, her face as radiant as if she'd just emerged from a cold lake.

"It took me another year to grow into my new body. Everyone treated me like I was a different person." Gaining seven inches and thirty pounds was a sixteen-year-old boy's deepest wish granted—and the wish, too, of a dozen or so bright, beautiful girls who only months earlier had called him *friend*, if they'd called him anything. He drew looks from girls with pupils so dilated they might have been watching him from inside dark rooms, and what did they want from him? Only that his new body, his new *self*, fulfill the romantic expectations these girls learned from hundreds of love songs and movies. There were rewards for playing this role, which he'd collected like a bounty hunter.

Jane gave him a secret approving smirk that directed his wandering memory straight to their last year of high school, when she asked *him* to the prom, the two of them too cool, too punk to take the evening's pageantry seriously. It was a lark, he'd told his Jane-coveting buddies, a chance to play bodyguard for a girl whose face all the school freaks sketched in their gloomy notebooks. He even half-believed his own shtick until he got to her family's apartment and saw her prom dress, a strapless indigo gown tailored from a single bolt of cloth supported, as far as he could see, by nothing more than her body's curves. Her hair was heaped into fertile bunches, and he wanted to kick her kid brother when he cracked a joke about her high heels. He stayed by her side all night, recklessly funny, drunk as a pagan warrior on the eve of a battle that could not be won. Later, on a hotel-room balcony, the after-party blaring inside, the city lights spread out before them like a flotilla of lanterns, he pressed her against the railing, the loosened cones of hair tumbling down her shoulders and falling eighteen storeys to the ground for all he cared.

He couldn't help saying it out loud: "Prom night."

"Can you believe it?" Jane turned to Franny. "Your father took me to the prom."

Liz laughed and Julian clapped his hands together.

"He kept the weirdos away that night," Jane said.

This was it then, their first night together revised for public consumption. He took a swig from his beer. What was it about being in on a lie that made him want to drink?

"You were at that prom too, eh, Julian?"

He didn't like Mike's faux-innocent expression. Mike hadn't met Liz until almost ten years later, but he knew the prom party ended in Julian's dad's hot tub at five in the morning. Very soft-core, but it put Jane and Joseph in the same vicinity.

"I was there, in my powder blues," Julian said.

"And that ruffled shirt." Liz laughed. "Like cotton candy."

Franny and Rebecca leaned in closer, sensing intrigue.

"Did you rent a tux for the big night?" Franny asked.

Joseph nodded, not trusting himself to elaborate. He didn't need Franny overhearing any cherished stories from his wild youth or even wilder early twenties, the details filling a biographical hole with the very Party Boy antics he needed to warn her off of. Dad with a dated haircut prowling the rec rooms, video arcades, and park parties of yesteryear, stoned, drunk, and on the make. Liz might as well hand Franny a photo, and by the end of the weekend she just might—even in the maelstrom, Liz had packed a camera.

Luckily Jane mentioned dessert, and the boys reminded their mothers about a promised after-dinner movie. She shrugged as the kids ran to the fridge, followed by Franny and Rebecca, signalling the end of her formal parenting duties. Joseph took the hint and went to retrieve his belated housewarming gift, two bottles he'd picked up at industry events.

When he got back to the table, Alex was telling an anecdote that tweaked Joseph's memory. It was from when Alex was still living in the city, slogging away on another reality TV show, this one about downtown home renovations he'd nicknamed "The Shock Troops of Gentrification," working fourteen-hour days without paid overtime. He'd tried to organize his fellow crew members into a union, a plan that went over as well as a recruiting drive for the Khmer Rouge and got him blacklisted after someone ratted him out to the producers. Alex had worked himself into an uncharacteristic fury when he found out, raging about his co-workers to Joseph with a torrent of personal contempt that Joseph mistook for drunkenness at first, lambasting their stupidity for supporting a system that would eat them up and shit them out at an accountant's whim. And yet he'd left the bosses who blacklisted him unscathed, as if he expected no better from the executive class.

"After I picked up my severance pay I just wandered around the west end," Alex said. "I was on this side street that looked very familiar, and I didn't understand why until I saw an old Baptist church that I'd walked past when I first moved to the city with Jane. I remembered it because I'd seen a man planting a young oak tree on the side lawn. He was having trouble fitting the tree roots into the hole, so I stopped to help him. Turned out he was the minister.

"He'd been sent to the parish to try to raise the congregation numbers. The neighbourhood was changing, he told me, young families moving downtown because they wanted to walk to local stores and talk to their neighbours. They also wanted to tap into the traditions their parents had cast aside. The church could provide some of that, the minister said. He gave me a tour of the building—the daycare, the meeting spaces they were making available to community groups, and the hall where they had a soup kitchen. Finally, he took me to the top of the bell tower and showed me the bells. They were all rusted and pushed into a corner, bathed in purple and red light from the windows. He told me he wanted to restore the bells. 'People love the sound of bells on a Sunday,' he said, 'it sets the day apart and reminds them to spend time with their family and their community, that there's more to life than work and entertainment. What's wrong with that?' he asked me."

"Nothing," Joseph said, picturing the earnest minister's face.

"If we'd lived closer I'd have checked out a service," Alex continued, "but I didn't return until the day I got fired. I was so angry."

Talk about an understatement.

"But I felt a wave of calm as I looked up at the bell tower. The stained-glass windows had been restored, the brick-work sandblasted, the roof re-shingled. And his oak tree was still there, twelve feet high and surrounded by perennials. The church must have looked like that a hundred years earlier, when the first service was held."

He let them linger over the image, of young families and elders in their best clothes, walking in dignified groups to the church they'd banded together to build.

"When I looked at the tower I thought, *At least somebody has made their community a better place*. Then I realized what should have been obvious. The building wasn't an actual church anymore. Some developer had converted it into condos. I felt like I'd been kicked in the gut.

"Why did I feel so gutted? Churches were closing all over the city—why shouldn't the beautiful buildings be put to use?" He gripped Jane's hand. He was struggling to articulate a swath of emotions he couldn't wrestle into the usual categories, and he instinctively sought her help. "I saw that it was a continuation of a bigger pattern. When the manufacturing jobs went overseas, developers turned the factories and warehouses into lofts and office spaces—you can't compete in the new knowledge-economy without an address in a former foundry or dry-goods warehouse. Once the industrial buildings were converted, they went after the old churches." He shook his head, chastising himself for not seeing it coming, and took a swig of his beer. "You know how suburban streets are named after the natural landmarks they paved over? It's the same with church condos: Abbey Lofts, The Priory, Glebe Space. This place was called The Rectory! Never mind if the actual rectory was torn down decades ago—it *sounds* churchy."

Joseph felt exposed by the clarity of Alex's outrage, but the rest of the diners weren't feeling it. Jane stared blankly—back at her early days with Alex, or maybe forward into the evening, when she could drink with her friends. Mike was reading a text message. Even Julian and Amber fidgeted in their seats.

"It was a glimpse of the future," Alex said, a little more desperately. "In ten years, when the loyal soldiers of the global management class have filled up all the old churches, the developers will turn the legislature buildings into condos. Why not? Politicians would love the cash infusion from selling off the real estate. Democracy Towers, Legislature Lofts, Ordinance Hall—turrets, columns, period light fixtures, and wainscoting memorializing the democratic impulse." He lingered on the face of each guest, as if to acknowledge their shared plight.

"Last time I checked we still live in a democracy," Mike said.

"True." Alex gave the *r* a short roll, mimicking the acrobatics of his parents' mother tongue. His family had moved back to Finland for a few years when he was five, long enough for him to acquire a faint, floating accent that Mike accused him of using like an eighteen-point font—*Finnaca sans serif*—to underscore a point with European gravitas. "But when people have no say over economic decisions, they no longer live in a democracy. Every major economic decision for the last quarter-century has been made in anonymous towers in Brussels, Hong Kong, Davos, Houston." His face had a strange, sweat-less glow. "Power has liberated itself from geography."

Never had the word *geography*—Joseph's favourite subject in grade school—sounded so ominous. Alex was right, but why dam the stream of good feelings by rubbing everyone's faces in the evils of global neo-liberalism? Did he want to hear their own despairing anecdotes? They all had them—they were the first downwardly mobile generation since the Great Depression.

"The government buildings are still standing," Alex said, "but the officials inside have as much power as a McDonald's branch manager does over the menu."

Jane slipped her hand from Alex's. She wanted an intervention. This was *her* night.

"I've brought gifts from the city," Joseph said in a boisterous tone he'd pulled from his quiver of voices. He brought out the cloth bag he'd stored beneath the bench. "A new tequila from a Mexican fair-trade collective. And a Russian vodka distilled from the tears of former Politburo clerks."

Mike went to get fresh glasses, and dinner plates were pushed to the centre of the table as Joseph poured drinks, ignoring Alex's wounded expression. There'd be time to make it up to him later. Time to talk to Franny. Time to figure out his money problems. But now it was drinking time.

He lifted his shot of tequila and said, "Fellow adults, old friends, visitors from enchanted lands: the children have retired, let us talk freely."

"Oh God, he's going to get deep."

"We'll finally make it into his column: 'The Splendours of the Dinner Hour.' A three-part series."

"A toast!" Joseph said. "To our fat savings accounts!"

Jane let out the first bitter laugh. Personal debt was their generation's only taboo topic, but the liquor made them brave.

"To our RRSPs!" she said.

"To our pensions!" Mike said.

"To juggling 'til I'm eighty!"

Liz wasn't ready to spit in the face of her real estate career, but she poured everyone another shot. "To my sagging ass!"

"We'd all better stay in shape 'til we're old," Alex said.

Amber agreed. "Fitness is important."

"Franny gets my maxed-out gold card."

"She will, actually," Alex said.

"They'll have property," Liz said.

"They'll have *mortgages*." Alex was making a last run up his favourite hill. "If we're *lucky* our kids will inherit a half-paid-off property—which they'll have to divide between them."

"Our inherited capital spread ever thinner," Joseph said, "until the Lord of the Manor asserts first-night privileges on our great-great-granddaughters. But this is more of a hangover conversation."

Amber's beaded braids and the distant roar of movie pirates dispatching foes with corny tag lines smoothed the silence but not the sight of Alex's flushed, hurt face.

"When we're old and poor we can share Julian's beautiful teeth."

Julian high-fived Joseph.

"Shit, man!"

"I know!"

"I can't believe we're all here!" Liz said.

Jane cackled. "Oh God, remember the football team?"

Of course—a girl fell for Julian at a house party. Turned out she was the quarterback's girlfriend. Team spirit came in the form of the offensive line chasing Julian into the ravine.

"I thought I'd have to sleep down there. Wouldn't have been the first time." Julian's big smile pinched the creases around his eyes into agreeable bunches. "Those boys were only doing what they thought was right."

"Remember Linda Cheever's party?" Joseph let the name hang in the air. "Liz was only doing what *she* thought was right!"

Big laughter.

"You crashed the party," Jane said, exaggerating Joseph's former bravado.

"I was invited."

"Like hell you were!" She fixed on Joseph an expression he recognized from the old days. *Bring it on*, she was saying. *Bring it on*.

Because it was still light out, the flaming logs looked artificial, like a video installation commenting on the cultural practice of building bonfires on summer holidays. Joseph was giggling. They'd gone behind the shed to sample the dope Mike had bought from Derek that afternoon, then dragged the lawn chairs to the unnecessary fire. He wanted to tell Jane the thing about the fire, but his thoughts kept floating away like clouds with pleasing shapes. Where had he heard that before? He was giggling again, because after being away from dope for years he found the giggles and the trippy connections right where he'd left them, like a shelf of knick-knacks in a childhood bedroom. Mike handed him a bottle of microbrewery beer—nice hoppy flavour, no preservatives, brewed with local spring water.

"I'd endorse this beer," Joseph said.

Jane was in the chair next to him, her calf against his, their ankles warm where they touched, as though their feet rested in the same fire-warmed pool. They'd danced in the living room after dinner, Joseph exploring the curves he'd known as a covetous young man, and even now he could feel where their bodies had been pressed together, as if the blood were still pooled there under his skin, in his hands, his chest. Everyone had danced except Alex, who watched from the doorway, too pissed off about his failed dinner speech to join them. Then the jangly opening chords of "Sweet Child o' Mine" sounded, still able to call a packed room to such desperate life you thought the furniture would start dancing, and Jane pulled away from Joseph to dance with Liz and Amber, because the girls had always danced to that song with one another. Now Julian, two lawn chairs away, was trying to tell Jane what those long-gone days of high school meant to him.

"I always felt very comfortable around you. Even at that age, we understood things people *never* get, without even *saying* anything. You really impressed me, without any reservations."

"Get out the incense and purple light bulbs," she said, watching Alex return to the fire with a load of wood. "I'm amazed we got in two words to each other at those parties." She spoke loudly enough for Alex to catch this minor historical revision.

"I will always follow you and Liz, at any point in my life. I know I can come to you when I want to touch my root."

"Which root is that?"

"I'm *sincere*."

"Presses stopped," Mike chirped.

Jane patted Julian's leg. "You were always a sweet-talker."

Amber was resting her chin on Julian's shoulder, their

black shirts merging so that two heads seemed to spring from one broad torso, the first head a lion's—wide in the face, proud, and scarred—the other an old hunting bird's—dark-eyed, sharp, riding updrafts into strange heights.

"Jane, I say this with no reservations." The lion paused, calling for a full hearing of his heart's contents. "As a musician, I never forgot, through *everything*, hearing you and Andrea Wilson harmonizing to Human League at those park parties."

"Human League!" Jane couldn't believe it. She leaned across Joseph's lap to tap Liz, her breasts pressing against him. "I heard Human League at work the other day! It's still good music!"

"It was wicked when you sang," Julian said. "I say this sincerely, you had a major impact—*major*—on my musical development."

"Sing!" Amber's black eyes were already three mood swings ahead of everyone. "One song!" She gestured at the fire and the fields and the white dome over the low sun, set pieces for an outdoor concert celebrating the coming nightfall.

Jane took a quick glance at Alex across the fire. "Trust me, no one wants to hear me sing."

"We *do*, Jane," Amber said. "I see you holding on to something." This fact seemed to hurt her more than Jane. "Something that won't let you express yourself, a *blockage*."

*Yes, his name is Alex.* Joseph fought down a giggle. He was being mean, but really, Alex had to lighten up—glaring at Jane's friends when he should be flattered they wanted to hear his wife sing.

"*Go* with it, Jane," Amber said, the sun highlighting her high curving cheekbones and almost-slanted eyes. Joseph imagined her as lover to the brilliant guitarist, frontwoman of the art-school punk band, muse of the poet. Tonight, she radiated on Jane's behalf.

Julian had taken out his guitar, and a single chord cut the air with a sound as sharp as lake ice cracking. Joseph's senses sharpened at the sound, flexing against the booze and the dope as Julian strummed the first hurting chords of "Me and Bobby McGee," timeless staple of kitchen-party singalongs, now transformed by Jane's clear voice into the chorus of a Greek tragedy, the Kentucky coal mines framed by Doric columns. Everyone except Alex sang along, but Jane left them far behind when she reached the chorus about freedom being another word for nothing left to lose. How could Joseph have forgotten Jane's *voice*? It made him feel like he was leaning out of a car window doing eighty through cool mountain air, and when she sang about letting Bobby slip away to find a home, he was flooded with vivid pictures—an unspoiled green valley, a winding riverside, a beautiful woman waiting by a campfire, scenes from an imaginary life.

There were cries of "Wicked!" and "That's scary!" as Jane brought the song home. She tried to retreat into the rickety lawn chair but it was like trying to fold a peacock in full display into a handbag.

"You've got it, Jane," Julian said. "The Gift. I say that sincerely."

Jane shot Joseph an "Oh, *please*" expression she believed less than he did. He blinked away the wetness. The woods seemed closer now, and he saw shapes moving in the trees. The breeze shifted smoke into his eyes, and when he opened them again the shapes were gone.

Julian strummed a few blues chords.

"Another song? *Great*." It was Rebecca's voice, close behind Jane. She and Franny had been standing there long enough to hear—what? He pulled his knee away from Jane's.

"What's up?" Jane said. She turned in her chair to face Rebecca.

"Nothing."

Jane sighed. She knew her job was to question Rebecca until "nothing" turned into a request for money or an extended curfew.

"Are you going to sing again?" Rebecca might as well have asked if Jane was going to parade naked down the town's main street.

It was Alex's job to step in here and play the peacemaking father. Instead, he studied his wife and daughter with defiant passivity, as if he was resisting a persistent interrogator. Joseph tried to lock eyes with Franny, who was standing slouched behind Rebecca, but she'd trained herself to shut down at the first sign of familial tension. Liz gripped his arm and pulled him closer.

"I've missed you Joseph." She had the singularly happy face of a children's toy.

"I missed you too." He looked down at little Sam, half-asleep in her lap. "You're very funny. I didn't always appreciate it." It was the nicest thing he could say to her.

"I'm not sure I'm funny anymore."

Her sudden deadpan expression made him laugh.

Julian strummed a nervous chord, and Joseph thought he heard Jane whisper, "You little bitch." Or was it *witch*? Alex must have heard it too. He stepped back from the fire. His long cheeks, flushed and heavy, had gone the colour of uncooked pork. The man was fucking *high*.

"It's Sam's bedtime," Liz announced in a suddenly chirpy voice. "I'm putting him in the boys' room."

Sam clung tighter to his mother. He'd danced with Liz to an old love song in the living room, holding up his head to gaze at her, as proud as a groom who has scored a wife way out of his league.

Julian stood up to give Sam a friendly pat. "Sam I Am. Little man! I'll stay in touch—for the rest of my life."

"We'll take him upstairs," Franny said, lifting the suddenly compliant Sam and guiding his lolling head into the crook between her neck and shoulders. *She is a good kid*, Joseph thought. He'd talk to her tomorrow, work things out—and he'd better, because she'd be living at his apartment every second week starting in September. Martha's orders.

"Kids—fucking amazing," Julian said, now back in his chair. He squinted at the sun. "I'm so happy to see you folks again, and to finally meet Alex. Especially now that I got my teeth!"

"Teeth made this country great!" Mike was giggling.

"How *did* you lose them?" Alex said.

"I hooked up with the wrong people out on the Coast." Amber rubbed his back. "I did so many drugs I went into a coma. No one brushes your teeth when you're in a coma."

That got Alex's full attention. He stepped around the fire. "How long were you asleep?"

"Four years."

*Holy shit.* While Joseph and Jane were flirting with addiction and self-annihilation, Julian had followed the Dionysian impulse down as deep as you could go without dying. Imagine it—nodding off one day with a needle in your arm and awakening from a magic sleep four years later: toothless, skinny, and sponge-bathed, no memory of the years spent wrapped in white linen, the nurses moving your limbs like a doll's, or the prayers and accusations of family members and ex-lovers at your bedside.

"How did you feel when you woke up?" Alex asked, as though he'd been pondering the scenario for years. "What were your first thoughts?"

It was a great question. What *would* it be like to inhabit the silent pause between thoughts for four uninterrupted years—to wipe clean the stale patterns of your mind and overstimulated senses? What if the whole world went to sleep for four years?

Jane half-stifled a laugh but it was too late to stop the giggles spreading. Only Alex and Joseph didn't get the joke.

"I'm sort of kidding," Julian said, staring into the fire. "I was a junkie for four years—sincerely. I might as well have been in a coma. I ate nothing but candy." He hugged his guitar, awestruck by the memory of his candy consumption—chocolate mountains, candy houses behind marzipan fences. "My teeth rotted out."

Joseph shifted in his seat. Alex had stepped back, but his sour, betrayed face showed through the smoke like the sun through the haze. The guy had to lighten up for fuck's sakes, learn how to let things go.

"We've all done time in a coma." Joseph wanted to move on.

"Amen, brother," Julian said. "We all fell asleep on the way to Oz."

Alex was at a disadvantage here, having made few journeys down chemical yellow brick roads in his youth.

"At least the Wizard gave me back my teeth!" Julian called out. "It's great to be awake!"

"And what are you taking to stay awake these days?" Alex asked.

Joseph felt Jane tense up at the sound of Alex's baiting tone. Julian shrugged and took a small pouch woven in a Central American pattern out of his shirt pocket, dangling it from his fingers by a loop of string. He removed a tiny glass vial filled with micro pills, and a tiny envelope folded with autistic precision.

"I've become a man of letters, like my father wanted. I've got my *A*, my *E*, my *K*."

"And your *H*?" Alex said.

"No, brother—*H* is for *hell*."

"And heaven."

"Not in my alphabet." Julian spoke in the ex-junkie's penitent tone.

"I guess I should have had more of that joint."

"Someone had to get the placebo tokes." Julian examined his own stained fingers. "What you need, brother, is the One Night in Bangkok joint. If you're up for it."

Alex edged forward. The sun was now skimming above the treeline, and the heat from the fire laid a sheen over his body, setting him outside the group, as if he were grafted onto a scene from an old movie, the one about the wronged man forced into a showdown. No one saw this coming: Drug Fight at the O.K. Corral. Julian opened his guitar case. Three taps to the lid of a small compartment produced a joint as thin as a nail.

"I'm fine," Jane said, staring at the joint as Julian lit it.

"We can do better than fine," Amber assured her. She *knew* this dope and where it could take you.

"I'm here," Joseph whispered to Jane, catching the smell of her hair. "Let's get high. We'll ride out the waves together. Like old times."

Jane did an inventory of her old friends and then fixed on Alex. "Don't expect me to make everyone an omelette later," she said.

"Fucking hell." Joseph didn't mean to say it out loud.

"Amen, brother."

The One Night in Bangkok joint had knocked seven adults on their asses. Joseph kept losing pockets of time, falling into a buzzing hole as he and Jane walked through the pasture behind the farm. They stopped to watch the setting sun, a layer cake of conch-shell pinks and oranges that gilded Jane's face, drawing her wet pupils half-closed.

"I'm *too* high," he said.

"We'll ride it out together."

She slipped her hand into his and squeezed, and he reflexively glanced back at the farm, finding the shed that stood next to the white board fence. No sign of Alex. He'd asked Jane to stay behind with him, then skulked back to the house when she refused. A car glided down the road, and bats flaked off the farmhouse roof to take to the sky, the top-floor windows glowing like a jack-o'-lantern's eyes.

Jane and Joseph slowed their steps, letting the two other couples get even further ahead, through the grass as thick as a mop. Above them, the sky was darkening, as if the bright colours had been thrown against the western sky by centrifugal force.

"This is the first time we've been alone since the night you told me you were marrying Alex," he said, almost sure he was right.

"Yes." Her languid voice extended the word. "What did I tell you? That Alex gave me what I *needed*."

"Yeah, me too." He didn't mean it as a joke, but he and Jane were laughing so hard his stomach hurt. "Maybe *I* should have married him."

"No, no—I said he gave me what I *needed*, not what I *wanted*." She wasn't laughing anymore. "I said I was sick of what I wanted because I wanted everything."

"I remember." Was that also the night he followed Jane's lead and decided to marry Martha? He watched the thought slip by, safe to think anything he wanted. Jane was beside him, not Jane the wife or mother or protective friend of his ex-wife, but *his* Jane. She looked up at him, the puffy half-circles beneath her eyes like ceremonial smudges. The farmhouse felt miles behind them, Alex and the children under glass, curios in an exhibit. They leaned on each other and kept walking, and then it started, the high mewling and barking of coyotes from the woods.

"They have an animal cornered," she said.

They turned to stare at the throbbing black line of trees, hearing the animal thrash and struggle as the coyotes' howls cut the humid air to ribbons.

"They sound almost human," she said. "Would you join them?"

"I'd leave tonight."

"What if you wanted to leave the pack one day?"

How could he have forgotten them—Jane's "what if" permutations? What if you could be invisible for one hour, what would you do? What if my face got horribly burned, would you still want to fuck me? Another yapping tremor went through the pack, followed by a sound like a huge ball rolling through the undergrowth.

"They're relentless," she said, not without admiration.

He put his arm around her waist and pulled her closer.

"I don't know about things anymore," she whispered. "I know where I've been, but it feels like the tracks in front of me have run out."

He didn't know what she meant but her tone of renunciation excited him. He kissed her cool cheek.

"I love my husband and kids," she said, shifting her face to bring her lips closer to his. "I just want them to go away for a little while."

He'd waited years for this without knowing it. He could hold off a little longer. They followed the line of the forest, hand in hand, the sky still pulsing as they reached the second pasture, where the freshly cut grass was gathered into round bales, giant cheese wheels in the orange light. The pasture climbed gently toward a horizon made jagged by copses of trees, and they saw the two other couples in the distance, moving beneath the sky like revellers in a seasonal procession.

"Follow me," Jane said.

They turned and walked toward the forest, touching and kissing until the trees loomed over them as if they'd pulled up their roots to meet the old lovers halfway, even extending a welcoming gap that opened onto a dim, warm clearing, the air scented with pine and cedar. He found Jane's neck, a wave of warm white milk that poured down into her shirt collar, and the treetops swayed, filling the clearing with a sound like water flowing over rocks. He felt obliterated, his life in the city a fading, unpleasant mirage, and he sensed in her desperate kisses the same shrugging-off of a life. The trees closed around them as she eased him down onto the ground, pressing him into the soft mulch. It kept slipping between his fingers, the murky picture of the strong, focused man of purpose he could have been, but he gladly let the image go. They undressed and they gave in, laughing at their altered bodies, grunting when they found what still worked, until a while later they heard it, a branch snapping as the breeze picked up. Jane sat up and glanced around the clearing. The sky glowed purple in stained-glass shards on the canopy of leaves above them, and the forest throbbed in Joseph's peripheral vision, pulsing as gently as a vein in a sleeping child's wrist.

"You'll always want me," she said as she got to her feet. She pulled up her pants. "We can't do this again."

"I won't tell anyone about this."

"Damn right you won't."

He understood: she had more to lose. A marriage, a home,

an intact family. The gap between them yawned open again, and as they stepped out of the clearing and into the pasture, she walked two steps ahead of him. He felt lightheaded and shaky, and when he looked back at the forest he couldn't find the opening, as if even the trees that had parted for them were denying what had happened.

Eventually, they met up with the others on their way back to the farm.

"It's a good night to be a coyote," Julian said.

"Not so good for the roadrunner," Mike said.

Liz giggled, stoned clean of real-estate figures, and they joked about old times as the last light in the sky faded, old friends guided by visions of warm beds and plates of toast. The farmhouse appeared warm and solid, its lit windows a beacon in the twilight. They were almost at the white board fence when Alex stepped out from the shadows behind the shed.

"Did Rebecca and Franny go with you?" He leaned against the creaking fence, his face bloated, eyes puffy. "Did they?"

"Of course not," Jane said.

"Did you see them on your way back?" His limbs were moving in rigid bursts, like a ghost forced back into its old body, wobbly at the controls.

"They're in the house."

"No, they're not," he said. "I've looked." He grabbed the top fence board. "If they didn't go with you, then the girls are missing."

# GODS

It was that sensation of tripping over a root in a dream and jerking awake in bed, of falling out of one world and landing roughly in this one.

The girls were not missing—why tempt fate by saying it?

Joseph climbed over the fence, his feet hitting the yard with too much force, as though his centre of gravity had dropped to his knees. Everyone had gathered around Alex, their bodies massing in the dim blue light, a sinister bulk of summer clothing and bare arms and faces.

"They're not missing," Joseph said. Hiding, maybe, or walking in the fields, taking in the drama of the sunset, the coyote howls affirming their rebellious mood. Two kids pushing the boundaries, hoping to piss off their parents. The stuff of sitcoms. "Just out of sight," he clarified.

No one was listening to him. The conversation was already topped by sharp peaks.

"What do you mean they're *missing*?"

"You didn't see them leave?"

"They're not *here*," Alex kept saying.

"For God's sake, where would they go?" Jane swept her arms wide to dramatize the lack of destinations for two teenagers: fields, a rural highway, thousands of acres of dark forest.

"I've searched everywhere. I'd know if they were here."

Typical Alex: ambushing them with bad news, then grabbing the role of the strong, rational type—shoulders squared, arms folded. But his face betrayed him. It looked raw, as if stripped of at least two layers of skin.

"Listen, Alex," Liz said. "It must have freaked you out when you couldn't find the girls."

"The first half-hour of searching didn't freak me out, but the *next* half-hour did."

"We weren't gone *that* long," Joseph said, startled by the shrill tone in his own voice. "Half an hour, tops."

"Oh, were you keeping time?"

Joseph saw it in Alex's eyes: the urge to punch him so hard he'd be drinking through a straw for weeks. What was happening here? He turned to face the pasture behind the farmhouse. It would take ten minutes to reach the second pasture, another ten to get back. Factor in hand-holding time and stopping-to-kiss-and-chase-the-vapours-of-youth time—and he and Jane had gone much further. He reached for his BlackBerry to check the time. *Shit!* It was sitting on his kitchen counter. Never mind that Franny hadn't texted him in months—she might have tonight.

He scanned the fading landscape, terrified by the lack of visual detail—he could have been looking at the pelt of a giant animal.

"Did you check the fields?" Liz asked.

"Not *every* field."

"The Johnston brothers' place alone is two hundred acres," Jane said.

Never mind the Johnston brothers. They were standing on a two-acre plot, small by local standards, but expansive enough to hide two girls.

"You were here the whole time," Liz reminded Alex.

He stepped closer to her. "Yes. I was the one person who *was* here, with the kids."

"We went for a fucking walk!"

Alex nodded, as if she'd handed him all the rope he needed. "Listen," he said, addressing the group, "I wasn't in the house every second. I sat by the fire. I went for a walk to clear my head."

He actually lifted a finger to enumerate each point, leaving out the most important detail, that he'd been pissed off at their nostalgia and their dancing in the living room. He'd even tried to guilt Jane into staying behind.

"After my walk, I came back and sat by the fire. The girls could have left while I was gone, or they could've slipped away while we smoked that fucking joint. We would have missed a parade going by."

"Don't blame the dope," Julian said, defending his departed friend.

"What was in it?"

"Just good Thai hash, brother."

"Do you want a fucking ingredients list?" Joseph said.

"Are we really having this conversation?" Jane almost shouted the question. "What about the basement?"

Alex hesitated—he hadn't searched the basement. Why would he? The girls were too old to play haunted house in a damp basement. "They're not in the house."

"The corridor beside the house?"

Already the pout, like Alex wasn't getting enough credit for his hard work. *What a prick*, Joseph thought.

They were getting ahead of themselves. The girls had been at home when the adults left for their sunset walk—Joseph *saw* them by the fire. No, that was earlier, before the Bangkok joint. Wasn't it? The dope had reassembled the evening's timeline into a collage. He remembered going behind the shed to smoke the Bangkok joint, then Alex boycotting the group walk to prove a point now lost to antiquity. While they were gone, the girls went missing. Where would they go? Where *could* they go?

"Hold on," Jane said. "Did you look for a note?"

"Of course I did! Twice. The kitchen's a fucking *mess*."

"What about the dogs?"

"Napping on the back deck."

"The boys!" Mike said, as if he expected a gold star. "They might have seen them."

"They're in bed."

"You didn't ask them!" Jane was furious. Nothing bad could happen in sight of those fierce eyes.

Mike put his hands up. "I'll go check on the boys."

Joseph watched as Mike faded into the darkness beside the house. He must have reached the front door by now. In three seconds he'd turn the doorknob, step into the sunroom and go through to the kitchen.

If the girls had just gotten home, Mike would see them *now*.

In thirty seconds he'd appear with them at the side of the house.

Mike and the girls would appear *now.*

One, two, three—*now.*

The door might be stuck.

He will see Franny *now*!

Why was it taking so long? Liz and Julian and Amber kept glancing at him. He knew what they were thinking: *Poor Joseph, goes for a walk and comes back to find his only child missing. Christ, what he must be going through.*

When Mike finally appeared at the side of the house, he was alone. The crickets sounded like a giant rusty wheel grinding against its axis. The sunset had dimmed to purple twilight and the first stars were out, shimmering behind the fading heat haze. What was Joseph missing here?

"They didn't see the girls leave," Mike said, his words pushing Jane back on her feet and out of the circle. He turned to Alex. "Sean said you yelled at them."

"I did. I told them to stop playing video games and go to bed."

"He was very upset."

"He's not made of fucking glass! You'd know that if you ever fucking parented him."

"It doesn't matter," Julian said, stepping quickly between the two men.

Joseph saw the pinched ends of a smirk disappear inside Alex's mouth like two worms retracting into their holes. He must be sure the girls would be home soon, and was compiling a list of several failed role models to blame their transgression on, Joseph's name near the top.

Jane didn't share Alex's confidence. Her eyes made a quick circuit—forest, pasture, road, farmyard—before returning to stare at her feet, as though a pack of worst-case scenarios were running her to ground. The other adults stared out of closed faces—*their* children weren't missing. Julian and Amber didn't even have a child, though it would have been beautiful—tall, blond, with high cheekbones. Julian caught Joseph staring and nodded as if to say, *Don't worry, brother, we'll find them.* Liz seemed to be backing away without actually moving her legs, retreating into a safe space closed to the afflicted parents. Everyone but Jane was looking at him. Was he mumbling? Liz started doing something with her hands, making a box in the air—*open it!*

He cleared his throat and paused, impersonating a man capable of choosing his words carefully. "We have to establish a few probabilities." He sounded like a stoned teenager playing straight for his parents. Alex crossed his arms, resisting the absolute bullshit about to exit Joseph's mouth. The group had formed a circle around Joseph when he wasn't looking. *Wasn't Looking*—he finally had the title for his autobiography. "We were gone for about forty-five minutes."

"It was longer." Alex's voice was sharp enough to carve the words on Joseph's forehead.

"We're all missing something important here. The girls can't . . ." Joseph paced out of the circle and back in again. He was forgetting something. Jane and Rebecca had crossed swords by the fire, a tussle that ended with Jane calling Rebecca a bitch. She didn't say, "You're *acting* like a bitch," as the parenting manuals recommended—Jane had ascribed *bitch essence* to her daughter. Or was it *witch* essence? Whatever Jane called her, Rebecca had stormed off, playing the adversarial role handed to her. Kids were like that these days. Can't go two minutes without a cue, usually electronic, to tell them who they are.

"Franny has a cell phone!" Joseph said. "She has a fucking *cell* phone. It gets service when she's near the highway. She was texting this afternoon." *God love Franny for texting!* "I'll phone her. She knows to keep her ringer on."

"What if she doesn't want to be found?" Alex said.

*It's your daughter who doesn't want to be found*, he almost said. *She's sick of your life lessons and truth telling.*

"I'll leave a message if she doesn't answer. I'll convey the seriousness of the situation." He forced out a public laugh, a honking sound he heard in the air to his left, as if a lackey was positioned there to appreciate his jokes.

"Good plan, brother," Julian said. "We'll check the yard while you're gone." He'd know the best hiding places.

They were one phone call away from relief.

*Franny, where are you?*

*Just out for a walk. Where are* you?

It made sense: Franny and Rebecca couldn't find their parents, and minimum effort expended, they went for a walk. He could already hear himself joking with Jane and Liz, Jane doing Rebecca's voice: "We went for a walk, *Mom*, like you're always nagging me to do." He forced a smile, and then he was scissor-stepping the last ten steps to the house, his knees wobbly from the adrenaline surges electrifying the backs of his legs.

Alex was right about the kitchen: dirty plates were shuffled into drooping piles on the table and a broken glass lay on the floor. They must have been pretty drunk, even during dinner.

He picked up the phone receiver from the mount on the wall and stared at the numbered buttons, zero through nine. By rearranging permutations of those numbers, scientists had launched spaceships and connected voices across continents. Franny was a phone call away. He pressed her number into the keypad, enunciating each digit as though he were calling out the voyage coordinates to fellow crew members. If she'd left her cell behind he'd hear it ringing. What was her ring tone? He'd heard it this morning, the chorus of a dance track, not as cheesy as "Who Let the Dogs Out?" or "I Like Big Butts" but just as harmlessly sexual, or so he'd thought at the time.

"This is a long-distance call. Please dial one—"

"Cocksucker!"

He hung up, pushed *1*, and entered Franny's number again.

"Please enter your long-distance password."

Of course they had a discount long-distance plan. He bit the phone, the pain in his teeth somehow reminding him of the long-distance card in his wallet. He took it out and tried Franny again.

The call went straight to her answering service.

"Good news: you've reached Franny. Leave a message. Or *not*."

He interrupted her recorded voice with a grunt, trying to startle it free from whatever machine kept it on message, then he hung up and dialled the number again. The call went through to her voice mail, the familiarity of her recorded voice almost tricking him into speaking before the greeting finished.

"Hello chief, it's your dad," he said, aiming for an urgent but not shit-scared tone. "We're wondering where you guys went. There's no note here. I'm sure it's cool." Did he really say *cool*? "We're getting a little worried. Can you phone the farm when you get this message? You'll see the number on your screen. Wait. I'm using a phone card. The number is . . ."

There was no number on the phone mount.

"Just a second, Fran."

He searched his wallet for the slip of paper with Jane and Alex's number.

"One more second, chief. Da-da-da-dee-dee."

*That's right, talk to her like she's a friend from the fucking office.*

He found the piece of paper, read out the number, and after he hung up he stared hard at the receiver, willing it to ring, imagining the *exact* sound of the bell, his mind mimicking the duration and the humming intervals between. He was getting the sounds right—why didn't the phone ring?

The girls must be walking through a no-signal zone. Rebecca wanted to talk about a boy, the Facebook "stalker." What was his name? It didn't matter. She needed to talk, and it was a nice evening, and she didn't leave a note because she was mad at her mom. The girls left the house and walked up the driveway and down the road, staying on the shoulder, avoiding the passing cars. He could even see them, walking along the side of the road, hardly noticing the black car that glides past them and stops just up ahead, engine idling. Inside, the barrel-chested, bearded driver checks the rear-view mirrors; his skinny, sweating friend pats his concealed knife; the driver throws the car into reverse and stops with a jerk beside the girls. The doors swing open in unison like the wings of a vulture, disgorging the men.

Who is there to protect them?

It was pointless, but he replayed the terrible scenario—the men, the car, the doors opening in unison—until he could have picked the driver out of a police lineup.

A gauzy halo surrounding the phone reminded him he was drunk and high; his recollections derelict; his hands unsteady. A little corkboard on the wall near the phone was covered in bills and cards, but no note from the girls. They probably weren't planning to be gone long enough to leave one. That was a possible clue, a little white stone to guide the story clear of a bloody Brothers Grimm ending. But what did it mean? He took a few steps toward the living room, as if the TV would have an update on the ongoing crisis, then stood in the middle of the kitchen, feeling watched by a masculine presence that assessed his efforts, assigning minimal points for ingenuity, self-control, and diligence.

*Another man would have figured out where Franny was by now*, the presence said. *But look at you, spinning the hamster wheel in your mind.*

"Leave me alone!"

*Why don't you make yourself a sandwich while you're waiting?*

"Why don't you *help* me?"

*You know where this is going.*

He did: he was directly responsible for Franny's disappearance. It was crazy, but there it was: his transgression had taken form as a monster, silently loping up behind his daughter like a giant spider, paralyzing her, and carrying her body to its lair.

"I don't believe in you," he said. He nodded briskly to confirm this fact, obeying a need to be seen in action, then picked up his jacket from the kitchen bench. He had extra pockets now: they could only help.

"I'm not doing any good here," he said. "I'll see what the others are doing."

Outside, the yard was dark, loud with crickets. A car passed on the highway, its brightly lit interior displaying a female passenger poking at a road map that had burst open like an air bag. He imagined her as an actress in a dashboard-GPS ad, and he smiled as he watched the bubble of light float by until the car's red tail lights blasted him with a feeling of complete desolation.

As he walked down the front steps he heard a rustling deep in the hedge beside the stoop. The rustling got louder when he stepped on the ground, as though his weight had jarred loose a board beneath the topsoil, then it stopped. Was there enough room in there for a girl to hide? Why would she? He peered into the hedge but it was like staring down a dark well.

Two of his friends were watching him from beside the fire, as if waiting for the conclusion of a practical joke, the girls jumping out of the bushes to surprise him, revealing Joseph as the ridiculous city boy. He stood up, watching the silhouettes of the other adults moving against the last light in the west, calling out the girls' names, voices as lonely as train whistles in the night. Had he ever heard a real train whistle in the night? No. He'd picked up the image from a song, and it rose up now to underscore his loss.

Not that anyone was using the word *loss*.

Julian moved along the edge of the garden and met up with another silhouette. The shadows conferred, and then Amber and Julian were calling the girls' names, their bodies so close together that he couldn't match the silhouettes to their respective voices, a disconnect that sent him running back to the phone.

Franny hadn't left a message. She might be using her phone. He imagined her saying goodbye to a friend and noticing the flashing red light announcing a new message. He punched in her number, connecting so quickly to her voice mail he was sure they'd called each other at the same time. Later, when they recalled these moments in a cautionary anecdote, they'd laugh about the overlap.

God, how they'd laugh.

He tried again. When he heard her message he smashed the phone against his thigh. A strip of flypaper hung from the ceiling above him, coiling like a DNA strand encoded with hundreds of fly corpses. He leaned against the kitchen wall, convinced that it would collapse without his support. Franny was going to call any second. He counted backward from ten because countdowns manage the chaos of time.

She would phone in ten seconds.

In three.

One ring and he'd answer, run outside, tell everyone the good news, and return to his real life. He would get on top of things, be the father that Franny needed, pass on his life wisdom to her.

It was back again—the watchful masculine presence. *Pass on your life wisdom?* The man's tone was blatantly sarcastic, as though he'd just finished reading Joseph's personal file. *What wisdom do you have to teach her?*

Point taken: Joseph had no trove of proverbs and songs and myths to bequeath her, only his Party Boy stories: "Joseph, son of Don, did drink his portion at the meadhouse, and loins girded he bedded the fair Joanne, daughter of Loretta, who did leave him her phone number in the morning. But Joseph, spying treasure on a far shore, did not call Joanne." And fatherly advice? "Don't mix your white and dark alcohol; a hash joint *isn't* the perfect complement to the evening's final pint; and Pink Floyd's 'Comfortably Numb,' with its operatic self-pity and jaded romanticism, will guide you through the bleached-out finale of an acid trip."

Why didn't she call? He pressed phantom digits on his palm to reach Franny's phone, then started on another familiar number.

*Martha, it's Joseph. No, everything's not fine. Franny's missing. She and Rebecca . . .*

*An hour, at most.*

*We don't know. We were out on a walk.*

*I know, I fucked up. Again. I'm going to fix this.*

*Look, it wasn't just me.*

*Why is it always* my *fault?*

He couldn't make that call.

Put a gun to his head. Break his fingers.

Outside, his friends had gathered around the fire, giving up on the search of the yard. He walked down the stairs, ignoring the rustling in the hedge this time.

"She didn't answer, and there's still no phone message," Joseph said. They were already deep into Plan B, as if they'd known he wouldn't reach Franny. That was a big conclusion to jump to. If he'd phoned six minutes earlier, her line might have been free, and he'd be standing by the fire laughing at the misunderstanding.

"If we'd given Rebecca her cell back we could call *her*," Jane said to Alex.

"Yes, that's the problem here. Rebecca doesn't have a cell phone."

"Did you see anything in the kitchen?" Liz's eyebrows pinched together like she wanted to squeeze loose an important detail from Joseph's memory. "No clues?"

"Clues? What, like 'Mr. Mustard in the parlour'? There's no fucking clues!"

The low fire bristled with shifting colours: orange and ash grey and blue. Was the world always so rich in concrete detail, every burning coal so *of itself*? What a terrifying thought. So much pointless detail, and they couldn't find two teenage girls. A broken beer bottle lay next to the fire—they'd been *that* messed up earlier.

"Go back to square one," Jane told Alex. "Tell me everything you did."

He rolled his eyes. "I needed to walk off my high. I walked down the road and thought about going for a swim at the neighbour's place—a fucking *swim*."

"You didn't say anything about a swim before," Joseph said.

"I didn't go for a swim! I thought about it!" Alex paced around the fire, waving his arms like he was pushing through a crowd. Why was he, the sole adult who hadn't gone traipsing into the fields, being made to answer so many questions?

"The pool," Jane said, her voice wispy, as though afraid to trigger an avalanche of emotion. She held up her hand, then shook her head. "The girls wouldn't go for a swim."

"They might," Joseph said. "They were high."

She turned on him. "How do you know?"

His groin seemed to clench, pulling up his testicles. "Alex and I—"

"I tried to tell you earlier," Alex said.

"You tried to *lecture* me about Rebecca."

"I tried to tell you that we saw them getting high with Ruby."

"What was Derek doing here, anyways?" Jane was staring into Mike's petulant, defiant face, but he refused to feel guilty about buying dope on their property.

"We have to check the pool," she said.

"Jane, I'm sure it's fine." It was worse that Liz said it so calmly—she had nothing to lose here.

Joseph walked beside Jane as they crossed the road onto the opposite shoulder, his steps falling into rhythm with hers no matter how hard he tried to break the pattern. Farmers' fields stretched off to their right, a distant farmhouse and some outbuildings the only points of electric light.

He tried to focus on the lights but a terrible thought broke through: *If one girl has to drown, let it be Rebecca.*

Jane and Alex would be devastated. Nothing's worse than losing a child—the guilt, waking up turned inside out, all bone and gristle on the outside, frayed skin and nerves within. It would be awful, but they'd get through it. They'd have to, for Liam's sake.

If Franny died they might as well cut Joseph open and spill his guts beside the pool.

He let Jane get a few steps ahead and whispered quietly, enunciating every syllable: "Please God, take Rebecca. I'll die without Franny." Or worse, he'd keep on living—the shambling ghoul haunting the local schoolyard, The Man Who Lost His Daughter.

*Can you imagine living with that?* parents would say.

*I know I couldn't.*

*I heard he was high when she disappeared. I'm not saying it was his fault—oh God, he's coming this way.*

They came to a bungalow set back about a hundred feet from the road, on a massive suburban-style lawn. No one ran up the driveway. Later they might run. They'd scream and implore the heavens, they'd rend hair and gnash teeth, but whatever had happened in the pool was long over.

The pool was above ground and surrounded by a chain-link fence at the side of the house.

"I hate that fucking pool," Jane said. "It's a death trap."

Joseph wanted to clamp her mouth shut, silence her from using that last phrase again.

"Rebecca's a strong swimmer," Alex reminded her.

*So Franny isn't? She's a great swimmer, actually. Won a silver medal.*

She would not be floating face down in the water. If anyone drowned, it wouldn't be Franny.

Jane got to the fence first. The unlocked gate opened onto a staircase that ascended to a wide wooden deck. Joseph leaped up the stairs behind her and nearly tipped into the water to avoid crashing into her back.

There were no bodies. He thought he heard Jane whimper with relief. Alex was standing beside her now, staring into the calm water, riveted by his own reflection. Joseph kneeled down before his legs could collapse beneath him, and dangled his fingers in the water, watching the ripples roll out into the pool and expire. There was a feeling of inevitability about all of this, as if for years he'd been walking across a frozen lake, and only when the ice broke beneath him did he notice the hundreds of cracks he'd passed along the way. He was the kind of man who wrote columns about the challenges and foibles of fatherhood in the twenty-first century and then got stoned and lost his daughter in the countryside.

"I knew they wouldn't be here," Jane said.

"We had to look," Alex said. "Just to be sure."

"Now we're being thorough?" She glared at him, not having to say it. *How could you have missed the girls leaving the property?*

"At least I was *there*, at the farm." Alex's upper body was swelling with fury.

"I'm *always* there!" she screamed at him. "You fucking try it some time!" She took Joseph's arm and turned him away from the pool as Alex watched, stoned and horse-faced. More lines were being drawn.

They were back at the fire. Why always the fire? Were they cavemen? Jane was grilling Alex again, making him walk through every detail.

"The boys were playing video games, which made me wonder where the girls were. I searched the *whole* house."

This was good. Alex was following a rope back into memory, pulling tight any slack.

"I checked, but there was no note, no phone message, no sign of them."

Everyone just stared into the fire, the residue of the drugs and booze hanging before them like a thin mist they couldn't see through clearly. What were they missing?

"Rebecca's trying to push me," Jane said. "That's what this is about, trying to get a reaction from her bitchy mother."

"She wouldn't drag Franny into it," Liz said.

"If Rebecca went off in a huff then Franny would want in on the drama." Joseph knew that much about Franny. "She can be *indignant*. You should hear her and her mom fight." Actually, *he* should have heard their fights—heard them, refereed them. "Franny gets moody. Hormones." Was he really blaming this on hormones, as if they were the magical key to all female behaviour?

Amber spoke again. "They might have gone for a walk in the woods. Just to be alone. Girls need their space to grow." Was Amber going to lecture them on menstrual-based initiation rites in pre-industrial societies? She had a point, though. Kids wander off without thinking, caught up in their own mood.

Joseph imagined Rebecca sneaking up the driveway, followed by Franny. They close the gate behind them, but which way do they turn? Why were they leaving? They were all overlooking something, a clue that might be right under their noses. It was like trying to piece together the bones of an animal no one knew the shape of. "Does Rebecca have friends in town?" he asked.

Jane nodded.

"Could she have gone to see them?"

"She doesn't drive."

"I'm trying to bring in more possibilities."

Alex sneered at Joseph's detective talk and stepped away from the fire, his expression fixed, set in defiance against the crushing, deep-sea atmosphere they were descending into.

"If they were planning on going somewhere, they'd have left a note," Joseph said. "They're not ready for that level of 'fuck you' yet."

Liz agreed. "They're practically kids."

"To us the girls look like kids," Jane said. "But not to the perverts."

Joseph wanted to disagree, but he remembered Derek

assessing the girls' bodies and his own silent complicity.

"Jane, we're in the middle of the country," Liz said.

"*How* long have you lived here?"

"We know most of the locals."

"How does *knowing* help? Half of Rebecca's teachers are moral retards. Mr. Jenkins still lives with his mother. He *understands* what girls are going through. That's how they get to them."

"You really think Mr. Jenkins came out here?"

"You know his type, Liz. What they'd do to a girl if they could get away with it."

Joseph knew where Jane was going. He read about it all the time. The troubled teenage girl drawn into an online relationship with a middle-aged man posing as a wise, caring friend. The secret rendezvous at a motel. The obscene trophy photos extracted along with her virginity and dignity. Would Franny get sucked into that? He should *know*! She could be on her way to meet her online soulmate right now, accompanied by Rebecca. But then why not leave a note to cover their tracks?

"I don't think they were planning to be gone long," he said.

"Maybe they were frightened by all the noise around the fire." Alex's face flared in the orange light. "You sounded like a bunch of fucking idiots!"

"Hang on there, brother," Julian said. "We sounded like a bunch of kids—*big* kids. The gals wouldn't be scared."

Mike agreed.

"Maybe *your* kids would be fine with it, and *his*." Alex pointed at Joseph. "But Rebecca doesn't usually see her mother stoned out of her mind, singing like—"

"Singing like what, Alex?" Jane said. "Go on, tell me the *truth*."

"You were pathetic." Alex wanted to blow this wide open, but Jane's willing expression seemed to make him back off.

Mike tossed a fresh log into the flames, the surge of heat and light blurring Alex to a suggestive smudge, like one of those ectoplasmic faces in a seance photograph. Joseph inventoried the pinched mouths around the fire. Things were bad. If the girls had gone for walk, they'd be back by now or else they would have called. Everyone knew it, but there was power in not saying it, as if silence could keep the evil at bay a little longer.

"Let's expand the search," Julian said. "We'll each take a direction and *yell* their names. We can cover a lot more ground if we, like, fan out."

He gave them a team leader's nod and ran toward the work shed, calling the girls' names. Alex, drawing from a dwindling reserve of protective contempt, set off diagonally toward the back fence, while Jane and Amber took to the field, where only this afternoon Joseph had watched Franny and Rebecca walk. When Liz told Mike to check the phone for messages he looked like he'd never been so glad to be given a job—and why not? *His* kids weren't missing.

Joseph headed for the stretch of scrubby land running beside the highway, passing Alex's chicken coop and stopping to peer inside. The girls could be in there, playing a practical joke. He stepped through the low doorway, making out the hay-filled but chicken-less shelves along each wall. Even stooped over in the tiny house he could hear the adults calling the girls' names. He'd be the last to add his voice to the chorus, making this an official *search*, a nightmarish word from the 24-hour news cycle. How many times in his life had he heard the increasingly desperate updates?

*Police have begun a search for a missing nine-year-old girl.*

*Police have expanded their search to include a nearby golf course.*

*Police are narrowing their search to a stretch of shallow creek bed.*

*The search for Carrie Wilson*—by this point the victim's name is cited without referencing the case—*has ended, along with the hope of an entire community . . .*

All that searching, when the police knew the girl was already dead. They even had a rule of thumb: if a missing child wasn't found within forty-five minutes of disappearing, the abductors were already miles from the scene, safe in some motel or suburban basement, the child's body awaiting violation. Never mind if someone spotted the child stepping into a white sedan or holding hands with a woman wearing a parka—after forty-five minutes those clues are about as useful to a child's recovery as autopsy details. Where did he pick up this urban lore? The media, which once again had conditioned his responses without providing any helpful information.

But Franny was *not* a child. When a child disappeared the police searched the local ravine, where a man walking his dog had found her mitten. You saw the girl's picture on every network—always the same photo, the child smiling eagerly, beaming innocence and milk teeth and hope. No one gave the police a photo of their kid melting down at a birthday party or pushing their sister off the jungle gym.

Franny was a teenager, immune to the logic of the Forty-Five-Minute Rule. You were talking about a victim potentially *accepting* the invitation into the white sedan. Not a willing victim, but one lured to her death in a moment of misplaced independence. As if that made it better.

He felt a sob welling up from his chest and stood up straight, smacking his head against the peaked ceiling, the giant in his lair crying like a little boy.

He added his *Franny*s and *Rebecca*s to the net of voices trawling the night, turning his head on every *Franny* to extend his voice across the road. The girls were out there. No one could tell him otherwise. As he repeated the names he noticed that Franny's name made his voice rise with a piercing force, paternal love expanding his vocal range. Of course it did—he'd been one of the first to speak Franny's name when she was born and he'd spoken it tens of thousands of times since, in whispers, in playful accents, in the voices of imaginary characters, in soothing tones when she awoke from nightmares.

He stopped calling Rebecca's name and put everything he had into *Franny*, imagining the word as a magical bird flying free to seek out ears trained from birth to hear its call.

*Franny*—it flew from his mouth, out over the dark fields and into the trees.

He wasn't supposed to believe in magic or a spirit–matter divide. Matter was neutral, an atom in your child's heart no different from its counterpart in a tree or a worm, but he didn't believe that—*no one* did, not where a parent's love was concerned.

He walked on, launching a flock of magical *Franny*s from his drying mouth. Where was she? He did a 360-degree scan of the terrain, taking in the pointless geometry of black and navy blue stretching to every horizon. He was getting closer to the forest. The girls might have gone for a walk in the woods. It made sense. He approached the trees, calling Franny's name again and again until the word became meaningless, the component syllables slipping apart into nonsense words:

*Fraaalllyy.*

*Flaaaanee.*

*Fwaaalllly.*

He switched to *Frances* until he got his little girl's name back, but he seemed to be speaking phonetically, as though reading a foreign language out loud. Then her name disintegrated in his mouth again. What kind of man can't keep his daughter's name intact?

*Franny*: what *did* her name mean? What is a *Franny*? An old-fashioned party hat? A cakey dessert? A sexual euphemism?

"Shut up!" he shouted.

He stopped and listened to his friends' raw voices calling out, leaving no spaces between the names, as if they were afraid of silence. Where was she? The right answer must be buried deep in his brain, behind some obstructing cranial fold, but as hard as he tried he couldn't squeeze it free. He fell to his knees, mumbling fragments of prayers from his altar-boy days, imploring God to take this cup from his hand and he'd—what? Do God a favour? Take someone else's burden? If so, he'd gladly take Franny's. Maybe that was the deal: *God, take this cup from my hand and replace it with Franny's*. What was he asking? He couldn't even get his prayers straight.

Joseph groaned into his hands. The forest was about fifty feet away, the dark wall of trees looming over him like a raised drawbridge. He stood up and stepped onto a stretch of almost-bare earth sectioned by tire tracks extending from the highway to a cleared area in front of the woods. Some of the tire tracks were deeper than others, but he didn't know what that signified. A break in the trees marked the beginning of a wide path, probably the one Alex had emerged from that afternoon. Rebecca and Franny must know about it. They might have followed it into the woods and then got lost when the sun set. They could be a hundred feet away and not know how close they were to home. He shouted their names through cupped hands and waited for a reply. Nothing.

The moon had risen, fat, milky, and neutral, turning the bare ground a faintly glowing silver, like a fish's belly. The forest towered higher with every few steps, pulling him into its wake like a ship passing silently in the moonlight, and when the wind picked up, the rustling treetops became the silhouettes of rats running along the decks.

He slapped his hand over his eyes. He could not enter the woods. He called Franny's name, giving his full attention to the word. She had to hear him. She had to. She was out there.

The bright kitchen was as unchanged as a photograph. The light bulbs glowed at their appointed levels, the appliances were still off, the dial tone unbroken. Joseph punched in Franny's number and the message started on cue, her voice coming to him from a distant computer server, where it resided with billions of other information bits—corporate banking documents, medical records, video clips of rapists working out their fantasies on young female bodies.

He slammed down the receiver. He would not look at the clock or wait for the phone to ring. His head buzzed. The kitchen was losing its solidity—the wall would disintegrate if he touched it, revealing a hidden alternative reality, ancient and pointless. He ground his palms into his eyes to stop the awful pictures taking form, and the mocking voice started in on him again, laughing at his useless efforts.

He rushed through the sunroom and out the door, catching his foot on the bottom stair and nearly falling into the bushes. There it was again: the rustling noise, accompanied now by a soft crooning—animal, human, he couldn't tell. He shook the branches and heard movement in the lower branches.

"Franny! Is that you?"

He plunged his hand in until he touched something warm and yielding—*Franny*, alive, cooing like an injured bird! He wrapped his fingers around—was it a limb, a finger maybe? The limb shifted its downy flesh as he raised it from the ground, his elbows pushing aside the web of branches. There was a moment of resistance, then the branches erupted with a high shriek. Sharp claws slashed at his hands, raking his nose and cheeks. A rough hand or finger poked him in the eye and he staggered backward, still clutching the small living parcel as it gouged his wrists.

A chicken! He was holding a chicken, thrashing its wings and screeching, its phonetic range hinting at rudimentary language skills. It started to peck at his left hand with the uncanny focus of the lower animal orders, biting the same soft spot between his thumb and index finger, striking and withdrawing its tiny head, black dinosaur eyes unblinking. What could he, a stoned city boy, bring to match such singular purpose? He might as well try to stop the grass growing.

He squeezed the chicken's chest hard with both hands until the head sprang straight up like Jack from his box, the bulging eyes catching little diamonds of light, those soulless black eyes—instinctive, stupid. Why was it safe while Franny was lost out in the dark? Why should it be allowed to live unharmed? Did the world need the eggs that badly? He took hold of its feet and with a running step swung the body into the door frame, riding a rush of release and elation, swinging the body against the hard wood again and again until it went limp. The chicken's head was a bloody mush, and the body seemed to have shrunk to half its former size. He was afraid to drop the corpse—it might hit the ground running, the headless torso zigzagging toward the fire, announcing Joseph's crime.

The vision passed and he threw the body into the dark grass on the front lawn. He wiped his bloody hand on the door frame and decided to check the bushes again, knowing he'd never stop thinking Franny might be in there if he didn't. He reached between the branches, body tensed for a second attack, until his fingers came up against the warm, smooth surface of an egg. He lifted it up to the dim light, marvelling at the perfect shell as if it were the first solid thing he'd touched since Franny went missing, and he carefully wrapped the egg in a handkerchief he found in his jacket pocket, branded with the logo of a Caribbean rum, another media freebie. He put the bundled egg in his pocket and vowed to keep it safe until the girls returned, when he'd place it beneath the warm, feathered belly of a new mother.

When he got back to the fire Jane said they should try Derek's number.

"If he was over with Ruby today, the girls might have walked there. It's an hour's walk."

"What about Derek's cell?" Alex asked.

"I'll try it," Mike said. "He's probably out somewhere on a run."

Liz and Jane rushed off to call Derek's house while Mike texted his cell. This was good. Joseph imagined Franny's return, the desperate hug on her arrival, anger disappearing at the sight of the girls' faces, the exchange of stories. It was madness to tease his imagination like this, but he was weak, his nerves shredded. He checked his fingers for blood. There were flecks under his nails. He'd pulverized the chicken's head.

A few minutes later Jane and Liz returned. Liz had her arm around Jane, whose face was sickeningly white, even gaunt, as if she'd suffered the effects of a three-day flu in the time she was gone.

"We had a scare."

"*I* had a scare," Jane said, grabbing Alex's arm, her earlier anger replaced by shock.

"We went into the house to make the call." Liz did that box-making thing with her hands again. "No one's home at Derek's, but I left a message. Jane was going down the front stairs."

"I stepped in blood!"

"Not human blood. We searched."

Joseph wanted to run away before they said it but it was too late.

"We found a dead chicken."

"Its head was ripped off!" Jane's face in the firelight was demonic—hooded eyes and sunken cheeks, a slit mouth quivering.

Joseph caressed the egg in its handkerchief. It was cool to the touch. He should tell them the truth, that he'd murdered a harmless creature because he couldn't find his daughter, but they'd be angry, and scorn him for acting according to type, mistaking a chicken for a monster.

"The head was just . . . gone," Jane said. "The body wasn't touched. Whatever killed it didn't want to eat it."

"Or it was interrupted."

"You don't know what it was, Liz. Don't say you do." Jane buried her face in her hands. "Oh God. It gets worse. There were three lines *drawn in blood* on the door frame!"

Alex pulled Jane into his arms, agitating her further.

"On the door frame," she said, pulling away. "Three lines the width of a man's finger. Three stripes, like a message, a symbol."

"What kind of sick fuck—"

"It's probably a coincidence," Joseph said, thanking God they couldn't dust for fingerprints. "An animal killed a chicken, and in the struggle blood splashed onto the door frame."

"Three fingers!" Jane spat the words at him.

"You don't know it was fingers. We're all fucked up, so we see patterns." He wasn't getting his point across. "It's like those faces of Jesus that appear on the side of barns. It's just random lichen growth—"

"So Jane *wants* to see blood on a door frame?" The fury was back in Alex's eyes.

"I meant, in our state we're bound to be *predisposed*."

"Something bad's happened. I know it has." Jane spoke with prophetic certainty. Abandoned by her feckless father for a second marriage, left with an embittered, depressive mother who died of cancer when Jane was nineteen, she'd been waiting ever since for the final pillar to fall and bring the sky crashing down on her. *We made it through another day*, she used to whisper to Joseph after sex, lying beside him on his futon in that hot, cramped apartment, reminding him of the daily miracle. Now the long-awaited catastrophe was upon her, and she was no better prepared for having anticipated its arrival.

"God, it was so *blatant*," she said. "And then we heard something in the bushes by the fence."

They couldn't blame *that* on Joseph.

"We heard twigs cracking," Liz said.

A thought began to nudge into Joseph's mind, gently but firmly, like a body pressing against a locked door. Something about the twigs.

"You probably surprised a raccoon," Alex said. "It ran into the bushes."

"What about the message in blood?"

"You don't know—"

"Stop fucking patronizing me, Liz."

"Jane, listen." Alex spoke to her as if she was awakening from an anesthetic. "All we know is that you found a dead chicken and heard a noise in the bushes."

There it was again, the pressure in Joseph's head, the *almost* memory. He stared into the fire, a glowing orange-and-black mound faintly throbbing like the hide of a sleeping tiger. What was he forgetting?

"What are we going to do?" Jane shouted, pulling herself free from Alex's grip. She turned to Joseph. "What are we going to do?"

He moved his lips without speaking, matching her husband's uselessness.

"Call the police," Jane said.

"Hold on a second." Alex nodded slowly, his head making

a strange circular motion, a snake charmer's trick. "There's got to be an explanation."

They'd all seen this in the movies, the rationalist trying to ward off catastrophe with disclaimers:

*This boat has got through worse storms than this.*

*Werewolves are just an old wives' tale.*

*No man can take three shots to the gut and survive.*

"Jane, let's talk this through."

"The girls are *missing*!" she shouted into Alex's face. "You said it when we got back: *The girls are missing.* I believe you now. Happy?"

"What?" He raised his hands as though to freeze her words in the air.

"You wanted me to admit that we're in a fucking *crisis*! Well, it's a crisis! And it's all my fault."

"That's not what I meant."

"So whose fault is it? You're so good at assigning blame."

"We all made mistakes."

"I didn't," Mike said.

"You have to be alive to make a mistake," Alex said.

"God, what are we even doing in this fucking place?" Jane was pressing her fingers into her temples. "In the middle of fucking nowhere!"

Alex's hands grasped at the air as if he were searching for guard rails to hang on to. "You *wanted* to move here."

"*You* wanted to!"

"But we—"

"There was no *we*, Alex. Never! I went along with it. What was I going to say? *You can't get a fucking job in the city now, but we'll be fine . . .*"

She was knocking inches from Alex, every sentence passing through him like a freshly sharpened thresher. Joseph wanted to feel sorry for him—first his daughter rejected the life he tried to build for her in the country, and now his wife was turning on him—but the pity wouldn't come. There was blood in the water. They all smelled it.

"We should call the police," Joseph said.

"The nearest cop shop is twenty miles away."

"What's the matter, Mike? Afraid a visit from the police will tarnish your and Liz's *profile* in the community?" Joseph was crossing a line. It felt good.

"You know that's not it," Liz said, refusing to tolerate another attack on her husband after he'd embraced the safe role handed to him by the crisis. "It's too early for the cops to treat this as a missing persons case."

"It's *dark*!" Jane said.

"It's barely past eleven o'clock."

"Okay, *don't* call the cops. Let's just wait until whatever's happened to our daughters is over. Good plan, Joseph?"

"We have to do something," he agreed.

"Hear that, Alex? We have to *do* something! You're always saying, *Why doesn't anybody* do *anything*?"

"Look, even if we do call them—" Alex began.

"Don't *if* me. Call the police!" Jane nearly tripped into the fire. She recovered and held on to Joseph's arm.

"Okay," Alex said. "But it'll be at least a half-hour before they get here."

A knot popped in the fire, the embers cooling into ash and freckling Jane's tight, pale face. Joseph reached out and brushed the ash away with his thumb, leaving a grey trail against her cheek, before she pushed away his hand as if to say, *Don't touch me in front of these people, not so soon after . . .*

A memory loosened deep in his mind, so close to consciousness he could see its outline. He saw trees. Shadow. The fire popped again, a loud snapping noise that riveted Jane's body into a fight-or-flight stance. He almost had it, what he so badly needed to remember. Trees. Shadow. A twig snapping.

Joseph remembered, and he wished he hadn't: he and Jane lying naked in the clearing. They hear a twig snapping. Jane sits up and peers out toward the pasture, still faintly lit by the sunset. She sees something move, a shadow or a silhouette. Her body tenses.

He couldn't take the scene any further. He'd been looking at Jane when the twig broke, and he had as much chance now of seeing what she'd seen as a bug fossilized in amber did of turning its head.

It didn't matter. He knew. Jane had seen the blur of Franny and Rebecca running away from the clearing after snapping the branch. The supporting details rushed into place: the girls had followed the stoned adults into the fields, keeping just out of sight as they cracked jokes about the adults' stumbling progress. But then somebody's daddy went into the bushes with somebody's mommy and what was *that* about? The girls walked to the edge of the clearing, and what did they see but Jane and Joseph fucking on the ground. Where could the girls go after they fled the scene? Back to the house to wait for Jane and Joseph to return and pretend nothing had happened? No, they needed a safe place to talk, so they walked until they found a path to follow into the woods. The story scanned.

Liz was guiding everyone through a compromise plan to search the road and *then* call the police. Jane listened, shaking her head "no" at every point and ignoring Alex and Mike when they repeated the plan like a pair of disaster-relief workers. It was all pointless. The forest was a black strip beneath the dark sky, and behind the wall of trees Franny was afraid, in shock, unable to find her way out.

"Call the police or I will," Jane said.

Joseph studied her stricken face. She didn't remember seeing the girls, not consciously, but her *mind* knew—how else to explain that pucker of flesh on her forehead, as though an invisible finger was pressing there with force?

"Did you guys see anyone following us?" he asked. "When we were out walking." Everyone but Julian and Amber frowned at him. "Well, did you?"

They wanted to know: *Why this question, why* now?

"Are you sure you didn't see anyone?" He couldn't help but direct the question to Jane. "Did you see anything?" he asked Julian and Amber. "The girls might have followed us. They wouldn't want to be seen—they wanted to, you know, sneak up on us."

Julian nodded. It was possible.

"Why would the girls follow *you*?" Alex said, so angry his bottom lip quivered.

"I don't know. Why would they go for a walk on the road? It's just as likely they decided to follow the old folks for a laugh." He had to monitor his tongue here. The urge to confess was strong. "Maybe they followed us and then got bored and went for walk in the woods. It was still light out."

No one knew what to say. Did he sound too sure of himself? Only Jane stood near him, her face turned down toward the fire, their proximity like the mark of Cain on their foreheads.

"Jane, did *you* see anyone? Can you remember if you did?"

"Why?" Why was he picking on *her*?

"You and I walked a little behind everyone else," he said, pushing her through a plausible version of events. "*I* didn't see anyone, but my eyes aren't that good."

He tried to bore words into Jane's eyes: *You heard the twig snap. You saw shadows move.*

"You said you saw movement, near the trees. You thought it was a coyote."

*Just tell them you saw something. We have to give them a reason to search the woods.*

"When everyone else was up ahead looking at the sunset."

*You're the best liar I've ever met. You can talk your way out of anything.*

"You said it was probably nothing."

*Do I have to make up the whole fucking story for you?*

"Jane, do you remember?" He was trying to sound like Liz and Alex—firm, focused, patient—but there was a squeak in his voice.

She was still staring at the fire, but she seemed to stand straighter, as if a surge were moving up her spine. "You don't think . . ."

"When we *stopped*!" He was almost shouting. "We were near the woods and you saw something." He was too deep into the story, the roles too established, to suddenly remember that *he* might have seen the girls following them.

"Joseph, I don't think she saw anything." Liz, being helpful.

"If you saw anything—*anything*."

*Just say you saw a shadow. I'll take the story from there.*

Jane was bending toward the fire.

"Think!"

*Our girls are lost in the woods.*

Jane knelt on the stones and released an almost-languid sigh that might have come from deep within the fire. She touched a smoking log to test its heat. She was composing her story. She would roll the log back into the fire, then stand up and tell them, *Yes, I did see something moving near the treeline.* She hadn't thought about it at the time, but it was probably the girls, and yes, they might have detoured into the woods. *We should start searching there right now.*

Jane stood up holding the log, which was honeycombed into glowing orange cells at the far end, her eyes still locked on the fire. He followed her gaze, trying to find what had fixated her. He didn't see the log coming until it was too late to stop it.

When Joseph came to he couldn't remember the words she'd howled at him before the log struck his head. She'd set her mark upon him—a bloody lump behind his ear—and now the log lay on the ground, still smoking with righteous anger. And there was a terrible noise. Jane screaming. Liz was holding her by the waist, and Alex by her shoulders. Joseph sat up, the band of pain shifting in his head like a heavy box.

"Why did you come here?" Jane screamed at him. "Why didn't you leave us alone?"

She was right. This was all his fault. She started to say more but her face collapsed and she screamed again, a high, heaving shriek that seemed to freeze the fire, hush the crickets, and still the breeze. Her eyes grew so wide they would have swallowed Joseph if she hadn't collapsed into Alex's arms and started weeping, a wailing moan from ancient days when women keened over the bodies of fallen sons and husbands.

"Oh God, oh God, oh God," Joseph mumbled. The pain

clamped his head even tighter as he tried to think about how to fix this. He struggled to his knees, a sob expanding in his lungs that a cough could knock loose. He choked it down. Not now. No tears for him. He stood up, his brain encased in a second, heavier skull. His friends turned to look at him, amazed to see him standing. He felt a wave of nostalgia for their concern, as if it were already deep in the past. He was alone in this. He knew what he had to do.

"I'm going to search the woods for the girls," he said. He nodded, the pain and dizziness almost tipping him backward. "I think the girls followed us to the pasture and then went into the woods. It got dark, and now they're lost. I'm going to take that path near the highway."

Alex lifted his head from the tangle of Jane's splayed hair, his mouth pinched shut like a scar. His eyes locked on Joseph, but he was also seeing through him, or into him. The intimacy was unnerving. It made the iron wall of pain in Joseph's skull hum.

"I'm going with you," Alex said, finally breaking the connection.

"I'm going alone."

"You won't last twenty minutes in there. You don't know your way around."

Alex did know the woods. He was resourceful, strong, even-keeled. Joseph nodded. He needed him. Alex was already doing an inventory of the available cell phones. Mike and Liz had theirs. Alex and Amber had freed themselves from cell phone plans, and Jane had given up hers to save money. Julian's phone was out of batteries, and Liz's was close to it.

"Mike, give Joseph your iPhone," Alex said, taking charge of the operation. "Take Liz's cell and drive to Derek's place to see if the girls are there. If no one's home, check the highway alongside the woods. If you see *anything*, call your cell, which we'll take with us. Liz, you call the police from the land line and wait here with Jane. Julian, you and Amber keep searching near the farm."

People were moving, performing the tasks assigned to them by Alex with a new sense of purpose. Joseph wasn't ashamed to admit he was relieved. Alex rushed over to him and guided them away from the fire, Joseph's legs still feeling slightly foreign, as if they'd been transplanted from another body while he was knocked out.

"I saw someone standing in the trees earlier," Alex said. "A man, in khaki."

"A soldier?"

"A little quieter, please. He was wearing old army pants and shirt, at the edge of the woods, just after we smoked the first joint."

"Why didn't you say something?"

"You guys would have made it into a joke."

"I would have locked the girls in a bedroom." *Maybe.*

"It's not unusual to see people near the woods."

"I thought I saw movement in the trees," Joseph said, remembering his stoned ruminations by the fire.

"You probably did. One of the main paths exits at our property line, near the road."

"I was there!"

"Exactly. The forest is full of paths. People get up to all kinds of stuff." Alex leaned closer. "I've seen a couple of guys on my walks—too young for Nam or the first Gulf War."

"In *those* woods?" He glanced over at Mike.

"Mike lives in town," Alex said. "Those trees could be stage scenery and he wouldn't know the difference." He pressed Joseph's shoulder. "I didn't like the look of the guy I saw tonight. His eyes weren't right. Reminded me of a couple of my officers who were in combat and never really came back. I need you to keep your head. The others would freak if they heard this."

"Franny doesn't talk to men she doesn't know." A post-traumatic stress disorder victim in khaki wouldn't get within twenty feet of her, and if he did, she was a fast runner.

"That might not be the problem."

Joseph started to blubber something.

"Listen," Alex ordered. "If we leave now we can still catch up to them."

Franny in the woods with a crazed war vet—could it get any worse?

"We have to be prepared," Alex said.

"The gun! Bring the gun!" Joseph didn't want it to have to come to this—not a gun for God's sake—but it *had* come to this. There was always going to be a gun.

"There's nothing we can do here," Alex told Julian and Mike, who'd walked up to them. "If the girls are lost in the woods, anything can happen—quickly."

"I'll go with you," Julian said.

"No. I need you to keep searching near the farm. And to be here when the cops arrive."

None of them said it, but they wanted a man to stay behind and guard the place. Julian nodded, the selfless obedience coming naturally to him. Joseph was moved, but he didn't want to start finding the good in people. God no. He and Alex were going to find the girls before anyone hurt them.

Mike handed over his iPhone. Joseph almost asked him why he'd switched from BlackBerry, the need for banal conversation still so deep. He reached into his pocket. The egg had survived the fall. It was a good sign.

"There's not much battery time left," Mike said.

"We'll be out of range a few hundred yards in," Alex said. "But it can't hurt."

Mike gave Joseph his passcode and mumbled generic good wishes, unable to summon a working persona for such a profound crisis, then half-ran to his car.

"I'm going to get my rifle," Alex told Julian. "If we're out of phone range and we find the girls, I'll fire a shot. If you hear it, call off the search. Two shots means we need help, but it won't come to that." He ran toward his shed to get the gun.

"Your head . . ." Julian said.

"It's fine." Joseph touched the lump. It was kidney-shaped and raw and it gave off heat.

"Shit, man."

"I know. I know."

An engine started. Mike's car crawled up the driveway as Liz and Amber helped Jane into the house. The world was spinning too fast—he'd see light streaks trailing the stars soon. When did the night slip from his grasp and go hurtling down a slope? In the clearing with Jane? When they smoked the joint? At dinner? He could trace it back further if he tried, back to his betrayal of Martha and

Franny. He touched the egg in his pocket, then the lump behind his ear, but he couldn't connect them to what was happening. He'd lost Franny when he wasn't looking.

Alex returned with the rifle and two flashlights, the smaller of which he handed to Joseph. He stepped close to Julian. "Listen, don't tell anybody, but we think we saw someone hanging out at the edge of the woods earlier."

"What?" Julian looked at Joseph and recoiled when he nodded in assent. "Who?"

"It doesn't matter," Alex said. "One or two guys in khaki. But we're not taking any chances."

"Wait!" An idea had finally crossed the moat of pain in Joseph's head. "What about the dogs? They can track Rebecca."

"They don't remember the smell of their dinner," Alex said, but Julian was already running toward the dogs, who were sitting in the light from the back porch, ears perked, tongues folded into their mouths like bills in a wallet. Alex followed Julian, picking up a sandal from the mat beside the sliding doors and presenting it to the dogs. As he unleashed them, Alex spoke softly into Lady's ear, then Tyler's.

Julian took the other sandal and waved it in front of the dogs. "Hey boy! Where's Rebecca? Hey girl! Go find Rebecca!"

Lady paced the porch, some Law of Boundaries preventing her from breaking routine, but that didn't stop Tyler from taking off and jumping the back fence. The three men gathered, leaning against the fence's top board, and watched the husky cut diagonally across the field toward the forest, stopping every few seconds to pick up Rebecca's scent from a teeming reef of night odours.

"I think I know where he's going," Alex said. "There's a path into the woods, where the second pasture begins."

Alex jumped the fence and started to run, but Julian stopped Joseph from following. Julian's face and posture exuded frustration, even agitation. He shook his head but got no closer to what needed saying.

"I don't know, man. Something's not right."

Joseph nodded, despite having no idea what he was talking about.

"Be careful," Julian said. He reached into a side pocket of his baggy pants and took out a small knife in a moulded plastic sheath. He slid the knife free and held it up. The short blade was almost triangular, with a serrated section running along the top like a ridge of fish spines evolved to shred the mouth of an attacker. The bottom edge was almost as thin as a razor.

"Keep it to yourself. Only take it out if you need it." Julian paused for a few, long seconds, driving home his point. "I don't know, man. Just be careful."

"I will," Joseph said, pocketing the knife.

Julian put his hands on Joseph's shoulders. "You're in a dark place, brother."

"I know." Thank God someone had finally said it.

"I've been there. I saw some things, and I had to fight for them not to change me—essentially . . . *inside*."

Joseph thought he understood. "You're a good man, Julian." It was important to say it.

"I'm just one of those sad clowns, brother. You're a dad."

"Am I?"

"Of course you are. That counts for a lot. Remember that." Julian gave a big smile that wrinkled all the worn places on his face and he hugged Joseph, patting him on the shoulder blades. For thousands of years men had said goodbye like this, linking in a last embrace before the chosen one set out to prove himself in the hunt or on the battlefield. The trick was to let go before you chickened out, and even here Julian helped out, letting go first.

Joseph turned and put his foot on the fence's middle board. The last time he climbed over to the field, Jane had been waiting for him on the other side to take his hand. He'd made a joke about falling. He couldn't remember it now.

MEN

Joseph and Alex watched Tyler pacing in front of the woods, his oversized dog smile like a dollop of pink clown makeup slapped on dull grey fur. What had he found? Joseph squinted to bring the trees into focus, but they only blended into suggestive shapes—unlit houses, low buildings, and alleyways, peaked rooftops against the navy blue sky, their occupants long gone to escape the marauding armies of bandits and rapists and pillagers. These things happened all the time—towns and villages fell off the map and out of memory. The moonlit pasture was no better, offering the stock scenery of a nightmare—the boulder not quite hiding the mangled body, the sapling revealing itself as an animated skeleton. Any moment a coyote would emerge from the woods, its jaws clamped around a dead baby with a monkey's face.

Alex cradled the gun in his arms and watched Tyler pace, oblivious to the dog's excited whimpers. What was Tyler so excited about? Had he followed Rebecca's footsteps back to the same clearing where Joseph had fucked Jane? How was Joseph going to explain that one?

"There's a narrow path there," Alex said, pointing to where the dog was waiting.

"It makes sense the girls went in there." Joseph noted a tinny edge to his voice that any good interrogator would catch. "We went further into the pasture."

"How far did you go?" Alex's cheeks and forehead seemed to gather the milky light, throwing his eyes and mouth into shadow. It was like staring at a second moon.

"Probably another hundred yards, up to that rise, to watch the sunset." Joseph screened himself for confessional intent. "We were really high."

"I didn't ask that."

He looked away from Alex's terrifying face. The grass seemed to brighten, and he raised his eyes to catch the last ribbons of a long, fish-shaped cloud as it passed over the moon and deposited the orb behind it like a shining egg. He was pretty sure they were nowhere near the clearing. He'd be spared one horror this evening.

"Go on boy!" Alex shouted, his commanding tone bringing Tyler's keen animal senses to a joyful focus. The dog ran straight at the trees and dived in, his tail and hind legs vanishing in a faint silver flash.

"Don't use up the flashlight batteries unless you have to," Alex said. "We don't know how long we'll be."

Joseph followed Alex until they were a few yards from the trees, then stopped to watch Alex part a wedge of leaves like a stage curtain and step into the forest.

They were really doing this. Two girls were missing. Their fathers were searching the wilderness for them. These things *happened*. You read about these personal catastrophes, relieved that *your* kid wasn't missing, but also secretly disappointed to have missed out on the experience, because how often in this bloodless age do you get the chance to test your mettle against the elements, against the bad guys? You imagine what you'd do in the parents' situation, how you'd act with courage, sacrifice, and resolve right up until the final scene, when your dirt-streaked child jumps into your arms, crying, "Daddy, you found me!"

Alex was calling from inside the woods—a real voice issuing a real summons. Joseph took a last peek at the pasture beneath the moon, feeling like an intruder on the beautiful scene. He wasn't a bad man. He'd always meant well. That had to count for something.

He followed the path for a few minutes before stopping to adjust to the darkness, which was leaking into his peripheral vision like black smoke. He closed his eyes. The forest gave off a faint background noise, a pulse without bass that he could almost see against the deep velvet curtain of his eyelids. Other sounds appeared, each with its own shape and motion—the ruffle of an owl's wings, like a magazine flapping open in the wind, and the breeze in the treetops like a stream frothing over stones. With his eyes still closed he took a few steps forward, his arms stretched out, hands open, nerves and ears straining to detect the particular sound-shape of a tree in front of him before he reached it. He walked on, sensing a block-like structure beyond his outstretched fingertips, and when he opened his eyes he was standing before a tree. He hadn't cheated—he'd *sensed* the tree with his eyes closed. If Franny was near he should pick up her presence like seeing a plane on a radar screen. Why not? Who better to sense her body's unique frequencies than her father? Atoms can communicate across time and space, the scientists and mystics agreed, so wherever Franny was now, his atoms need only contact hers and close the space between them, reeling in the miles like fishing line.

He closed his eyes again. The trick was to get past the feeling that every blind step would drop him on his face. He could do this. The powers he was tapping into could not perform under the bright lights of rational analysis, but there were historical precedents. The mother who "miraculously" lifted a city bus off her child's pinned body. The cop who calmly stepped out of the way of a bullet after time slowed to millisecond increments. He had Love working on his side, and Love moves mountains, makes the broken man whole. Finding Franny should be a minute's work for Love.

He should have sensed the rock—it was the size of an ottoman. His scraped shin made its own inner noise as he came down hard on his hands. He got up and moved down the path, eyes still shut, sensing some obstacles before contact but missing too many others. He just had to open up and *feel* for Franny's presence. When his hand scraped against a ragged tree trunk he stopped, desperate to sense any vibrations in the air. There was nothing. No vibrations. No sound-shapes. No magic.

How could he not know where his daughter was? A father should know—*always*. How terrible to learn that his love for Franny was confined to the limits of his five senses.

Shouldn't some higher function be kicking in here, sixth and seventh senses that pierced the limits of time and space? Why endow humans with such a deep capacity to love their children when it was so easy to lose them? How did this serve God or Nature's plan?

"Who caught her when she fell?" he shouted.

*He* had. She was three years old, climbing the ladder to the top of the tube slide for the first time, and when she fell he was there.

"Franny!"

The forest muffled his voice to a polite, dinner-party level. He tried to project his voice further down the path, but it was like shouting into a tunnel lined with cinder blocks. He walked with his eyes open. No more magic. He had to catch up to Alex. They had a plan. Follow Tyler, who was on to Rebecca's scent. Watch out for any strange men. Preserve the batteries.

"Alex and I went into the woods to look for the girls." He was talking out loud to an imaginary companion, a forty-something professional in a beige jacket and expensive jeans, face tilted forward in concern. "I was starting to panic a little."

The man understood—he was a father, he would have felt *exactly* the same way.

"It was terrifying, actually."

"Of course," the man said. "But did you *know*, deep in your heart, that you weren't going to find her?"

"What are you talking about?"

"Franny: did you know she was gone, forever? You must have—a father *knows*."

"Shut up!"

The man vanished. Joseph ran deeper into the forest.

How had he lost Alex so quickly? Joseph was pinned in place by this impenetrable bush. He tried to squint the dark into recognizable shapes but it was like trying to mould water with his hands. He passed his hand before his face, and when it did not stir the liquid blackness he had to assure himself that his hand had not disappeared. He was sunk in a darkness without surfaces, or a darkness *made* of surfaces—all depth or depthless, he didn't know which.

It wouldn't have been this bad for the girls. Guided by the fading sunlight to the big path, they'd be walking between the trees now, the moonlight showing them the way forward. What did Alex say earlier? Head east, north, or south and you'll hit a road eventually. Rebecca would know that.

Joseph just had to find his way back to the path, but he felt trapped inside a giant pair of dry lungs holding in a stale breath—he didn't want to be around when they exhaled. How could anything survive in here? Even mosquitoes must need wider flight paths. He lashed out at the nearest branches, scratching his hands as the blackness settled back into place.

Stupid—he was *so* stupid. He'd been given a simple task: take Franny to the country for the long weekend. Feed and house her. Do not send her weeping into the wilderness, where she could die of exposure. Martha had pulled it off dozens of times, but he couldn't make it to Day Two.

He had to calm down. The path couldn't be far away. He chose a direction and pushed through the foliage, the close humid air parting and closing behind him like a tent flap, the lump behind his ear throbbing again. He called Alex's name but the bush swallowed his words. Of course it did—nothing yielded to him in this place. He stepped wildly from left to right, flailing at the leaves and branches, his uselessness on display in an entirely new environment. What was the point of this goddamned *bush*, crusting the land like non-aquatic coral? Franny could pass twenty feet from him and he wouldn't hear her cries for help.

He should turn on the flashlight, but if he drained the batteries this early Alex might send him back to the house in disgrace. Typical—kicked off his daughter's rescue team after twenty minutes.

He had it: Mike's iPhone! It would make do as a flashlight. There wasn't much battery time left, but they'd be out of range soon anyway. He took the phone from his pocket, punched in the passcode, and tried to choose the app that would throw off the most light. There were several video games—no surprise there—but his eyes were drawn to the phone icon. He brought up the dial pad, illuminating in black and white an area the size of a phone booth, the digital light making the swaths of vegetation look like blurry security footage. No direction appeared more promising than any other, though he was standing on a mild slope. Sweeping the phone around, he saw that he'd walked into a furrow even more overgrown than the woods, his feet typically having followed the path of least resistance downward. As he brought the light closer to the ground, he caught the flash from the twin reflective stripes on his un-scuffed hiking shoes, which he'd bought from an outdoor-equipment store equipped with a rock-climbing wall. God only knew what attempt at self-improvement had driven him there. He vowed to burn the shoes after he found Franny.

Joseph walked up the incline, the bubble of light leading him back to the narrow path, where he turned right and started jogging to make up lost time, to prove to himself that he could solve a problem without panicking. He heard Tyler's distant barking and followed the sound until he came up against a wall of branches, which he pushed through, stepping out onto the big path Alex had promised. It cut through the forest like a road, wide enough for four people to walk abreast. Above him, patches of sky were powdered with stars, and as his eyes adjusted to a light with no visible source he distinguished the outlines of trees, boulders, and bushes bunched on either side of the path like stone border-fences. Tufts of grass mottled the path, but the sandy surface drew the moonlight to the forest floor like a mist, illuminating the way between tracts of unimaginably dense wilderness.

Franny must have passed this same way less than two hours ago, the forest pressing in on her from both sides, as if she were skirting the base of two cliffs.

He'd fucked up again, worse than ever this time, but even a condemned man was entitled to a last call. Mike's iPhone informed him he was still within call range. A good man would phone Martha and apologize for everything he'd done wrong, but he didn't have the heart for that. He wanted to hear the voice of an infatuated lover, a woman who still believed in him enough to tell him not to blame himself too much, to stay on the path and keep his head up until he found Franny, which he would—of course he would! She couldn't have gone far.

But there was no one to call. No lover or lifelong friend to ease his journey. What could anyone he knew back in the city understand about his plight? He'd passed beyond the range of their experience hours ago, and he might have so much further to go.

The phone rang, the rock anthem's tinny synth chords so incongruent against his surroundings that he experienced them as a supernatural visitation, like a Paleolithic hunter confronted by a freight train. Then awe gave way to a desire to punch Mike for downloading such an irony-drenched song riff as a ringtone. The phone sounded again. Someone might be calling to say they'd found the girls.

He finally found the right icon and said hello.

"What's with the whisper, Mike? You doing lines on the back of the toilet again? *Hey, Liz!*" The caller made an extended snorting noise. "*Just having a pee.*" More snuffling. "*Be out in a minute.*"

It was a man of their demographic—eager for a laugh.

"Who is this?"

"Who is *this*?"

Joseph held the phone away as if it were a leech he'd peeled from his cheek.

"Dude, what's up?"

"*Dude*?" Joseph slapped the phone back in place. "How old are you?"

"Mike?"

"Seriously!" A vital truth was at stake here. "How fucking old are you?"

"Old enough to kick your ass."

"I'll cut your foot off!"

The guy was laughing. "You a buddy of Mike's? Hand him the phone, man."

"You're going to die one day! Think about it." He had nothing worse to say. He was about to throw the iPhone into the bush when he noticed the message icon was illuminated. Would Mike really update them by text? Did he bear that deep a grudge against him and Alex for all the teasing and put-downs over the years? Theirs was a passive-aggressive generation—you never knew how deep a grudge a friend bore you.

The first text was from *dingleberry71*, probably the same handle the sender used for his Gmail and Twitter accounts. Not "Jacob, son of Zacharia" or "Ulrick the Manslayer" but the seventy-first grown man to stake his claim in the digital world as "dingleberry." It said he'd be at Derek's place for the rehearsal next week. He wrote in lower case and called Mike "bro."

There was a second message—a text—from Derek, sent at 2:37 that afternoon, about an hour before he'd visited the farmhouse: *Swinging by soon. Will get info tonite on yr piece. The PieMan*. Piece of what? Joseph stared at the screen, awaiting the Magic 8 Ball message to swim up from the depths. Why had Derek come by Alex's that afternoon, knowing he'd piss him off by making a dope deal on his property? Mike could have just as easily picked up from Derek's place. Had Derek wanted to talk to Mike, or to

Alex? Joseph returned to the phone's app menu. The bright, ergonomic boxes were useless to him here, and for the first time in years he was about to step out of call range.

He started to walk. The path's faintly glowing surface revealed a slight curve that veered deeper into the wilderness. Soon a shadow moved up ahead and stopped. Joseph had lost his glasses over a year ago but hadn't bothered to replace them—who needed long-distance vision when the important things in the city happened within three feet of your face? He called Alex's name and got a sharp *shush* in return. Alex was a pale smudge against the trees ten feet away, crouched low to the ground. Joseph walked as quietly as he could and stood beside Alex, following his sight line into the dark woods. The forest emitted a faint rustling of restless life stirred by the breeze. Alex stood up, the rifle held across his chest, his dim face pondering Joseph's.

"Where were you?" he said.

Joseph flushed with shame before he understood what Alex was asking. "I got lost in the bush. Wandered off the path."

Tyler barked from inside the bush, and they heard him running toward the path.

"Did he find something?" Joseph asked.

"I doubt it."

The dog stepped out from the trees, stopping long enough for Alex to pat him on the head before he rushed down the path. They were catching up to him just as he shot back into the woods, his barks growing more frantic as he hurtled through the undergrowth. Alex turned on the big flashlight, a canopy of brightly lit branches spreading over their heads like the ceiling of a suddenly inflated pup tent, the light stabbing at Joseph's eyes. Alex pointed the flashlight into the forest, sending shadows cartwheeling across the illuminated trees, the illusion of movement drawing Joseph off the path. They heard branches snapping beyond the light's range, and deep, aggressive barking that sounded like a warning.

"What is it? Has he found the girls?"

Alex shushed him and turned off the flashlight, pulling the night back over them. Bright yellow after-images danced against the flat darkness, but slowly the outlines of trees and rocks appeared, then the path itself, materializing beneath them like a school of tiny fish drawn to the surface by the moonlight. They heard rustling and high-pitched dog noises. Tyler was closer now. Alex stepped into the forest, leaving one foot on the path. Joseph could barely see anything. Why didn't Alex switch on the light? A low, threatening snarl moved toward them, slowly at first, then Tyler was crashing through the woods at desperate speed, a train of high canine yelps in pursuit.

"The coyotes!" Alex shouted. He handed Joseph the big flashlight. "Point it into the forest."

Joseph gripped it with sweaty hands as Alex pumped a shell into the rifle's chamber. *The gun*—already the gun, loaded and cocked.

"Stand back!" Alex swept Joseph behind him with an arm as firm as a closing door.

Joseph took another step back, pointing the swerving light beam at the trees to the left of Alex's back. A wave of yelping shrieks rushed at them, the sound pitching him onto his ass and sending the flashlight flying into a rut in the path—the light slanting up into the air like the search beam of a half-sunk boat. The ancient instinct to run rippled up his legs, commanding him to leave this place.

"Point the flashlight!"

Joseph couldn't do it—he *wouldn't* do it. He was safe on the ground, his fingers digging into the sandy path—he'd dig his way to China if that was the only way out.

"Point the fucking flashlight!"

He rolled over, grabbed the light, and aimed it at Alex.

"Joseph, get up!"

Alex raised the rifle, his body poised for a kill shot into the forest's massive, impersonal depths, the black barrel merging with the shadows beyond the path—he could have been a shaman raising a staff against intruders from the spirit world. A desperate shriek sounded in the woods. Tyler and the pack swerved to the left, thrashing through the undergrowth, the dog's phlegmy growling answered by jibbering barks like laughter. Alex waved the rifle at the trees as if he could flush out a target, then looked down at Joseph as though he were an obscene stain on the ground. He was about to speak, but instead he picked up the flashlight and ran into the forest, a mini-lightning storm marking his course between the trees.

Joseph couldn't get up. He stared into the black woods and pressed the swelling behind his ear, making the world bend and keen like a tune played on a saw blade. He had to find Franny, and to find her he had to catch up with Alex. He got to his feet and turned on the smaller flashlight, its soft yellow beam seeming out of place, as if he'd turned on his bedside lamp to find himself in the wilderness. He stepped off the path, following the yellow beam like a golden thread as it led him between the trees and deeper into the forest. Soon the trees thinned out enough for him to risk jogging. The coyotes yapped in the distance, and Alex's flashlight sparkled far ahead and then disappeared. Joseph pushed his body, ordering it through the forest, dodging the brightly lit trees that tumbled out of the night like blocks of scenery falling from the back of a moving truck. He jumped over a boulder and went careening into a thicket of saplings, their springy trunks rebounding him back to his feet. The beam of Alex's flashlight showed in the distance again, and soon the chase took them up an eroded hill face, tree roots protruding from the ground like the ribs of a whale, patches of exposed rock trying to sweep his feet out from under him. The pounding in Joseph's head had started again, and when he reached level ground he stopped to rest his spasm-riddled legs and to drag air into his lungs. How did he get so out of shape? Did he really think he'd never have to put his body to use for anything but fifteen-minute city walks and twenty-minute fucks?

Once he was able to stand straight, he saw Alex about a hundred feet away. He was in front of a cluster of tall evergreens, the flashlight hanging at his side, throwing a skirt of light around his legs.

"They chased him into that grove," he said, pointing the light down one of the even rows of trees, likely the legacy of a reforestation scheme. Alex strutted into the trees expecting to be followed, the flashlight's beam bouncing ahead of him like a hound on a long leash.

How far off course had they gone? Joseph didn't want to ask, didn't want to consider why they'd left the path the girls were following to chase Tyler through the bush. It was not the time to second-guess Alex. He was a former soldier. He'd been trained to read maps, assess dangerous situations, survive behind enemy lines. If he said that Tyler offered their best chance of finding the girls, he must be right. Tyler was a dog. He would track Rebecca through any peril if his master so commanded.

*Master*—there was a comforting word! Joseph could use a master right now, someone to unburden him of his autonomy and put him in the service of finding Franny. Never mind the price at night's end.

He stepped into the grove and followed Alex, the air quickly closing in on him, the treetops swaying in the steady breeze that did not reach his face. Soon a silhouette appeared in front of him. Alex had turned off his flashlight and was straining to hear something. The grove was quiet, save for the blood racing to Joseph's head. The sharp scent of tree resin collected in the back of his throat like a paste, making him want to spit.

A shrill canine howl erupted not far away, answered by that bloody, gleeful yapping. The fear seemed to follow a cable up Joseph's legs into his bowels, raising every hair on his body. He started backing up, but Alex stood his ground.

"They're killing him," Alex said. "Let them know we're here!" He started shouting—"Fuckers! You fucking assholes!"—in a savage military bark and ran toward Tyler's howling, hurling his invective into the dark.

Joseph turned on his flashlight and followed, shouting the familiar schoolyard sex words, wishing he had a store of more blasphemous language to hurl at the coyotes. The ground was sloping, and as he raced between the trees the downward momentum tugged at his legs, dangerously stretching his stride. Alex let out a volley of Finnish before careening into the lower boughs of a massive blue fir tree that had escaped the loggers' saws. Joseph tried to stop but only slowed enough to take a running leap over Alex into the branches. Tyler was shrieking, or maybe it was one of the coyotes. The sound wrenched the hope from Joseph like a bone from its socket. The two men rolled from side to side, trying to gain purchase in the springy branches, Alex refusing to let go of the rifle or the flashlight, as if a point of pride was at stake. Eventually, he got to his feet. Joseph couldn't see his face, but Alex's sagging shoulders and the lowered rifle told him there was no point in hurrying. Alex stared down at the flashlight in his hand as though it were a baton with no runner to pass it to. Joseph stood up, trying to fight a fresh rush of panic.

"Alex, we've got to find Tyler."

Alex started walking. "It's too late."

They emerged into a large clearing and edged forward, sweeping their flashlights in wide arcs, illuminating old tree stumps and patches of chest-high evergreens. Ahead of them, a swarm of fireflies glowed and faded, clustering around a high, solid block, its outlines barely visible in the moonlight. Alex let out a soft grunt. This wasn't good. As the men drew closer, the block slowly revealed itself, first as a black slab at least fifteen feet tall, then its true form: a massive tree trunk scarred by shredded bark and burrow holes, piles of fallen branches forming a jagged ring around its base. Alex moved his flashlight beam up the trunk to the tree's crotch, which had been blasted by a lightning bolt that shattered the rack of branches, cleaving the charred boughs like the halves of a 3-D Rorschach blot. What power had visited this place? Joseph imagined a giant axe smashing through the branches to split the tree, the mangled stump left standing to warn interlopers, and his mind connected the image to earlier that day, when Alex had split the damp log with a single blow of his axe. A feeling of violence frozen in time permeated the atmosphere, a crystallized catastrophe, and he smelled copper and an under-odour of shit.

The beams of their flashlights played over the tangled, leafless branches until they converged on a patch of dark liquid beside a small mound. Joseph looked away before his eyes could process the details. Not Alex. He staggered toward the mound and fell to his knees, letting out a low groan. Joseph took a deep breath. He had to see for himself. A dog-sized body lay crumpled in front of Alex, who nodded his head with eerie regularity, reconfirming the same brute fact: the coyotes had completely gutted Tyler, strewing his intestines as far as the organs' length allowed. The husky's head was wedged against one of the knobby tree roots, his eyes locked on the bright stars, mouth lolling. Worst of all was Alex's face—he was devastated but also confused, as if he couldn't place this slaughter within a believable storyline. Tyler might as well have been torn apart by a werewolf.

What was the proper reaction to this? Joseph didn't know, so he followed the trail of blood splatters away from the scene. So much blood. They say blood is actually blue, that oxygen in the air makes it red, but he didn't believe it—why didn't your cheeks blush blue? He pondered this riddle, trying to block out Alex's hiccuping sobs. A man loses his dog and weeps—classic stuff, but why did the sound make Joseph feel even more numb? He had to keep moving. He ran his flashlight over the downed branches, following one contorted bough up and over his head, where it bent into a jagged arc spiked with sharp stumps, like a monstrous tentacle rising from the wreckage.

*Just step away*, he told himself. *Move your legs.* He obeyed the order and stepped onto a yielding mass that sent up a gagging gust of blood and shit. It was another casualty of Tyler's Last Stand, a coyote with its throat torn out. This time Joseph couldn't stop staring. The coyotes had gone for the soft spot below Tyler's ribs; Tyler attacked their faces. The coyote's sensitive black nose was almost entirely chewed off—muscles and tendons showed in places, and a tube protruded from its throat like a pipe clogged with grease, as if someone had frantically torn it apart searching for a misplaced object. Its wide-open eye was almost serene, an expression of submissive wonder imprinted on the filmy lens like a watermark, as though the animal had welcomed death at the end.

Alex came up beside him and pinned the dead coyote under his powerful flashlight beam.

"Fucking cocksucker," he said, in full dialogue with his rage. Joseph envied him. Anything was preferable to the numbness that had scattered his emotions. Alex's flashlight found the hollows and rises in the coyote's body and *it* became *he*—the pack alpha, now shrunk by blood loss and deflated lungs, stripped of whatever essence had made him fierce in life. Alex swept the beam along the corpse, from head to haunch and back again, creating an eerie illusion of bristling movement. He did it again, accelerating until the dead body seemed to flex and ripple like a monster in a stop-motion movie, the coyote re-animated long enough to answer for Tyler's death. He homed in on the coyote's mangled head. There was something brazen, almost pornographic, about the exposed tissue, the molars, and pink gums naked in the light. Alex pushed the rifle barrel against the exposed mouth, forcing the coyote to smile.

"I'm having a great day," he said in a bouncy voice.

Again, Joseph's nerves ordered him to run. He had no words for this.

Alex adjusted the mouth to a curling frown. "I'm having a *baaad* day." He made the coyote smile again—"I'm having a *great* day"—then frown—"I'm having a *baaad* day"—the coyote so earnestly somber, so unaware of the joke that it got funnier with each repetition, until Joseph felt a roll of laughter break through the numbness. It spread to Alex, whose dirty face was lined with tear tracks.

"I'll show you a bad day," Alex said. He prodded the coyote's torn throat with the rifle, making the head loll and the tongue jiggle, then he kicked the coyote so hard its head snapped into an impossible angle. Joseph started to applaud, the same involuntary muscles that had set him laughing now moving his hands to reward Alex's sight-gag. Alex gave the coyote another kick, knocking the head free of its connective socket and extending the neck.

*This is what you get for sticking your nose in*, Joseph thought. *You end up a piece of meat.*

Joseph kicked the coyote's stomach, excited by how deep his shoe penetrated the soft flesh. He brought his foot down and broke the coyote's ribs, the sound of breaking bones so much sharper than in the movies. Alex gave the body a punt that broke one of the front legs, and he kicked the coyote's bottom jaw so hard it completely dislocated, making the battered head look like one of those deep-sea fish, all jaws and teeth and squishy eyes. Alex nudged Joseph aside and stepped into the next kick. It was decisive. The head flew off and vanished in the darkness. They heard it bounce off a rock with a wet slap.

It was over. Joseph walked back to the tree stump and pressed his fingers against the crumbling bark, craving the resistance of a solid object. He could hear Martha asking him how he could have done such a terrible thing to a dead animal. "It was surprisingly easy," he told her. What surprised him was being spared the experience for so long, the dumb luck of making it into his early forties without having mutilated a body—canine or otherwise.

*What glorious times we live in! Our grandchildren should be so lucky.*

*No one made you do it*, Martha said, long immune to his pontificating.

*If I couldn't desecrate that corpse I might as well have run back to the farm. Those are the rules out here.*

*Typical—fucking typical. Hiding behind words again.*

Then she was gone, replaced by an image of Franny. His breath caught and fluttered in his chest like a moth in a spider web. He told himself there was no connection between the mangled coyote and Franny's predicament, but the more primitive part of his mind answered with a stream of terrible images: sharks killing each other in a blood frenzy; a rabbit swallowed by a snake; an animal in a trap chewing off its own leg to escape; drunken soldiers tearing a naked woman limb from limb. This was no good. He was slipping into the deep pit beneath shock. He needed to see a human face.

Alex was wiping his boots on a branch with long, slow strokes, like a barber sharpening his razor. Joseph cleared his throat, then coughed and sniffed, but Alex ignored him, slowly turning away to stand over Tyler's body in blaring silence, the rifle hugged to his chest, the scene missing only a bronze commemorative plaque: *The Hunter Bids Adieu to a Faithful Companion.*

"I tried to give Tyler away last year," he said. "I already miss him."

He rested the rifle against the stump and crouched down, offering a final goodbye. His hand must have brushed the dead dog because he recoiled, the shock sending him scuttling backward, knees bent and arms extended as if he were performing a traditional dance. He regained his balance and held up his blood-coated fingers. His face was lit from below, making craters of his eyes and cheeks. He rubbed his fingers on a branch, scraping the bark until his skin must have burned, and when he stood, the rifle slipped through his hand, the barrel pointing straight up at his head. Joseph winced, awaiting the gunshot and the splat of Alex's brains against the burned tree. It might as well be Joseph's finger on the trigger, Joseph's teeth that had ripped out Tyler's guts. He'd brought all this down on their heads.

"How did it come to this?" Alex said, his voice as denuded as the tree. "You think if you try hard enough . . . and then *this*." He shook his head, holding a defiant posture against the shudders that struck his knees, hips, and shoulders as if they were the blast points of a building demolition. He scanned the bleak clearing, his face quivering with rage and bewildered shock. Was he blaming himself for letting the girls slip away on his watch? Alex believed it was a man's duty to protect his family. Hadn't he done that for Jane and the kids, and even for Martha and Franny, whom he'd included on every nature walk, every fishing trip, as though she was his own child? And what did he get for his sacrifice?

Alex shifted the rifle to get a better grip on the barrel, muttering just loud enough for Joseph to hear: "Can't turn back." He started to lift the gun, his back and shoulders squared, the weapon seeming to weigh hundreds of pounds.

He was going to shoot himself.

"Wait, we'll find the girls!" Joseph said. "We have to stay focused. Keep our heads up." He didn't even know what that last line meant. Probably something he'd heard in a movie. "I just wanted to say . . ."

What he wanted was to finally tell the truth, to get it all

out in the open and hope for clemency. Maybe Alex would shoot him in the foot and call it even, knowing that every footstep would remind Joseph of his act of betrayal. Joseph was okay with that. Just let them find Franny.

"It's just . . ." What could Joseph possibly say? "It's . . ."

"What?"

"Jane is going to be okay."

Alex stepped back as if he'd been punched in the chest.

"I just meant . . ." What *did* Joseph mean? Why bring up Jane *now*? Why of all people *Jane*? "She's a survivor," he said, his tongue a fat, dry snake in his mouth. He saw what he was doing here: offering Alex a moment of intimacy as penance for withholding the truth about the girls' disappearance, as though they were tradable commodities. But to drag Jane's name into it?

Joseph stepped toward Alex, arms outstretched, eyes so fixed on the rifle that he failed to see the gopher hole. His right foot dropped into space and came down hard, buckling at the ankle and throwing him forward at Alex's feet. He lay on the ground, his ankle throbbing from deep inside the joint, shocked at how close he'd just come to giving himself away. This wasn't the time to try to set things right between them. They had to find the girls, and he needed Alex more than Alex needed him.

Joseph waited for a helping hand, but Alex didn't move, his expression hard and assessing, eyes half-hidden beneath a ridge of shadow.

"I can get up," Joseph said, needing to assert his basic usefulness. He stood and tested his injured ankle. The pain was vivid, unnecessarily intensified, as if the joint had been injected with a thick, cool gel that pressed against his bones and tendons, but his foot held. He tried more weight, wishing he had something to support him, then took a tentative step, bargaining with the slow, powerful throb in his ankle.

*Just hold out until we find the girls.*

Alex hoisted the rifle against his shoulder and walked around Joseph, the darkness flowing up and around the blasted tree trunk like ink pumped into a glass chamber.

"We're going back to the big path," Alex said.

Joseph reached into his pocket and ran his fingers over the egg's smooth shell, then took out Mike's iPhone: they'd passed out of signal range, the batteries were almost dead, and there were no new messages. He looked up in time to see Alex step into the bush, pulling the flashlight beam with him as if Joseph didn't deserve his portion of light.

Back on the big path, Alex and Joseph trudged deeper into the woods, Joseph handling flashlight duties, finding no clues, only litter and old ATV tracks, even a bike hanging from a tree, one rusted wheel protruding from the greenery like the fuselage of a crashed plane. They walked up and down low hills, skirting ravines and marshes, thickets of scrub, and patches of old growth, the boundaries of the path repeating like a wallpaper pattern of leaves and branches. Occasionally the pattern varied, evergreens replacing maples and birches, so that to Joseph's tired eyes it was as though they were passing from one narrow, wallpapered corridor to another without ever reaching a proper room. Through it all, his mind replayed reels of shrill interior voices, self-defeating memories, and violent images until they became as monotonous as the passing landscape.

Eventually the path led them to a barren plateau overlooking miles of black treetops rolling out to the horizon to merge with the night sky. The sunset was long over but a luminous glow pulsed in the west, as if the forest extended to the outskirts of a shining city just out of view. Above them the sky was crowded with stars, clustered so thickly that they looked, to Joseph's city eyes, like diamond brooches mounted on a velvet backing. It must be the Milky Way. God, if only Franny were here with him, on a camping trip, the two of them contemplating the stars, bonding in the silence far from the city. Never mind that he hated camping. For her sake, he'd learn to like it. Just give him the chance. He turned around to take in where they'd come from. The sky there was solid black, the stars cancelled out by banks of clouds that were following their trek into the wilderness like a silent flotilla.

He called Franny's name, hoping against reason that she was close enough to hear him. He remembered her at eight years old, just before he'd moved out, arranging her foreign-coin collection on the kitchen table, as absorbed in her work as a composer, placing the coins inscribed with animals in one pile, those with buildings in another, one-offs in the centre. She'd looked up at him, her face expectant as she waited for him to surrender his complete attention to her, but even there he'd failed her. He should have shared with her everything he'd learned as an obsessive stamp-collecting boy, flooded the room with that boy's enthusiasm, but his attention had been distracted, racing between the romanticized past, unsatisfactory present, and bright future. Had he ever given his full attention to Franny and Martha, even for an entire day? He'd read to Franny at bedtime, then comforted Martha after another grinding day at the legal clinic, but that barely added up to two hours. Why was his attention so precious that he needed to keep a portion in reserve? It wasn't like he put it to noble ends. It brought him no deep, lasting joy, and yet he protected it from the world as though it was a princeling—imperious, needing constant stimulation and novelty.

When the path brought them back to level ground, Alex took out a compass and held it up to his flashlight.

"Does it work at night?" Joseph asked.

Alex stared at him with a bewildered expression, as if he couldn't figure out how they'd ended up in the same place. "You don't know how to use a compass?"

"No."

"You weren't in the Scouts?"

"They didn't have them in my neighbourhood." He wasn't going to tell Alex he'd quit Scouts because the weekly meetings conflicted with the airing of his favourite sitcom.

Alex shook his head. Poor guy, stuck with a partner who was good for nothing but magazine-style commentary and ironic riffs.

"I know where we are."

Good for Alex. That left Joseph to focus on his scorecard of sins: getting so high and drunk that his daughter had disappeared from his care like a passenger over the side of a ship; his lusty idyll in the bushes, sending her and her best friend fleeing into a forest filled with crazed war vets; getting Tyler killed.

Impressive. Talk about following your bliss.

"Where are we going?" he said.

"To the commune. Where the vets live."

"You think the girls are there?"

"Maybe. This path ends very close to there, so either way . . ." Alex put the compass away, the indignant expression reclaiming his features. No wonder he was so angry—why was he, who'd always tried to do the right thing, being put through the same crucible as a chronic fuck-up like Joseph?

Joseph fought back a groan. What if the girls weren't at the commune? How would he and Alex find them in this endless forest?

Alex was already walking down the path, forcing Joseph to strain his wobbly ankle to catch up. The flashlight beam moved from one side of the path to the other like the arm of a pendulum, sweeping past the same pattern of dirt and branches. A few minutes later the light seemed to disappear into a gap in the woods not far ahead. As they got closer, Joseph realized the gap was an old dirt road that intersected the path, creating a lonely crossroads hemmed in by thick vegetation. Joseph turned on his own flashlight, picking out sinkholes and tall grass that nearly obliterated the road in places.

"Logging road," Alex said without enthusiasm. "Stopped using it in the late fifties when the logging companies pulled out."

"Where does it go?"

Alex pointed to Joseph's right. "That way probably joins up with another logging road." He motioned to the left. "Down there's an abandoned work camp."

Joseph pointed his beam in the camp's direction. The gravel on the road was scuffed in places, and there was a line of slightly bent grass going down the left side.

"Someone's walked there," he said.

"I doubt it. The camp is a ruin. The townies use it as a party site sometimes." Alex sounded irritated, like a child forced to suddenly change plans.

Joseph turned to face him. The men stood a few feet apart, their lowered flashlights throwing their upper bodies into deep shadow. It was like staring into a mirror that distorted Joseph's silhouette, masculinizing it by adding a couple of inches to his height and to the width of his shoulders. Above them, the moon dived into the mounting cloud banks before coming up briefly for air, losing the fight against the approaching storm. Joseph felt the coming of rain in the air as the wind set the branches rustling, rain that would fall on the girls, adding to their misery.

"If the girls found this road, why *wouldn't* they explore it?" he said. "And a camp is exactly where they'd hole up for the night." It was a long shot, but so was everything that had happened since sundown. The odds had to go in their favour eventually.

"It's a waste of time."

"We went miles out of our way to chase a dog." Joseph tried not to sound peevish. This was about finding Franny. "A ten-minute detour to check a potential resting place isn't going to make a big difference."

Alex's face bunched up like a cramping muscle, then just as quickly relaxed. "Okay. Ten minutes."

Joseph took the lead, his ankle holding up to the ruts and potholes. The garbage on the road collected into larger patches as they drew nearer to the camp—shoals of broken beer bottles and faded cigarette packets, condom wrappers and gutted snack bags. He saw, stacked beside a ratty suitcase, a pile of yellowed paperbacks so bloated with rainwater they wouldn't catch on fire even if someone still cared enough to burn books. On top of the pile was a mould-spotted staple of his family's single bookcase: Erma Bombeck's *If Life Is a Bowl of Cherries, What Am I Doing in the Pits?* He remembered his mother passing the tome of folksy wisdom to her sisters as if it was a family talisman, each hand-off increasing his shame at his mother's passive acceptance of her narrow reading, her narrow life. He picked up the bloated book, now feeling protective of what it had represented to his mother, a dutiful housewife and part-time accountant who'd placed her hopes on him, her brightest son. He even smirked at the title's now viciously ironic subtext. When he opened it the spine cracked, accordioning the pages and loosing their cargo of potato bugs and silverfish. He dropped the book and jumped back as though it had moved in his hands. A high screech sounded from the trees, remarkably similar to Tyler's dying cries, as if all mammals sounded alike while suffering a violent death. He felt the trees push closer, cutting off his escape routes, and the moon slipped behind the clouds, deepening the darkness outside his flashlight beam. He stumbled backward, bumping up against a hard point that pressed into the fatty flesh around his kidneys. It was the barrel of a gun.

Joseph turned and blasted a man's face with the flashlight. It was an awful sight. The man's features were grotesque in the yellow light—like the face of a creature that had evolved in a cave—pale skin, protruding lips, lidded-over eyes.

"Jesus, Alex. Are you okay?" Joseph said.

Alex pushed the flashlight down and lowered the rifle, his hands shaking.

"Of course I am. Are you?"

Joseph stepped away, his instincts warning him to keep his distance. "I was just . . ." He pointed down at the paperback. "My mom swore by that book. It was like the family Bible." Why was he explaining himself to Alex? He'd sworn to stop doing that years ago, but here he was, in the ruins, once again justifying his actions to stern, admonishing Alex.

"The camp's just up there," Alex said, as if each word cost him in flesh. "Let's make it quick."

The road ended at a wide, almost-treeless area pockmarked with old firepits, barbeques, tires, and other relics from the camp's second life as a party site.

"What happened to the camp?" Joseph asked.

"Once the forest's assets were plundered, the company abandoned it to the elements and to the townies."

The loggers were probably all dead, their post-industrial Dionysian heirs well past their flat-stomached primes and locked into awful service jobs, in town or far away. Men had lived and died here, their bones interred in the earth, where young townies later fucked and partied away the best years of their lives in the picturesque ruins, all that desperate life passed from memory into the numbing forest solitude.

Joseph walked through the central area, sweeping the flashlight across the ground and nodding after each pass, a rhythm he was soon afraid to break. There was no point in calling Franny's name. No one had visited this place for a long time. The elements had stripped the beer cans, bottles, and wrappers of their bright retail colours, and there were no footprints or other signs of recent human habitation. Further into the camp he found the foundations of several buildings reverting to an organic state, compost for saplings and ferns. He glanced back at the road, where Alex waited, refusing to waste energy proving what he already knew—the girls had not come to this place. Why did he have to be such a smug prick about it? If he was so sure about the girls' movements, why were they no closer to finding them?

Joseph's flashlight picked out the camp's single standing structure, a wide log-and-plaster building with no front door, its windows picked free of glass, the moss-covered walls sagging under the weight of the collapsing roof. A massive black iron stove was tipped on its side in front of the doorway and spray-painted with a pot leaf, a double-initialled heart, and an ejaculating penis. There was also a smaller symbol—four crossed lines forming a diamond, with a squiggle in the centre and topped by a crude human eye—an obvious bit of occult nonsense that still menaced his nerves.

He had to check inside. *You never know.*

He stepped through the gouged doorway into a room smelling of urine and rot. The place was stripped of its original contents except for a thick stovepipe elbow joint that lay on the floor, like an old diver's helmet calcifying at the bottom of a garbage-strewn sea. Sofa cushions, bottles, and disintegrating beer cases lay around the room, and derivative graffiti covered every surface, but the rotting party paraphernalia did not completely submerge the room's older function as a bunkhouse. Grooves had been worn into the plaster by the missing bunks, the long straight lines topped by scuffs and grease marks, a nocturnal record of exhausted sleep. He tried to imagine the loggers' faces, their sharp expressions and defiant facial hair, the bug bites, welts, and bruises mottling their bodies—a collection of second sons of farmers or sons of landless men.

Alex would see the same picture differently. He'd see men gathering in the bunkhouse after a day of work for a game of cards and ball-busting, or a dozy reading session with one of the books and magazines they passed around. It was a life, a place to be every day, with dignity and the total absorption of labour.

Joseph stepped on something soft. A thin futon was sprawled on the floor, its surface a mandala of sweat and other bodily fluids. A pair of rusty handcuffs lay beside the mattress, one cuff gaping open like a trap. He felt the breath leave his body.

He backed away, but it was too late, the image was ripping through his mind: Franny, her neck and shoulders ringed with bite marks, chained to a piss-smelling mattress while some rat-faced man raped her, all of it captured on grainy video to be posted later for fellow devotees. He ran back outside hugging his sides, trying to draw breath, dire conclusions massing just beneath his consciousness, rising up like a pod of whales about to smash their way through the ice. He'd gotten everything wrong. Would the sight of him and Jane fucking really have sent the girls fleeing into the woods? Even if it had, why didn't the girls just follow the path out to the highway when it got dark?

No, their journey into the woods spoke of intent. Of brute force. *Male* force.

The girls hadn't run into the forest, they were carried in by Alex's ex-soldiers, the lurkers at the woods' edge. Good men once, now hollowed out by combat, driven to regain from the female body the power stolen from them by the horrors of war. Fantasizing wouldn't be enough. They'd want total control, the power to debase, to break, to kill.

The scenario was too plausible to deny. Fleeing the scene of Joseph and Jane's betrayal, the girls run into the vet, his combat-trained hands tensed behind his back, his friend hiding in the trees. The girls know not to speak to strange men, but the vet puts on a meek expression, telling them he's hurt his leg. Can they lend him a hand? He just needs to use the phone. He even jokes about how he thought he'd end up as the coyotes' second course—serial killers are said to be charming. The girls hesitate, but the man reminds Franny of a beggar she passes on her way to school. They go to him, and when Franny reaches out he locks her thin wrist in the vise of his hands and pins her to the ground while his partner cracks Rebecca in the jaw. The first man hits Franny when she struggles, twists her wrists until she begs him to stop. Yes, she'll obey. The man likes that word: *obey.* He tells her to say it again. Yes, she'll do anything, if he'll just stop hurting her. The girls are carried off to a destination the police will never find, because the men have worked on their plan, supported it with alibis, a hideout, and a place to stash the bodies after the girls are used up. How long will that take? How many rounds do each of the men get with the victims?

The vomit shot from Joseph's mouth into one of the firepits. Where was he when the men snatched her? Walking back to the farm, or still rolling in the dirt with Jane? Franny's cries should have pulled him out of his lust, out of space and time, and dropped him in the evildoers' path, his flaming sword at the ready.

He staggered away and tripped over a root. The ground was soft, dead matter returning to dust—the mingled remains of leaves, coyotes, deer, birds, and bad fathers like him. He could see Franny's face, first stricken with horror, then the blank acceptance as the men hurt her. How was it possible to contemplate his daughter's violation without his mind shattering or his hair turning white? The world was letting him in on a horrible secret, that the real curse of being human is that you never stop thinking—even when you lose the most precious thing in your life, your mind keeps turning over ideas, making observations, your inner voice chattering like a prisoner handcuffed to your wrist. Even an animal forced to chew its own leg off to escape a trap is spared this torture.

"She can't be dead," he said to himself. "If she's dead then I'm dead!"

Someone better take that into account. You *can* die of a broken heart; it had to be true, even if history argued otherwise, with its millions of survivors of wars and death camps and natural disasters.

"I'll die. I will fucking die!"

Sobs rattled his lips but he fought them down. He slapped his own face, surprised he could inflict such sharp pain on himself. He had to focus. He forced himself to walk toward the road, ignoring the terrible images in his head, trying to see them as clouds passing, as the instructor had advised in the one yoga class he'd attended, where he'd hoped to meet a different kind of woman or become a different type of man. The resolution didn't last. Nothing did with him.

"Shut up!" he screamed. "Shut up!"

He was useless. Why, in this desperate hour, couldn't he shut up and focus? He had things to do. The police would want him and Martha to do a press conference, appeal to the public for help—as if that had ever worked, as if child murderers would be swayed by his and Martha's appeal to their morality and compassion. You wouldn't get him in front of a bank of microphones. If a reporter pointed a camera at him he'd roll up his sleeve, tear off a strip of his own flesh, and hold it up for the perpetrators to see. *This is what you've done to me*, he'd say, *and this is what I'll do to you when I find you.*

He slapped himself, harder this time. Alex was waiting. Alex had a plan. Alex had a gun. They'd find the girls, even if they were chained to a wall in a makeshift torture chamber. There was still time.

He made it to the logging road, the tears in his eyes blurring his flashlight beam into a yellow smear across a wet windshield.

"I'll die if you take her," he said. But he wouldn't. He'd survive. He'd see her face reflected in store windows and in crowds on the subway, her memory tormenting him to the point of insanity. Then, one day, he'd notice a beautiful woman on the street or enjoy the taste of a hamburger or lose himself in the book he was reading, and he would fail Franny again. *We all betray our will to perfection.*

"Shut up!"

He fell to his knees and stayed there, waiting for the judgment—for lightning to strike or the earth to open up beneath him. He rolled onto his side, giving in to the sobs.

"What are you doing?" Alex's voice was close.

"Leave me alone! I'm waiting."

"For what?

"Leave me alone." Let Alex figure it out for himself. "Go away!"

"Joseph, look at me! Look! I found something that belongs to Rebecca on the path!"

Alex stood triumphant, his right hand clenching a shiny bauble Joseph couldn't see clearly. A residue of anxiety left Alex's face as Joseph rose to his knees.

"It's Rebecca's," Alex said, holding a dangling gold-and-purple earring aloft in a pocket of electric light, as if his arm was reaching into a better world, one of warm bright bedrooms and playfully garish jewellery. "I just found it!"

"Are you sure it's hers?"

"Her favourite colour is purple."

"Most girls choose purple as their favourite colour. I read that somewhere."

Alex mashed the earring under his nose and inhaled. "You think I don't know what my daughter's perfume smells like?"

Of course Alex knew his daughter's favourite scent. Joseph didn't even know Franny's favourite shampoo—he bought whatever was on sale. Was anyone surprised?

"Wait, I remember these. Rebecca bought them when we were in Toronto this spring."

Joseph remembered the visit. The family came down to see a specialist about Liam's asthma, and Jane invited him and Franny to meet for lunch in Chinatown. Joseph dropped Franny off at the restaurant, waiting until the last moment before telling her that he had to be somewhere, which may or may not have been true. Franny told him not to worry, she'd tell them he had an important meeting. He'd thought she was being a loyal daughter, but no, she just knew not to expect better from him.

"She liked the gold thread on the purple." Alex brought the flashlight closer and illuminated the gold snaking around the purple glass, the Good Father following the golden twine through the Forest Perilous to find his lost daughter. And what was Joseph's role? Pack horse? The flawed sidekick who sacrifices his life to complete the hero's quest? He bit his lip, the pain focusing his attention. This was good news.

"It was lying on the path over there," Alex said. "They must have passed this way."

The story scanned, but he might as well have found one of Rebecca's limbs for all the comfort it brought Joseph.

"You don't believe me?" Alex stepped closer. Something in his voice, a vein of flint scraping against granite, made Joseph wince. "How else did it get here?"

"Okay, it's her earring." Joseph wasn't arguing: bad men had forced Franny and Rebecca down the path to their lair, knocking free an earring on the way.

"The path we've been following eventually crosses a rural road," Alex said. "It's very isolated, but there are a few farms there, and the commune. The girls will reach that road soon."

Joseph fought down a fresh wave of nausea. When the girls reached the commune it would all begin, the real nightmare.

"Alex, we both know the girls didn't go down that path of their own volition. You know what I'm talking about." He was afraid to look at Alex's face. "The girls must have been abducted."

He waited for the bolt of lightning. For Alex to contradict him. When he didn't respond, Joseph risked a peek at his face. Alex was staring into the dark logging camp, his mouth drawn tight.

"You've known it all along," Joseph said.

"I suspected. I told you I didn't like the look of that guy."

"There was more than one." Joseph remembered: that brief glimpse of men in the woods when he was sitting at the fire.

"Probably. They're on foot. They can't have gotten very far."

Joseph nodded. Thank God he wasn't in this alone. "Fire the gun. Twice."

"Why?"

"The signal. To tell Julian we need help."

"He won't hear it. Do you have any idea how far we are from the farm?"

Joseph didn't want to admit that for all he knew the distance they'd covered could have been one mile or ten. "We have to get back. We'll show the cops the earring. They've probably already sent out a search party."

"Have they?" Alex stepped even closer, as if he were examining a defect on Joseph's face.

"When we tell them what we know, the cops will call in everything they've got." Joseph could see it—the men, with their paper coffee cups and flashlights, methodically combing the woods, the search dogs, the helicopters. "They'll get a posse of volunteers. That's how it works."

"In the movies."

"On the news."

"So tell me, how long after the kids are reported missing does this *posse* show up?"

Okay, someone had to call the posse at home, and the posse would have to square things with dozens of bosses and wives. The posse had to make coffee and sandwiches.

"Listen to me, Joseph. They've cut the police budget three times since I moved up here."

"Posses are free."

"Liz already called, but nothing will happen until the cops are sure the girls are missing."

"How much more proof do they need?"

"Not proof—*time*. It's been four or five hours at most. With all the shit teenagers get up to around here, you think they'll blow the summer budget on *that*?"

"We have to go to the police!"

Alex bent down and put his hand on Joseph's shoulder, meeting him full on with his grave, searching eyes. Men did this in movies when the chips were down—now Joseph knew they did it in real life too. There was comfort in that.

"Of course you want to go to the cops," Alex said. "And that's just what those men want us to do. They know exactly how long it'll take for the police to get organized, and by then they'll have covered their tracks. You think they've never done this before?"

Of course they had. These men fed on women's pain and humiliation, survived on it. When one of them was caught, another took his place, as if the world demanded an annual offering of dead and broken women so the rest of us can live in peace. The odds against Franny being chosen for sacrifice must be a million to one, but someone had to win the lottery.

Alex squeezed his shoulder. "We should have gone into the woods as soon as we realized the girls were missing and left the others with their instructions. That's what they wanted—someone to tell them what to do."

He was right: what were all those stunned expressions around the campfire but the paralysis of indecision?

"We were afraid to take charge," Alex said. "It's the story of our fucking lives. Wait for somebody to act—the cops, the corporations, the politicians—then form a strong opinion about the actions. Listen, Joseph, we're here *now*. We're here and we know the girls are close."

"But the cops, they know how to do this."

"You see a search party?" Alex pointed his flashlight down the road and then up into the treetops. "Any helicopters?"

"What are you saying?" He needed to hear it said out loud.

"It's up to us, Joseph. No one can help us find our daughters. No one can help us find those men."

*Men*—weak, pathetic men making the world a hunting ground, an outlet for their flaccid cocks and mommy rage.

"Those men think they're going to get away with it," Alex said. "They think they've won. They *like* winning. It makes them feel strong."

Of course. Exerting absolute power over their victims wouldn't be enough—they'd want the same power over their victims' parents.

"They planned everything perfectly, but they made one mistake. They think men like us never *do* anything. They think we'll just take it, that no matter what happens to us, we won't act." Alex stood up and pointed the rifle at the black wall of vegetation, as if he was ready to take out the forest one tree at a time. "They think the worst we can throw back at them is a weepy phone call to the cops."

"They have a point."

"You're right! They *know* what kind of men we are—harmless, married to the system in spite of our constant griping about it. They're counting on us to call our surrogate daddies at the cop shop."

"That's what I would've done," Joseph said, eager to support this withering assessment.

"Of course you would have. And that's *still* what you want to do—hand responsibility to the police and hope they'll return Franny unharmed." He leaned down until their faces were almost touching. "They don't realize that we've changed. We walked into the woods with our fantasies of *decency* and *fair play*, afraid to even think about the kind of men who took our daughters. But we've changed. We're not acting according to type anymore."

"Yes." Joseph said the word tentatively, but he won the long-awaited big brother's smile.

"They don't know what we're capable of. What are you capable of, Joseph?" Alex spoke his name in a voice unheard outside movie theatres or private fantasy—the voice of action. "I know you've *imagined* doing things decent men aren't supposed to think about. You imagined punching the dumb-ass dad whose kid pulled Franny's hair in the sandbox."

He had, in great detail, right down to the dad's grovelling apology, which he did not accept.

"The asshole berating his girlfriend over his cell phone at the back of the streetcar—"

"I smashed his head into a pole! I broke his nose and his teeth. And the shithead who used to race his car down the street when Franny was a kid. Took a baseball bat to his face."

Alex nodded. "You waited by the car of your company's CEO and smashed his face into the windshield."

"Fuck yeah. Worse. I pushed him down the stairs, heard his leg snap."

"And you kneecapped the gutless politician who cut programs at the rec centre, and you beat to death the climate-change-denying talk-radio DJ."

"I lined up all the cunts who crashed the economy against the wall." Fucking right he did! "I made them think they could get a last-minute reprieve if they begged for their lives."

Alex was smiling. "It's time to do something, Joseph. Not to *imagine*—to act."

Joseph had been waiting to hear those words since boyhood, the call to action and consequence, and the words came to him on beer-scented breath, as he knew they would.

"We have our *kids* to protect," Alex said, watching Joseph's reaction. "Those creeps think *they* have nothing to lose? That they're the only ones who'll go all the way? No. *We* have nothing to lose. We're fathers. Everything is permitted."

"There's nothing I won't do," Joseph said, his voice as tentative as the first time he told a woman he loved her. Then firmer: "Nothing. I'll kill those fuckers."

Alex nodded, his squared shoulders and expert grip on the gun announcing the imminent demise of the men who'd taken Franny and Rebecca. No police, no courts—this fight began in the woods and it would end there.

Joseph got to his feet. His ankle throbbed, but the pain burned off the vapours of useless *talk* from his mind, opening up space, so much space, so much energy, flowing through him, from his heart out to his hands and feet.

"They've probably got two hours on us," Alex said. "We'll go to the commune and surprise them."

The commune: Joseph imagined a gabled farmhouse rising from a litter of sagging outbuildings and tarpaper additions; in the field a barn, converted to a meeting and dining hall during the commune's Eden period, reverted now to a pen for animals and human body parts. There would be a storm cellar, its earthen floor absorbing the blood and the screams. The men had Franny there. That might not be the worst thing. The killers' actions were dictated by pathological compulsions, but they were also good at what they did—they'd delay gratification until everything was in place. Franny was smart, she was adaptable—hadn't he taught her about adjusting to unexpected situations?

The shock of capture would have worn off. She'd be taking stock: she and Rebecca were at the mercy of Bad Men—worse than bad, these men were ghouls from the outer rings of humanity. There was no appealing to their "good side," but she might delay the inevitable by asking the men about themselves and the old commune. How long have they lived out here? Do they still grow crops or keep animals?

*Keep them talking, Franny, buy us some time.*

Franny started dreaming about a zombie apocalypse when she was nine, not long after Joseph moved out. Violent and monotonous in their hopelessness, the dreams locked her and her friends inside a public institution—school, hospital, police station—whose walls proved useless against the onslaught of the flesh-eating undead. The zeitgeist was lousy with zombies, standing in for personal and millennial fears, but only he, her wayward father, could talk Franny back to sleep after they attacked. Martha would phone Joseph after one of the nightmares, and he'd share with Franny his storehouse of weird facts and news stories—giant galaxies discovered by deep-space probes, lost cities uncovered by archaeological digs, giant squid sightings, UFO rumours—rattling them off until her voice grew calmer, softer, then faded out to soft breathing.

There was still time. The ordeal would leave the girls with terrible memories, hours of experience teaching them more about human venality than their friends will learn in a lifetime, but he and Alex could still spare them the worst.

The air was starting to sag, heavy with water. Soon they could add rain to the list of advantages working in their favour: rain, darkness, the element of surprise, a rifle, and righteous anger. And Julian's knife—he'd almost forgotten about it. The vets would be closing the commune against the approaching storm, the girls securely confined in the basement, the men confident that a visit from the police, if it came at all, was at least a day away. They knew how these things worked, but their detailed plan wouldn't take into account Joseph and Alex slipping into the yard in the night, Joseph drawing the guard's attention with an innocuous noise while Alex knocked him out with the rifle butt. The other kidnappers would be caught off guard and beaten unconscious, tied up and left to await their punishment while Joseph and Alex located the girls—frightened, in shock, but restored by the sight of their fathers.

Then they'll punish the men who took their daughters. They'll break the abductors' fingers and toes, then the major bones; limbs will be pulled from their sockets, eyes gouged out, testicles crushed. If drugs are available they'll inject the men to intensify the pain and terror. Then the prolonged executions, maybe a full-body skinning or a castration, the sheer range of violence so absolute in its retributive power that other sexual predators will swear off hurting children for life. Martha will be proud of him. She won't want the details. Knowing he finished the job will be enough.

Not Jane. *I hope you made those sick fuckers suffer.*

Joseph was up for it. "Did you learn how to kill other men?" he asked Alex. "In the army?"

Alex had to think about the question. "We fired guns."

What Joseph wanted to know was: Could Alex crush a man's larynx with an open palm? Could he break wrist bones with a quick twist? Because Joseph couldn't. He was not like his father, a bartender who'd considered steady employment, marital fidelity, manageable alcoholism, and the maintenance of a strong-but-distant paternal presence the limit of his life responsibilities. Now *there* was a man of the Old School, a guardian of boundaries and oaths, standing behind the long, polished hotel bar in a starched white shirt, black tie, and pressed pants, the red money belt around his waist a challenge to any bull mad enough to charge.

"Did they teach you how to take out an enemy *without* a gun?"

"I learned some nasty business in a special training course. None of this pin-the-guy-to-the-mat stuff. It was about inflicting maximum damage with the minimum moves."

*That's better*, Joseph thought.

"Only a few of us were invited." Alex didn't try to hide his pride. "Getting picked meant you had hard-ass potential." His voice had acquired a commanding, military edge—or so Joseph assumed. "The course screened for potential special forces recruits. They had to see if you could survive in any situation and act without conscience."

Joseph wasn't surprised that the officers had picked Alex. But how, over the course of their friendship, had Alex refrained from bragging about getting chosen to take a special forces training course? Joseph couldn't have gone fifteen minutes without reminding everyone of his army experience, yet Alex had kept this training to himself.

Maybe the experience didn't fit with his identity as an activist and family man.

"How did they test you?" Joseph asked.

"We went without sleep, did night hikes, learned hand-to-hand fighting techniques—skills you need to survive behind the lines. After the training they took us into the wilderness, split us into small teams, and left us to find our way to a rendezvous point thirty miles away. After four days we finally rendezvoused in a ravine. Only one guy was late, so the commanding officer decided to make an example of him. Showing up five minutes late could get your whole unit killed, he said. He ordered us to hide in the bushes and to mess the guy up when he arrived."

Joseph easily cast himself as the missing soldier, announcing his late arrival with excuses that would only make things worse.

"The missing soldier was *two hours* late. By then we'd have jumped him without the orders. Eight of us took him down, but he went into a berserker rage. Hit you where it hurt—knees, nuts, throat. Every time we pinned him he'd spring up and knock us down like bowling pins. Then the c.o. suddenly steps in and pins the guy in three seconds flat. He's got one foot on the guy's throat and he's twisting his arm like a wet towel. But the soldier won't give in. He pulls a knife on the c.o. That was it. The c.o. pulls out a pistol and puts it to the guy's head."

Maybe Alex *had* told this story before, because the details lined up in Joseph's mind a half-second before he heard them. He could have sworn the c.o. had a dog.

"What did you do?"

"I yelled, 'Don't shoot!' I was the only one—the rest would have let the c.o. blow the guy's brains out."

"Jesus."

"The c.o. wasn't *really* going to shoot him. It was all a test—the soldier showing up late and pulling the knife, the c.o. pulling the gun—they set it up to test our reactions."

Joseph felt betrayed. More than anything right now, he needed for Alex to have passed through the crucible of real violence.

"I failed the test because I second-guessed an officer and brought civilian morality to a situation that demanded ruthlessness."

"Maybe you knew all along, subconsciously, that it was a set-up," Joseph said, trying to coax back the man whose speech had raised him from the garbage-strewn logging road.

"No, I believed he'd kill the soldier—I *wanted* him to—but I was so horrified by my reaction that I yelled at the c.o. to stop."

"This is a different situation. Entirely different." He understood: Alex was afraid that he'd freeze up when the time came to pull the trigger, punch out the teeth, stick in the knife. Everyone felt like that these days—angry and frustrated, but afraid of confronting power and losing what little you had. "It's like you said, Alex: everybody imagines taking action, but when the time comes, can they do it? You can. You have to."

Alex nodded as if he was continuing Joseph's speech in his head. "I'd have let the c.o. kill him if I thought the guy deserved to die. That's what it comes down to: appropriate punishment, giving somebody what they deserve." Then he stopped, as though he'd reached the edge of a shore, his flashlight pointing at a boulder beside the path. The light set the boulder apart from the dark mass of rustling trees, catching seams of quartz that marbled the rock's surface like fat in a good steak, but Alex was staring beyond it.

"We have to do what's necessary," Joseph said, disturbed by Alex's wide blank eyes.

"I will. This time." Alex's voice was strangely inflected. "We should hurry. It's going to rain."

The wind picked up again. An animal ran across the path, proof perhaps of recent human passage—or just another random event in the wilderness.

There were about a dozen fresh indentations on the path, each a few inches wide, and the sandy ground was torn up by half-circle wedges and skids.

"They're bike tracks, probably BMX," Alex said. He was down among them with his flashlight. "They're fresh."

Joseph looked back in the direction they'd come from. The tracks did not continue that way. "They must have turned around."

"No," Alex insisted. He was standing again, his flashlight beam stabbing at patches of the criss-crossing tracks. "Look! The tracks *stop* here. Four sets of tracks come this way—you can see them approaching—then it's like they fell off the earth."

"So . . ."

"Whoever was on those bikes got off here. Look around you."

"We're in the middle of the fucking woods."

"Exactly. So why did they get off their bikes?" Alex was almost frantic for Joseph to reach the same conclusion.

"I don't know."

"Because something happened here. They ran into somebody. They must have."

"You don't know that." Joseph felt both his hope and his fear levels rising. He didn't like it. The resolve to confront Franny's abductors was slipping through his hands like oiled rope.

"This is what I *know*." Alex's tone was moving quickly from eager to angry. "You don't stop your bike in the middle of the night in the middle of nowhere without a reason. Joseph, the girls were on this path. They were heading this way. These tracks aren't more than a few hours old. The timing lines up."

"I know, but—"

"Put the fucking pieces together for once in your life!"

"But we're nowhere near the commune." Joseph was trying to keep the hysteria from his voice. What those sick men at the commune could do to Franny in a few minutes would take lifetimes to unremember.

"I know that." Alex was all firm reassurance now. "The commune's still an hour away. But something might have happened *here*. We have to take a look. It'll take a few minutes. Then we'll make our decision."

*Our* decision? Was Joseph ever going to stop taking orders from this cocksucker? What choice did he have?

"Just search that side of the path," Alex said.

Joseph turned on his flashlight and stomped into the

bush. There was only about ten feet of level ground before a hill began to climb into the dark. He walked through a corridor of ragged trees between the path and the hillside, winning an argument in his head with Alex about the stupidity of this change in plans.

On a patch of bare, dry earth, his flashlight picked out a few sets of faint footprints walking away from the path, toward the hillside. He kneeled down, careful to keep most of his weight on his good ankle. One of the sets of footprints looked small enough to be a teenage girl's. Maybe.

Joseph remembered the boy—*Dave*—Rebecca and Ruby had talked about earlier. He and a bunch of friends could have ridden their bikes out here to meet the girls—no, he'd been through all those scenarios. The girls would have left a note if they were going out to meet friends.

He needed to focus. There were at least three sets of prints and possibly a few tire tracks leading to the hillside.

"They went into the bush here," he called out.

After a few seconds Alex stepped into the bush, and crouched down to examine the tracks.

"They got off their bikes," he said. "That's why the tire tracks are so faint. I told you! Something happened here."

Joseph wasn't going to argue anymore. *Just get this over with.*

Alex reached the hillside in four steps and started climbing, Joseph struggling to keep up. The ground sloped up steadily, the trees and bushes thinning the higher they went. Occasionally, a short run of footprints appeared on the ground.

"Turn off your flashlight," Alex said, his voice almost manic with anticipation. "There's something up there."

Something was blocking the way a little farther up the hill, either a boulder or a fallen tree. Above the blockage, a faint light glowed in the trees, too white and cold to be firelight. Joseph checked the sky. The moon was buried in clouds.

"It's electric light," Alex said.

Joseph tried to line up the feeling of dread triggered by the mention of electric light with a plausible scenario, but he came up empty. What did this have to do with Franny and Rebecca?

"Does someone live back here?"

"No."

"Then what is it?" Joseph tried to get Alex to look at him, but Alex was fixated on the light, his lips silently mouthing words. He even shook his head, as though quieting a contrary thought.

"Someone's up there," he said. He pointed to the top of the hill, his hand grasping at air. "And they don't know we're coming." He stepped over a low bush, gently brushing aside branches with the rifle barrel, as close to silent as a man his size could be. "Let's keep that advantage."

Joseph tried to match his movements, easing branches back into place as if they were squeaky doors. He checked his pocket to make sure he still had the knife, and remembered Julian's vague but utterly sincere warning to *be careful*.

Alex stopped and put his hand up. He risked a quick burst from the flashlight. Joseph's guess was right. A pair of trees had fallen across the hillside. Alex must have guessed the same because he was nodding.

"Climb over."

Joseph made it over the trees without hurting himself, then stepped into a hole and nearly turned his other ankle.

"Jesus! Two trees and now a *hole*? Is this place fucking booby-trapped?"

"Keep your voice down."

Alex helped Joseph out of the hole and they walked up a narrow path that led to the top of the hill, where faint patches of light clung to the trees' lower branches like a phosphorescent fungus. A shack a little wider than a single-car garage sat in a small clearing, its outline shimmering in a caul of electric light that emanated from every wall but the one that faced them. Alex nodded them forward, and as they walked into the clearing Joseph felt as though he was stepping onto a self-consciously stark theatre set, the audience hidden in the trees, awaiting the spectacle about to begin. There were no obvious signs of danger, but the wall facing them, suspended like a black curtain against the cool light, made his skin crawl. Alex also stared at it, his cheeks slack, his mouth hanging open, as if his wide, unblinking eyes were siphoning the energy from his face.

"Don't worry, they can't see us in the dark," he said. "Just be careful. It could be a meth shack."

Joseph stopped. "Then we should get the fuck out of here."

"No. I'm going to get a better look."

Joseph grabbed Alex's arm. "This is dangerous."

"If it's dangerous for us, what would happen if the girls came here?"

"What? Now you're saying the girls are being held by meth cookers?" The forest was sprouting life-and-death scenarios like wild mushrooms.

Alex was too agitated by the possibilities, whatever they were, to tolerate objections. "We'll check it out, then we'll leave."

He ran along the edge of the clearing, shadowing the trees on the border, and since there was no point arguing about the plan, Joseph followed him. They stopped at a boulder that gave a view of a small window, mounted above the front door, which spilled a shadowless, fluorescent wash that reminded Joseph of highway gas-station washrooms. Kids might have built this place, nailing together drywall and sheets of panelling and lumber taken from family garages and building sites, the shack a summer's worth of theft and scrounging—Huckleberry Finn stuff. Then again, the workmanship wasn't half bad: the window frame formed a proper square and the door appeared to keep out the worst of the elements. Behind it came a rush of muffled talking and laughter, punctuated by a stranded, out-of-time laugh.

"Doesn't sound like they're cooking meth," Joseph said.

Alex continued to stare ahead with a piercing expression, as if he were trying to see behind the door.

"Why don't we just knock? They're probably just kids."

"Kids?" Alex didn't hide his contempt. "Kids with thousands of hours of hardcore porn and violence under their belt. God only knows what drugs they're on."

"What are you saying?"

Alex shushed him. "The chess club doesn't build a shack five miles into the woods. Just be prepared. If someone grabs you, bite their hand, gouge their eyes, bring your heel down on their foot until you hear the bones break." Drops of sweat beaded Alex's face like a spattering of melted wax. He wasn't leaving until they'd seen what was going on in that shack.

Joseph closed his eyes, reaching down to the bedrock of will that surely lay beneath his shallow, jittery attention. Alex must have his reasons for checking the shack. If it turned out to be a waste of time, Joseph would veto any future detours. If Alex's hunch was right, they could be a few minutes away from finding the girls. He reached into his pocket, slid Julian's knife from its case, and held it up to the light. The blade did not throw off horror-movie flashes—instead, the steel absorbed and dulled the light, except for the sparkling sharp line of the blade. The edge was so thin it seemed to fizz, inviting the skin to press a little harder—*there*, it cut his thumb, opening a little smile that oozed a fat drop of blood.

"That's the real deal," Alex said, impressed. "Keep it handy." He stood up and pumped a shell into the chamber. "I'll check the window on the big wall facing the trees. Try to see into the window on the far wall, but don't let them see *you*. Meet me by my window."

He moved off in a loping crouch into the trees across from the front door, the rifle swinging by his knees like a piston. Joseph imitated his stance as he ran in the opposite direction, staying close to the trees before he remembered that there were no windows on the wall facing him. He stepped into the clearing, every standing hair on his body a sudden receptor, the sheer volume of empty space pressing down on him as if he were chained to the bottom of an enormous water tank. The black wall, framed by the halo of electric light, looked like a doorway into a deeper darkness, but he was safe for now. Even if someone stepped out for a piss they'd be blind for the first twenty seconds. Plenty of time for Joseph to reach the trees.

He approached the side wall and gently leaned against the ridged plastic siding. Someone had put a lot of work into the shack. That could be a good thing or a bad thing. As he reached the end of the wall, the men in the shack unleashed a round of approving hoots. The voices sounded young, but he couldn't be sure. He turned the corner and stepped into the narrow space between the shack and the trees, the branches facing the shack frozen in a dull white glow. He eased his way toward the light's source, a crude window sawn from the drywall, and leaned his back against the wall. Franny and Rebecca might be in there. Maybe they'd escaped the vets and run into the guys who built the shack. He stepped away from the shack and stood in front of the window, which was covered from the inside with thick, translucent plastic. It was like peering into an out-of-focus microscope lens, vague shapes wiggling and merging behind a bright foreground. Inside the shack the guys laughed, one of them capping a cackle with a hearty "Yeah, bitch." They were using their "boys only" voices, amped up by recirculated testosterone. Franny was not in there.

He wanted to punch the wall, cut a hole in the window, smash something. Instead, he took a deep breath. They were boys, maybe eighteen or nineteen, he guessed, but they might have spotted Franny and Rebecca, or seen strangers in the woods. He and Alex would knock on the door, play the Concerned Fathers card, appeal to the alpha male. The boys might even join the search.

He made his way further along the wall, pausing to touch the knife through his jacket pocket before rounding the corner. About five paces away, Alex was staring into a bright window, an expression on his face Joseph had never seen before. How to describe it? Like a father who comes home to find his son hosting a raging party—stunned, disappointed, desperate for a trigger to unleash his rage. Joseph stepped closer. Alex's eyes were bright with moisture. He heard Joseph approaching and waved him over.

"They can't see you if you stand back from the window."

About a foot high and twice as wide, the window was positioned closer to the front of the shack, the dirty glass giving a decent side view into the single room. Two battery-operated camping lights sat on a Formica kitchen table crowded with beer bottles, and there were two glossy posters nailed to the far wall, the first of a cartoon pit bull wearing a diamond-studded collar emblazoned with the word *Player*, the other of a curvy blonde pole dancer—real aspirational stuff. A folded futon mattress leaned against the side wall next to a small wood stove and a stack of beer cases. Four teenage boys—kneeling, rapt, silent, all of them about sixteen—occupied the front half of the room, facing a large screen plugged into a laptop beside the door.

The porn they were watching was amateur stuff, the actors' skin shimmering in patches like fish scales. Onscreen, an orange-faced girl in heavy makeup lifted her head, dislodging from her mouth an average-sized cock that flicked in the open air like a hatchling forced to fend for itself. One of the boys shouted, "Viagra injection please!"—scoring big laughs. The girl stared into the camera with her glassy, drooping eyes and licked her lips, earning a "Dude!" from a boy with a faux-hawk, who called out, "A fucking star is born!" A boy in a jean jacket and a backward ball cap over his blond afro was high-fived by the skinny kid to his right. Then the biggest boy stood up too quickly and stepped back, claiming distance from the screen without looking away. He was a squat giant—broad and square under his baggy sweatshirt and cargoes—tagged with a tattoo of a Chinese character, a gold hoop forcing open a dime-sized hole in his earlobe. The three other boys sported a selection of tattoos, blurs of zigzags and Maori war markings, and there were goatees and a chunky silver thumb ring—obligatory tokens of pagan non-conformity.

"The future chamber of commerce," Alex said, any trace of sadness gone from his bearing.

Joseph watched the big kid, who seemed to want to will what he was witnessing out of existence. Onscreen, the girl grabbed the cock before it could wilt out of sight, and a panning shot caught a lip of baby fat pinched between her hip and ribs.

"Fuck, she's a kid," Joseph said, his head feeling as though it were being injected with carbonated water. She was Franny's age, at most.

The camera lingered on the baby fat, skin only the girl's mother had ever touched, before veering away to settle on the male actor as he pushed the girl's head deeper home.

"Piston-fuck that mouth!" a boy called out.

"Respect!"

*Respect?* Had a word ever become so utterly unmoored from its meaning?

The camera pulled back, revealing the actor as the boy with the faux-hawk and silver thumb ring. He appeared younger onscreen, and like any actor he didn't like watching himself. He turned his head until the camera returned to the oral sex, the prolonged blowjob clearing the room of joshing and high-fives.

"They *made* this movie," Joseph whispered. Yes, he'd jerked off to softcore skin mags at sixteen, but *this*—thank God he'd been spared the temptation.

Another cheer went up. Only the chubby boy kept his hands fisted and out of his pants. Joseph knew his type: the sensitive bruiser with a crush on a girl way out of his league—in this case, the film's younger and possibly drugged starlet. The story was there in his wincing face: his crush dating back to the girl's incarnation as a pony-tailed, school-activity keener with a rough home life, when he was so far off her radar he could only bow his head when she passed in the halls. His desire deepening and darkening the summer she "went bad"—her range of backseat activities earning her pride of place in the pantheon of bad girls. How he watched silently as she was passed from the top bad boy to his right-hand man to the third in charge and on down, her first onscreen blowjob consigning her to permanent slut status without knocking her from the lonely boy's pedestal. When the boy stared at the screen, he still saw the straight-A student, the notebook doodler, the shy girl playing at porn actress.

The camera shifted as another boy stepped into camera range, his muscular body shaved from knees to nose, his 1970s white-boy afro and hairless skin putting Joseph in mind of a best-of-breed poodle primped for a show. He too was sitting on the shack floor, rhythmically moving his hand inside his pants. Onscreen, the first boy moved over and motioned the girl to follow as the afroed boy kneeled behind her, his bigger cock needing no fluffing as he guided it toward her ass. Feeling its touch the girl looked up and mouthed "no," as in *No, I won't do anal.* No one cared what she wanted—not caring was the point, that and the stuffing shut of every vulnerable hole with male meat. The first boy grabbed her head and put her back to work, and the afroed boy buried himself in her ass and didn't clean himself when they did the switcheroo. When a third naked boy walked onscreen the boys in the shack shouted, "She's working for her protein shake!" The girl was gagging, the boys were laughing, onscreen and inside the shack—even the big sensitive lad, who now had his hand down his pants, working on his cock with all the joy of a father suffocating a deformed son with a pillow. The camera zoomed in on the girl's face. She was crying, but the tears were as mechanical as sweat. This was the money shot—her pain, her humiliation, her vacated face.

That poor girl. She was still a child. Joseph pressed up against the window, not caring if he was seen. He wanted to get closer to her. She was crying for real now, her sobbing face familiar to him. He reached for the knife, his hand brushing up against the rifle barrel. He pushed his face harder against the glass, daring it to shatter.

The girl was pushed onto her belly. The boys in the room started laughing, triggering a sharp snap inside Joseph's skull, like a high-tension cable torn by a heavy load.

His vision went red.

He grabbed the rifle and smashed the window with the butt end.

"That's my daughter!" he screamed.

Inside the shack: absolute mayhem, boys rolling on the floor, tucking their cocks back into their pants, the big kid a human battering ram aimed at the door.

"That's my daughter!" Joseph screamed again, the word *daughter* rising out of him in a geyser of wrath and love. "You fucking animals!"

He aimed the gun at the low ceiling and fired, and it was as if a bus had roared by and clipped him at the shoulder, the recoil throwing him onto the bikes stacked beneath the trees. Gunpowder stung his eyes. His right hand was numb. Alex took the rifle and mumbled—or maybe Joseph couldn't hear over the ringing—then he ran toward the front of the shack. Joseph sprung to his feet, his right arm hanging dead at his side, and followed Alex into the clearing, where the last boy was running into the trees near the path.

"You're fucking dead if I catch you!" Joseph yelled, wielding the knife with his left hand. No one had ever run away from him with such desperation. It felt good. He reached the path and took a few steps down the hill. Those fucking animals. He was going to do what their fathers should have—teach them fear, teach them the pain that comes of misusing their power, teach them what it feels like to have a stick shoved up their asses.

"We're going to waste you, man!" one of the boys shouted.

Maybe Joseph wasn't completely deaf. "Come on, tough guy!" he shouted back. "Maybe you want to come back and fuck *my* ass. Let's see how that goes down!"

"We saw your face, man!"

The boys kept running, smashing through branches and cursing. Joseph laughed. The terrible pain in his arm didn't bother him as he gazed at the silent, tall trees, his back straight, feeling like he'd just conquered a high summit.

*Where's Alex?* he wondered. They should be sharing this triumph.

*Alex*—the name induced a tingling sensation between Joseph's shoulder blades, as if he were being touched under his skin. He heard a metallic click behind him, raising the hairs on his arms and neck.

He took a deep breath, then turned around to see Alex, ten feet up the hill, pointing the rifle at him. Alex was going to kill him.

# BEASTS

He waited for the gunshot. Another second passed, empty of thought and as vast and looming as a cathedral ceiling. Only two details showed in the dim light: Alex's lips curled up tight with rage, and his shaking hands. He'd barely stopped himself from blowing a hole in Joseph's chest.

"I thought you were one of those kids," Alex said, lowering the rifle. He sounded genuinely shocked, even remorseful, too stunned to try for a more convincing lie.

"Yes." Joseph was unable to take the sentence further. He tried to smile but his mouth kept slipping back into a grimace, like a lock of hair that wouldn't stay parted. A casual shrug was defeated by his injured arm. He'd give himself away if he didn't speak soon. He had to play dumb, a game well-suited to his skill set. He finally got the smile in place and walked up the path, his eyes fixed on Alex, who smiled back just as eagerly.

They were both in on the game now, but only one knew the rules.

Joseph put the knife back in his jacket pocket, because that's what a man who trusted his companion would do. The egg in his pocket was broken. Touching it was like dipping his fingers into a tiny body cavity, sticky with mucous and thin shattered bones.

"You see those little fuckers run?" Joseph said, pushing out the words.

"They got what was coming to them. If I'd watched much more of that movie *I'd* have fired a shot, and not into the ceiling."

The rifle was now pointing at the ground, the butt inches away from Joseph's good arm. Did he have it in him to wrestle the gun from Alex? He hadn't been in a fight for at least twenty years. He also had a concussion and a twisted ankle, and his right bicep felt Popeye-sized, but with none of the sailor's strength. You imagine yourself in these situations, battling a villain in the scaffolding above a vat of molten lead or disarming a terrorist in a 747 cockpit, but your borrowed arsenal of fighting skills and tag lines—"Thanks for flying with us!"—no better prepared you for the real thing than sexual fantasies made a virgin a good lover.

As if reading his intentions, Alex lifted the rifle off the ground with a swift, natural motion and clutched it to his chest. The gun wasn't going anywhere.

"We better get going," Alex said. Was he playing with Joseph, like a cat with a mouse? Did a cat really toy with a mouse before killing it? The "Man versus Man" segment of his Grade Nine English class had insisted that only humans took pleasure from killing.

Joseph bit down on his bottom lip.

*Get a grip!*

He focused on the map of pain zones that now composed his body, moving from his head to his arm to his ankle.

"It won't be long before those kids come back." Alex was a good liar—men with strong convictions usually are. "We have to keep going."

*Until you find a better opportunity to kill me?* Joseph considered saying it out loud. It probably couldn't make the situation any worse, but he had to aim higher. He had to take action.

*The name of action*—where had he heard that before?

Joseph slipped the flashlight into his right hand, which still functioned just enough to hold the light in place. He couldn't let Alex know about his injured arm.

"I need to do something," he said, nodding at the shack's door, obeying a dim intuition that he'd be safer in the shack's vicinity, as if Alex *couldn't* shoot him in there.

Alex shrugged, unconcerned about time. He was not only less agitated than he'd been all night, he looked relieved—his back and shoulders unburdened of a physical weight. Maybe he was in shock, the magnitude of the aborted murder numbing his senses. Joseph stepped past him, running with this hypothesis, then rejecting it, embracing it, rejecting it again, fighting the panic by focusing on the pain, telling himself to breathe, to *think*.

Inside the shack, the flat light turned the space into a two-dimensional surface. The room smelled like beer, mould, and sweat, and with the elation of his averted murder passing, conflicting thoughts came flitting in and out of view like bats trapped in an attic.

What did he *know*? Alex wanted to shoot him. He could have gotten away with it, telling the police that Joseph fired the rifle into the cabin, then dropped the gun when he chased the boys. Alex grabbed it and followed, and in the chaos of shouts and threats, a man brandishing a knife stepped onto the path. One reflexive squeeze of the trigger and Joseph lay dead. A terrible accident, but who'd question the motives of a father searching for his missing child? Joseph would have believed it if he hadn't seen Alex's face and shaking hands. But *why* did Alex want to kill him? Joseph was no worse than most men. He was even better read and took the right position on the issues close to Alex's heart. Sure, Joseph had failed to live up to Alex's expectations from day one, but why try to kill him tonight?

"You installed a new skylight," Alex said, pointing at a triangular hole in the ceiling.

Joseph prodded the damaged plaster with his left hand, leaving a smudge of fingerprints that would place him in the shack, a detail that might incriminate Alex later. He walked to the pole-dancer poster and traced the pole with his finger, then laid his palms flat on the table, transferring prints onto the surface.

Alex didn't seem to care. He leaned the rifle against the wall and joined Joseph at the table, leaving four steps between himself and the gun. Joseph would need at least five to get there. Alex laughed as he poked at a flame-stained glass pipe lying beside an empty baggy, then he picked up a hand-carved pipe with a bowl in the shape of a skull and dropped it onto the floor. The neat pile of DVDs was next. He lifted one from the stack and smirked. The cheap, photocopied label showed a blurry nude stepping from a limo with *Gents Klub II* stencilled over the image. Alex laughed again—his daughter had been abducted by deranged vets and he'd nearly murdered a man, and the fucker was *laughing.*

"Her classmates and half their fathers probably pre-ordered copies." He gave Joseph a bitter smile. "Still, that was priceless. *That's my daughter!*" He rolled his head into his cupped hands and moaned and faked a barking sob. "That's my daughter! Turn it off! Turn it *oooffff*!"

Joseph didn't get the joke.

"Hardcore," Alex said.

"Porn?"

"*Hardcore*, the movie. With George C. Scott."

Joseph remembered the bare details: a small-town patriarch's daughter runs away to L.A. and gets caught up in the porn industry. The dad hires a detective to find her. He and Alex probably saw it together at one of the rep theatres back in the city.

"The scene where George C. Scott is shown a porn film starring his daughter. He says, '*Turn it off. That's my daughter!*' You shouted that before you fired the gun."

Joseph let him think the reference was intentional, and maybe it was, the buried celluloid memory breaking through his paralysis.

The big video screen was now leaning back against the wall at a skewed angle, transforming the porn film into a kid's show about a bubble-gum-pink fish exploring a bed of pale sea sponges, where it was swallowed by a shimmering orange blob. Joseph pushed the screen back onto its base, and squinted to bring the girl's face into focus. He knew now why she'd looked so familiar: she could pass for Franny's sister. Same big almond eyes and flat face, same cute pixie nose. The girl's eye makeup was streaked to Sad Clown grotesque. The boys had cum all over her face. Poor girl. Poor boys. Poor Joseph—he'd weep for the world if he could.

To keep the mood going he turned and did his impression of George C. Scott's General Patton: "Son, thirty years from now, when you're sitting with your grandson on your knee and he asks, 'Grandpa, what did you do in the great World War Two?' You won't have to say, '*I shovelled shit in Louisiana*.'"

He got the laugh. A vague plan was forming: keep Alex talking until he gave himself away.

"Her dad must be a real bruiser," Joseph said.

"Why?"

"The boys wouldn't have run like that if her dad was the local minister."

Alex smiled wider. "No, think about it: the mild-mannered father *pushed to the edge*, with nothing to lose. How many times have those kids seen *that* movie? Well played."

Joseph glanced at the door hoping to see someone, anyone, who'd confirm that he was discussing revenge films with a man who wanted to kill him. He closed his eyes and opened them, hoping beyond reason to see Franny appear. Where was she? Why were they wasting time in this place?

He took a deep breath and started exploring the shack again. If life had taught him anything, it was to play along until he caught up.

The old laptop lay beside the screen. He used Julian's

knife to pop the letters from the keyboard like corn kernels. The big screen cracked with a single kick. That poor girl. He kicked the screen again and then threw the computer across the room with his good arm, hitting the far wall. If any man tried to hurt Franny he'd gouge his eyes out and then cut off his balls and shove them down his throat until he choked to death on them.

Alex stood there, slyly smiling. He was rejuvenated, lifted high above the night's crisis by Joseph's violent rampage. There was more where that came from. Joseph tipped over the big screen and brought his full weight down on it, nearly re-twisting his ankle, then he kicked a hole in the drywall with his good foot. There were a couple of large cans of barbeque fluid and a hibachi under the table. Joseph splashed the lighter fluid on the DVDs and over the table, onto the wall and the futon.

"People will see the fire for miles," he said. "Cops, firefighters—the more the merrier."

Alex nodded—*set the whole fucking forest on fire*, his smiling face said. Joseph splashed more barbeque fluid on the back wall and window frame, careful not to soak his sleeves, then emptied the can on the chipboard floor.

"I need a match," he said.

When he turned around Alex was standing in the doorway, holding a pack of matches in one hand and an unlit match in the other. Another can of barbeque fluid lay near his feet, the nozzle leaking the last of its contents in a puddle that was spreading toward Joseph.

So that's how it would end. Twenty feet of floor separated Joseph from the door. He'd be a human fireball by the time he hit the open air, if Alex didn't slam the door on his face first. Alex would tell the cops that Joseph went nuts in the shack, doused the place in barbeque fluid, then lit the match too early. Joseph closed his eyes and locked in on an image of Franny, the one good thing he'd brought into this world. He remembered when they took the ferry to Vancouver Island. She was six, and she'd never been on a boat that held more than twenty people before, and when the ocean-going ferry loomed up to the dock her eyes filled with awe. "It's a *ship*! Daddy, it's a ship!" she shouted, her voice coming to him from a finer world, her eyes free of the doubt and self-consciousness that clouded them now.

*I love you*—that's what he'd tell her if she was here. *Never forget that.*

"Are you coming?"

When he opened his eyes, Alex was regarding him with mild annoyance, his nose scrunching against the gas fumes.

He wasn't going to kill him here.

Was the asshole going to run Joseph through a series of agonized Last Moments before finally finishing him off? Joseph put the knife back in his pocket, but not in the case. He wanted to keep the weapon handy. He was going to get out of this alive and find Franny.

He ran through the doorway, propelled by a rush of hope that felt like the first stage of madness, so elated that, as Alex lit the match, he shouted, "Goodbye Twenty-First-Century Cocks Studios!" The cornball joke seemed to trigger a loud *whoosh*, and a hot wind hit their backs before they reached the trees. Glass shattered, and they turned to see funnels of fire whirling up from the front door, carrying the glowing fragments of particleboard and plastic into the black sky.

"Burn you fucker!" Joseph shouted, the blood roaring right out to his fingertips, threatening to burst them like overripe fruit. The stars were gone, the trees bright and shadowless, the burning shack pushing back the encasing night. The men watched the flames, the orange light softening Alex's face—he could have been a child mesmerized by the old magic of fire. The blaze licked its way up the shack's outer walls, flames scrambling over each other to meet above the roof and join the funnelling cone, a beacon for the cops and a warning to Franny's captors that Joseph would scorch the dark places of the world to find her.

"We better go," Alex said at last, making a half-hearted attempt at the Leader of Men voice he'd used on the logging road. Had it sounded so rehearsed then? Joseph would have been desperate enough to believe even the poorest performance if it meant saving Franny.

"We just burned down the little fuckers' shack," Alex said. "They'll jump us if we go down that side of the hill." He pointed to the path, conspicuous now in the firelight. "If we go down this side, we should reach another path. It'll take us just north of the commune."

Another change in plans.

"We need to hurry." Alex stepped into the woods, leaving Joseph alone.

Alex was right, but why the sudden concern for their pace?

The adrenaline was draining from Joseph's system, the first signs of a monstrous hangover intensifying the pain and dizzying pressure in his head. Sentences seemed to lose their glue, scattering their words, and he felt himself sliding between narratives, each as compelling as the last while it reigned. In one, Joseph followed Alex to the old commune, where they took out the war vets and rescued Franny and Rebecca. In another, Alex led Joseph to a more suitable site to kill him. A third had the men fighting to the death.

Joseph touched the knife in his pocket, feeling the serrated edge. He tried to imagine stabbing Alex's belly until he was dead, a sequence of actions he couldn't complete because he'd be lost without Alex. People died out here, driven mad by bugs, missing the search party or the hunter's shack by a hundred yards. He needed Alex to lead him out, and more. *It never changes*, Joseph thought, *in the schoolyard or the old-age home, the willingness to hand fate over to a bigger, stronger male.*

He felt sleepy and passive, captive to the fire as it ravaged the shack, the flames burning yellow and orange and blue, leaping out to touch the edge of the forest. A forest fire—that would get the police and firefighters out here, maybe force the vets into the open. He should have set the forest on fire hours ago. He turned and walked into the woods after Alex.

The wilderness gradually assumed its own presence, trapping the two men inside a distinct atmosphere, as if they were piloting a bathysphere floating through a deep ocean trench, their feeble flashlight cutting a tiny wedge out of the blackness. They were safe inside their cramped craft, but if the light failed, the wilderness would pour in like tons of frigid water. Shapes moved into the light and merged back into the darkness, the evergreens bustling like pods of kelp, occasionally revealing a pair of pupils reflecting the light back like marbles.

Alex moved at a methodical, energetic pace, with Joseph trudging a little behind, wrestling with the facts as he understood them, his mind picking through the same open-ended conclusions and speculations. Alex had aimed the rifle at him, intending to pull the trigger, then didn't go through with it. An incriminating detail might have stopped him, a clue the CSI nerds would pick up on later. Then there were the kids—four local boys who'd testify to hearing a second shot only *after* they'd reached the bottom of the hill.

Was it Murder One—the charge, not the crime—that had stayed Alex's hand? Or maybe Joseph's reckless attack on the boys had saved him. Aiming the rifle at Joseph's back, Alex might have thought: *Here is another man, morally outraged enough to fire on four boys who filmed the gang rape of teenage girl.* How could he shoot a man who'd so blatantly demonstrated his moral worth? Whatever the case, Alex walked down the narrow deer path like a man unburdened of a crushing load.

*Look at him*, Joseph thought, watching his broad back, *like he's on a recreational hike.*

*Stab the fucker in the back*, a voice urged. *Stick in the knife before he finds another place to kill you.*

Joseph touched the knife, wondering what it would feel like to kill a man. Could he do it if he had to?

*It's him or you.*

Not yet it wasn't. He still needed Alex.

They finally reached flat ground again, the smell of pine resin saturating the damp air. Alex stopped to check the compass, clearly not in a hurry, then stepped to his right, pushing the branches aside so they didn't swing back in Joseph's face.

*What a guy.*

He was close enough to kill. It would be so easy.

"I found it," Alex said.

They were standing on a path, narrower than the big path but still wide enough for them to walk side by side.

"This will take us a little west of the commune."

Joseph was sure he'd said "north" when they'd left the shack. For God's sake, he'd better start paying attention if he wanted to stay alive.

"How's your ankle?" Alex said as they started down the path.

"It's holding up." He hadn't noticed he was limping.

"Good. We've got a ways to go."

*To where?* Joseph chewed the inside of his cheek to keep the words in. He felt apprehensive, alert and confused, but he didn't sense any immediate danger.

"Those boys will think twice about playing at porn kings again," Alex said.

"It was pure adrenaline." Joseph was too exhausted to play up the machismo of his earlier actions. "I could have just as easily run away."

"Your body knew what it was doing. It took action."

"The name of action," Joseph said, finding the phrase again.

"Hamlet."

"What?"

"*The name of action*—it's from *Hamlet*. I memorized that soliloquy in high school."

Of course he had.

"You fired that gun because your body said *enough*! You couldn't just sit back and take it anymore," Alex insisted. "It wasn't enough to comment or make a joke or send an angry email. You know what I mean."

In a general sense, Joseph did. Life had heaped a lot of shit on him—clean-scented, cost-analyzed, and justified from on high. And the more of it he ate, the leaner and broker and more debt-ridden he got—like everyone else he knew. But what did that have to do with tonight?

"How long until we reach the commune?"

"Can't be more than three miles."

"And the veterans live there?"

Alex waited to answer. "Some are vets, yeah."

Why did he pause? "Which war did they fight in?"

"The guys who started the place in the sixties are still around."

They would be Nam vets, nearing retirement age, still strong enough to overpower two girls but too old to drag them back to the commune. And if they'd been abducting local girls for forty years, wouldn't the police have caught them by now? Iraq or Gulf War vets were more likely culprits. God only knew what they'd seen over there, the kills notched on body-shredding rifles, their minds scrambled by experimental inoculation shots and uranium-spiked bullets.

"That guy in khaki, standing by the woods," Joseph said. "How old was he?"

"Hard to say. He was pretty far away."

Joseph had him! Alex had mentioned the vet's troubled expression earlier, now he couldn't guess the guy's age. But why lie? Was he so desperate to get Joseph, a risk-adverse city boy, onside for a dangerous nighttime search that he'd invented the crazed vet?

No—it had been Joseph's plan to search the woods. He glanced at Alex, who was already looking his way. His expression, lit by the flashlight below, was provocative, challenging, as though he wanted Joseph to know something. And did he? Had he been fucking with Joseph all night? Joseph had to keep him talking.

"Why did you join the army? You never told me."

Alex was ready with an answer. "I wanted to be part of something bigger than me. Not very fashionable."

"Understatement of the first order."

"Everyone I knew was trying to *find themselves*," he said, easing into memory. "I wanted to lose myself, or find a better self. I probably read too many explorers' biographies. Shackleton, Scott, Livingstone, men from the Great Age of Exploration—men who sacrificed everything for an ideal or a test of will. Since I didn't know any men of destiny, I thought I might find that spirit in the army. I used to lie in my bedroom and imagine what it would be like to be a unit in a single organism working toward the betterment of humanity."

"You wanted to be a limb." In spite of everything, Joseph felt protective of Alex's wounded faith in human progress, an idealism their hip friends used to laugh at as if it was an affectation, like a taste for obscure jazz records.

"I was sick of myself," Alex said. "Sick of hanging around the plaza and going to parties. I wanted to join a community that would force me to go beyond my boundaries. I didn't want people to *ask* what I was into, I wanted them to *show* me." He groaned. "I'd seen too many movies and read too many books—it always comes down to that."

"I didn't want to surrender my precious identity to any ideal at that age," Joseph admitted. The only earthly limitations he pushed against were erotic. Sex was his Great Western Sea—sex and the priestesses who guarded its mysteries.

"I don't know," Alex said. "I think you were always a closet idealist. You wouldn't have put it this way, but what you really wanted was a *cause*."

Why not just admit it: there was a time, after Franny was born, when Joseph would have been lost without Alex's idealism, his mentorship of the man Joseph wanted to be—husband, father, engaged citizen, and writer. Martha wasn't enough for Joseph, and neither was Franny. He remembered her as a three-year-old, skinny limbs and big eyes, climbing up his arm like a spider monkey to latch onto his waist, looking up at him with total trust, as if he was a god with no dominion but her child's world. She'd been easy to care for. She needed food, shelter, stories, and strong arms, a supportive tone and a few pet names—*Honey*, *Puppy*, *Fan*. And then. And then. In crept the old doubts, the old vanities, the boredom and yearning for new sensations. Had he really let himself believe that Franny would be better off without him?

Alex should have pointed a gun at him years ago.

"There was that crazy experiment you tried when you were a kid," Alex said, already laughing. "I'd call that idealism."

Joseph couldn't help it: he was flattered that Alex remembered the story. "I thought I'd figured out the secret to time travel. I just had to repeat my movements in the exact reverse order. If I walked ten steps across the room while swinging my arms, I would travel back in time by walking the same ten steps backward—same arm-swinging motion, same distance between steps. If I could just master my bodily movements in reverse, I'd move back in time to the original starting point, like rewinding a videotape." Joseph spoke in a self-mocking tone, but he was proud of the ambitious boy he'd been. "The theory fell apart at the dinner table, when

I couldn't work out the metaphysics of un-cutting my meat and rolling the peas back onto my fork."

"Do you ever wonder what would have happened if you'd stuck with the plan?"

"If I'd figured it out, I'd start walking backward right now." Joseph bit his lip, tearing the thread of conversation before it unspooled any further. "I tried to rewind time, but you actually joined the army," he said, obeying a strong urge to flatter. "You weren't messing around, man."

"The army turned out to be just another *dick* thing. I liked parts of it—the discipline, the travel. I loved being in those old halls and barracks and pissing in a washroom the size of a three-bedroom apartment."

"The officers must have liked you. They wanted you in the special forces."

Alex didn't answer.

"When you went on that survival retreat."

"Of course. It was crazy: they wanted me to shoot a dog."

Now Joseph knew why Alex's story about the C.O. in the wilderness had sounded familiar—it was lifted from a movie. He couldn't remember the title, but there was a platoon of soldiers on a special-ops training mission in the wilderness, and the hard-assed officer ordered the protagonist to shoot a dog. The soldier couldn't pull the trigger, and so failed the test. Later, the platoon was attacked by werewolves.

What about Rebecca's earring then? She might have deliberately dropped it as a signal, like that hobbit in *The Lord of the Rings*, but what were the chances of finding it in thousands of square miles of forest? Alex had probably picked the earring off the floor that morning and put it in his pocket, and seeing Joseph weeping on the logging road, put it to work. Why hadn't Alex just shot him at the logging camp? It was as good a killing site as any. No, for some reason he'd needed to keep Joseph moving, so he dropped the earring on the path, feigning curiosity when his flashlight beam picked out the shiny trinket, and then joy when he pretended to recognize it, rehearsing the story he was about to tell Joseph. Not that he needed to—Joseph had bought into the Hollywood Revenge Drama shtick from the first word. He was desperate for the call to paternal sacrifice, because what father doesn't want to risk his life for his child? Dying for a child was easier than raising one.

Alex stopped to examine a rusting beer can. What would he pretend to find next? A shoe? Broken teeth? Maybe he hadn't seen any war vets at all. Then why the *show*? Why the two-men-against-the-world speech? Why the gun?

Alex stomped down on the can, crushing it to the thickness of a coaster.

Joseph stopped as suddenly as though he'd bumped against a wall in the dark.

That's when he knew—that's when he knew *everything*.

It was Alex, not Rebecca and Franny, who'd watched Joseph and Jane fucking in the clearing. Alex who'd snapped a branch as he fled the scene.

Joseph's calves went rubbery. He forced himself forward on locked knees until he could walk normally again.

"Are you all right?" Alex said.

"Just a little dizzy."

Joseph saw how it must have happened: Alex fleeing

from the site of Jane and Joseph's betrayal, tearing at the air like King Lear, riding a tsunami of rage across the fields. One type of man, catching his wife of sixteen years fucking a family friend, would have killed the lovers on the spot. Another—like Joseph—would have slunk back to the farmhouse and gorged on righteous anger and self-pity until Jane returned, then berated her with belligerent questions that built to a thundering guilt trip: *I'm so disappointed, Jane, this is so beneath you, so beneath us*. If that didn't make her cry, his next move—the theatrical smashing of a family keepsake—surely would.

Not Alex. Back at the farmhouse—stoned, drunk, and blind with anger—he stalked through the kitchen pondering the important business of revenge. He noticed that the girls weren't home. Maybe Rebecca did leave a note, passively sarcastic, informing the adults that she and Franny were at a party or in town with friends. Seeing an easy way to punish Jane, her lover, her good-time stoner friends, *and* his own ungrateful daughter, he dropped the note behind a cupboard or under the fridge, creating a believable miscommunication no one could trace back to him. Then he waited at the back fence, where he lobbed the news of the missing girls at Jane and her guests like a hand grenade, enjoying the sight of his betrayers spiralling into panic when the misplaced note went unfound and Franny didn't answer her cell phone, all too happy to play an array of enabling roles—accuser, voice of reason, pot-stirrer—to accelerate the momentum.

Had more luck ever dropped into an angry man's lap in one night?

Alex had been lying all along. The girls hadn't gone missing: he'd made the whole thing up.

Joseph stopped putting the pieces together long enough to affirm the essential thing: Franny was not lost in the woods. She hadn't been abducted or raped. She didn't see her father fucking her oldest friend's mother.

She was safe—precious Franny—safe, *unbroken*. This madness had not touched her.

Joseph shut his gaping mouth, smothering the mumbles of joy. He now knew what it meant to want to fall on his knees and thank God, for sparing his daughter and for granting him a second chance. To show Franny how much he loved her. To build on that knowledge every day.

He just had to get out of the woods alive.

Joseph faked a stumble, grazing the rifle at Alex's side. If he got hold of the gun, he might get off one shot. If he missed, Alex would have no choice but to kill him. Joseph was a desk jockey with a patchy attendance record at the gym; Alex made heavy wooden furniture with his hands. The odds were bad.

"Do you need to rest?"

"I'm fine," Joseph said. "We have to keep up the pace."

He wondered if he sounded convincing, or if it even mattered anymore. His eyes fought to see into the moonless gloom beside the path. Large humps of quartz loomed into the light and there were boulders between the trees, the record of powerful and pointless geographical forces in flux millions of years earlier. The land was flat and rocky, the rocks suggesting the ruins of stone temples and sacrificial altars.

Wind whipped the treetops, making a noise of leafy tides, an atmospheric backdrop for the final stanzas of Alex's "Appalachian Revenge Ballad." The amorality of Alex's plan, its petty, narcissistic cruelty, fell within Joseph's imaginative powers, but his resolve to see the plan through was the stuff of song and legend. To silently watch as your wife fell apart, then abandon her to lament her firstborn child while you took her lover out to the woods to shoot him—to think that such men still walked among us!

Joseph was probably giving him too much credit. Somewhere in that first hour the plot had slipped from Alex's control. Franny didn't pick up her messages, Derek's phone went unanswered, and after panic tipped Jane into a breakdown, the cops were called to search for two girls who weren't really missing. Alex was looking at jail time and a wife who'd never forgive him.

Leave it to Joseph to call for a search of the woods, presenting Alex with an exit from the crime scene *and* an isolated location for an honour killing. When Alex dropped in the sighting of the war vet, Joseph ran with the implications and begged Alex to bring along the rifle. Perfect: he could accidentally shoot Joseph and they'd still call him a hero. You can lie on a couch for five years drinking beer, but risk your life to save a child and the world anoints you a great father. Only Julian had sensed, with a druggie's rewired radar, that something didn't add up. No wonder he'd told Joseph to keep the knife to himself.

Joseph dared a glance at Alex—his clenched, heavy jaw in profile, his bottom lip quivering like a leaf straining under the weight of raindrops. What was going through his head? Did he have his own internal chorus of voices?

*You should have shot him when you had the chance—he fucked your wife. Be a man!*

*You can still walk away from this. You haven't reached the point of no return.*

They were passing through a stretch of trees, stunted by an infestation of wild grapevines as thick as ship's rope, the trees bent and twisted as if collectively frozen in the midst of a violent attack. The trees were dead or dying, held in pose by the coiling vines, the branches fluttering against Joseph's body like protuberances guiding him toward some acid-filled digestive sac. He wondered what everyone was doing back at the farm. They too had been locked tight inside Alex's story, playing the roles he assigned them until the arrival of the girls set them all free. Franny was safe—she had to be—back at the farm drinking cocoa in her pyjamas, the cops long returned to the station.

Joseph could feel the words sliding into place like boxcars behind a powerful engine, a full cargo of confessions: *I fucked Jane. I know about your plan and don't blame you for putting it into play. Can't we just go home?*

That wouldn't cut it with Alex. He'd come to the end of what a man of conscience can accomplish with words. What had any of them done since they were sixteen but talk? And why would Alex trust Joseph with a secret that could destroy his reputation and his marriage? Without Jane and his kids, Alex would live out his days with the bluffers and conspiracy theorists who crowded his store on Friday nights. But if he walked out of the woods alone and stuck to his story, no one would ever know the truth. His alibi was sound, and the cops, knowing Alex from town as a man's man, would believe him. Those same cops did not read Joseph's column.

They took a fork in the path that led them beside a marsh, the air buzzing with frog noise and loud plonks along the murky edges. Every few minutes Alex turned on his fading flashlight to sweep the area, revealing scenes too primitive to believe: pools of stagnant water emitting tendrils of mist; waterlogged trees that resembled the masts of sunken ships; hillocks rising from the muck like the backs of sea monsters. A cloak of self-consciousness had descended upon the two men. They'd gotten ahead of themselves, presumed too much of an old friendship struggling back to life in inhospitable terrain. Or so Joseph hoped as they passed into a stretch of spindly trees and massive rock faces. Were they still pretending to search for the girls? What about the commune—was it now a discarded prop? Alex was giving nothing away. He looked almost serene, as if he wanted them to step into the final act like gentlemen—*no hard feelings, old boy, the whole thing couldn't be helped.*

"Alex, where are we going?"

"I want to show you something," he said. The gun hung freely at his side, bobbing like a kid's hockey stick. "We're almost there."

Was this how it would end: Alex pulling the trigger while Joseph took in a site of natural beauty? He'd been so open with Joseph a little while ago, like in the old days. Was it all a con to get Joseph's guard down? Alex couldn't be that good an actor.

Something caught Joseph's eye. He turned on his flashlight and pointed it at a mound the size of a small house not far back from the path. "What's that?" he said.

Alex stopped, his flashlight hovering on what appeared at first to be a pile of moss-covered boulders. Details emerged as they got closer: the boulder pile was actually a steep hill, and built into its base was a disintegrating wooden frame filled in with branches, boards, and other debris.

"It's an abandoned mine," Alex said. He sounded strangely shy but eager, like a boy revealing his trove of toy trains or science-fiction collectables to a new friend whose mutual enthusiasm is not guaranteed. "Probably a two-man operation. Semi-precious gems. There's a lot of them around here, all closed up."

Alex turned off his flashlight and rested the rifle stock on the ground, keeping one hand on the end of the barrel as he pulled a board free from the entrance, releasing a draft of cold, damp air that smelled of minerals.

*Put the rifle down*, Joseph mouthed. He slipped the knife from his pocket, concealing it at his side. He'd go for the throat if he got a clear path, the stomach otherwise. Stab and withdraw, stab and withdraw. Rip off a few more boards, push Alex into the mine, leave him to bleed to death. They'd never find the body.

Joseph's mouth was dry, the rush of blood in his ears louder than the wind in the trees. Could he kill a man? He had to, for Franny's sake. He had to get out of here alive.

Alex raised himself onto his toes to peer into the mine, his fingertips the only thing holding the rifle up. Joseph gripped the knife harder and took a step forward.

Alex turned around and, seeing something in Joseph's expression that either embarrassed or frightened him, carefully picked up the rifle, keeping the barrel pointed at the sky.

"Better get moving," he said, making his way back toward the path. "We'll be there soon."

Joseph let a deep breath escape as he slipped the knife back into his pocket. He didn't know why, but he believed Alex. This was all going to be over soon.

There was no commune, no country road, just another wall of trees, this one bordering a field of weeds and saplings, many growing out of stumps scorched by an old forest fire. They were close to the end. Joseph sensed it in Alex's resolved posture and in his own straining nerves. He couldn't wait much longer. He'd been pushed so far past any previous experience of exhaustion, shock, and physical pain that every thought and sensory impression glowed with hallucinogenic lucidity. Beneath this bright procession, a tremendous internal pressure forced his emotions to the surface with such force he felt them trying to escape through his skin. It was like trying to sweat stones. He was desperate for release. He wanted to talk to Franny—about the books they used to read together, about the cool, bleached-out techno music she loved, about anything she wanted. He would listen and ask the right questions.

Alex turned off his flashlight as they entered a grove, moving slowly past the skirts of the old evergreens. Alex's sure but cautious footsteps revealed that he knew what was up ahead. This was their destination. It probably had been the whole time.

The night seemed less gloomy, though there was no trace of sunrise yet, and as they walked the light grew stronger, gathering the quality of blue flame—chemical, single-purpose. Finer lines appeared in the tree branches, and far ahead a bright green line seemed to hang in the air like a thick mist.

Alex grabbed Joseph's injured arm near the bicep, and the sharp pain drowned out the light. "I think somebody's here."

"There are *people* here?" Joseph had never wanted to see another human face so badly. "What is this place?"

Alex let out a rush of air. "A grow-op. A big one."

"Derek!"

"Yes, and it's not just pot he's into."

"If Derek's here, he can drive us home." Joseph's imagination had already raced ahead to the reunion scene with Franny.

"Do *not* try to talk to him," Alex said. "Out here, he's a different man than the one you met. This is *his* place."

"But he thinks you're a fucking genius. I'll tell him we got lost searching for the girls. We don't give a shit about his dope plantation."

"Don't we?"

"I don't."

Alex chewed that over. "He's not what he seems. He's all business."

"Come on—his *business* is playing the badass drug dealer. It's like being a rock star all over again. He'll do the right thing."

"Don't be fucking stupid!"

Joseph stepped back from Alex's rage. "Is he working with those vets?"

"They're not the problem. He told me he needed investors to help grow his business." Alex stepped closer. "He asked me to come in as a partner. He said *someone* has to grow the stuff, so why not us, and create some jobs while we're at it. I told him he'd ruin the area by bringing in organized crime and the cops. He's been paranoid ever since, thinking I'm going to rat him out."

"Then this is perfect."

Alex frowned.

"He helps you out by driving us home, and then you owe him." Joseph waited for three seconds. "I have to see who's there." Joseph wasn't going to budge. Not if it meant finding out the truth about Franny. He was sick of playing this game of half-confessions with Alex.

"Okay, if it's just Derek, maybe we talk to him." Alex was giving in too quickly for Joseph's liking. Maybe he just wanted an ending to the story he'd put into motion God knows how many hours ago. What a relief it would be, after so many nightmarish twists and reversals, to put down the pen and hand over the narrative to someone else.

"You go a few paces to your left and walk to the light," Alex said. "I'll go to the right."

So Alex wanted them to separate. Had *that* been his plan all along? Take Joseph to the grow-op, where they come upon bad men. Shots are fired. Joseph gets killed and Derek goes to jail, eliminating two of Alex's enemies with one shot.

It added up, but Alex had seemed genuinely surprised when he saw the lights.

"Watch out for booby traps," Alex said. "If things go wrong then *run*—that way, east, toward the sunrise. Run that way and you'll reach the highway."

Run to the east, to the sunrise, to the highway—Alex left Joseph to puzzle the meanings as he loped into the trees. Joseph moved a few paces to his left and started walking toward the light, trying to maintain a mid-crouch posture to minimize his body mass. Soon the stripes on his shoes were reflecting the light like miniature aisle lights. He stopped to rub dirt on them and heard movement in the trees to his right. Alex was close. What had he told Joseph? *Run to the east*—right into the path of his rifle sight.

Joseph squeezed his eyes shut. What did he really *know* about Alex's plan? Everything that had happened after they smoked the One Night in Bangkok joint was as open to interpretation as a dream. Joseph had his evidence—Alex's lies, the earring, the raised rifle at the shack—but that didn't prove Alex rigged any of the night's disasters. The possibility of the girls being snatched by war vets was a long shot, but so was the backstory to any abduction.

*We turned our backs for ten seconds.*

*We'd known her soccer coach for five years.*

*She never took a shortcut before that night.*

He patted the knife in his pocket and kept walking. There was only one story that mattered: getting out of here alive and back to Franny.

About fifty feet ahead of him the woods ended at a wide grassy area lit by powerful halogen lights. He moved from one tree to the next, his eyes wincing at the widening bands of light between their branches, some of which trailed what he guessed were spiderwebs. He reached a maple tree a few feet from the clearing, one of the few non-evergreens in the grove, and waited for his eyes to adjust. Soon he distinguished Derek's blue pickup truck in front of the solid wall of pulsing light. It was parked on the far side of a work area the size of two tennis courts, the headlights illuminating a garden shed draped in pine branches and a large shack beneath the clearing's single remaining tree. The shack was made from plywood and painted green, with two metal chimneys protruding from the roof and a metal door that hung open, revealing a barrel of chemicals and one end of a gleaming steel table inside. About twenty yards from the truck the pot field began—a dazzling green sea of waist-high plants and the odd pine tree standing out against the surrounding darkness. One of Alex's vets, an old hippie in khaki with a bushy ponytail the colour of rat fur, stepped out from behind the shack carrying a garbage bag and went inside.

Maybe this was Alex's Plan B—having destroyed the local gonzo porn studio, he and Joseph would end the night on a morally uplifting note by burning down the county meth shack and setting the pot fields on fire. Then why had Alex still led them into this lion's den after he realized that Derek was here?

No, he'd been the one to insist they check out the grow-op, not Alex.

Joseph clamped his thoughts shut. It didn't matter. He'd picked a good hiding spot. Three quick steps would take him back to the safety of the woods. Or he could step into the clearing, giving Derek a full view of his unthreatening, ragged figure.

*Derek, it's me. Alex's friend from this afternoon. Rebecca and Franny went missing. Alex and I are lost.*

Derek would help—anything to impress Alex—and if Joseph walked into the clearing, Alex would have no choice but to put down his gun and follow. Joseph could pull it off. He'd partied with plenty of drug dealers over the years. He knew how to ingratiate himself with tough men. Don't suck up to them, and don't challenge them at what they think they're good at. His only enemy was himself—his deep need to know, indisputably, if Franny was okay. He couldn't appear too desperate, too weak.

He heard derisive laughter coming from beyond the reach of the lights, and then a man materialized at the edge of the field, followed by two others who stepped out of the bright green sea. The two men were bikers in jeans and black T-shirts under denim vests. The man in front was Derek, looking very pleased with himself, beating a rock anthem against his thigh as the two bikers exchanged a private nod. The bikers weren't wearing their colours, but they didn't have to—an extraterrestrial would know they were hard men, their molecules packed tighter than a normal man's, like sharkskin. The skinnier one was the leader. He had a predator's face, all wedged power and black eyes.

"I still do the odd acoustic show," Derek said to the other biker, a large bearded man, at least six-foot-four and a yard wide at the shoulders.

"*Unplugged.*"

"Exactly, bro." Derek was using his raconteur stage voice.

The bigger man was secure enough in the role of the Muscle to do the talking while his boss sized up the operation, his head moving while his eyes remained as still as windows. They'd probably been partying at a strip club, the bikers indulging their new business partner in an all-access sampling of the local wares before heading to the grow-op.

The lead biker, his assessment completed, hooked his thumbs in his belt loops and said, "rock and roll," a cue for everyone to appreciate the field of pot plants. He rose up onto the balls of his feet, a posture that showed his sinewy body's coiled strength—even his thin ponytail could do double duty as a weapon. He *was* a weapon, a long blade of a man, and when he turned his gaze toward the trees, the exact distance between him and Joseph—twenty strides—impressed itself into the soles of Joseph's feet.

"That's prime botanical, buddy," he said.

Derek nodded too many times. "We're miles from the highway, ground's higher here, drains well, good tree cover." His lurching voice made him sound like an actor two rehearsals behind the rest of the cast. He'd probably done too much coke and too much talking—exactly what the bikers wanted. "No one comes back here. I put the word out."

The leader's expression said he'd be the judge of the security arrangements.

"How many more weeks?" the big biker asked.

"Eight, tops."

The biker turned to his boss. This wasn't good.

"It was a dry spring," Derek said, his agricultural report reluctantly confirmed by the old vet, who'd come to join the men. "Driest in fifty years."

*Stop talking, Derek*, Joseph thought.

"It was a bitch getting the water tank down that logging road."

"That's a *road*?"

Derek's face reminded Joseph of a fish in an algae-choked tank, eyes and lips bulging for oxygen. "It *used* to be a road," he said. "No one uses it, especially since the forest fires."

"No?"

Joseph leaned back into the safety of the dark.

"I'd know if anyone set foot on that road," Derek said, staring at the ground. "One of us is usually out here, and we have this big . . . big wall, made of branches and leaves, at least ten feet tall." He was trying to make the wall sound almost mythical. "It slides right into place so you can't even see the break in the woods from the main road. Jimmy here designed it."

Jimmy, the old hippie, was reluctant to take the credit.

The leader shrugged. "Every bud is sold," he said. "You deliver the goods, we take it from there. And we get a cut of the meth, but you know that."

Derek clearly didn't, but he tried hard to hide his shock. "I've got some boys who'll help out with the harvest in exchange for a share."

The leader smoothed his flat hair and frowned—amazingly, Derek didn't disintegrate in a cloud of smoke. "What are you telling me, buddy?"

"They put in a little money up front, I give them a cut. Of *my* share."

That explained Derek's "piece of the pie" text—Mike had

invested in the harvest. No surprise there. Mike's salary probably couldn't even keep up his half of the mortgage payments. The money must have been tempting for Alex too, with his store struggling and two kids to put through university, but he'd never participate in the gangsterization of the local economy.

"You better be able to handle them," the leader said.

"I got it covered."

"Hey man, you guys planning a reunion?"

Derek turned to the big biker, who lifted an air guitar and sang, "*Talk to me laaater.*"

Derek smiled because he had to do something.

"*Talk to me laaaaaaater!* That was a good track!" The big guy started dancing with surprisingly nimble feet, though his thick, tapering legs barely bent at the knees. "*Talk to me laaater!*"

Derek finally recognized the chorus of Hardwar's one near-hit, and he easily assumed the modest ex-rocker pose. "The boys are scattered to the four winds. Gavin's gone all Mister Corporate."

The Muscle ran Eddie Van Halen finger trills down his air guitar: "*Dee-dee-dee—nannel, nannel! Dee-dee-dee—nannel, nannel! Talk to me laaater.* Sing it, man."

"It's 'Talk *About It* Later,'" Derek corrected between fake laughs.

Joseph had had a pothead roommate in first year whose one party trick was to flick his lighter in people's faces and ask if he was freaking them out. That and his hearty fake laugh, which Derek was conjuring with eerie accuracy as the biker baited him.

"Sing it!" the big man shouted. "*Dee-dee-dee—nannel, nannel!*"

"We got some clubs up north," the leader said, disintegrating the air guitar. "Shitholes, but money pits if you know how to work them. Your band could headline on Saturday nights. Bill it as a reunion tour."

Derek stared down at the ground again as the leader assessed him with the melancholic expression of a man long disappointed by the privileges of power. Joseph stepped further back into the darkness, his fingers brushing another hanging spiderweb.

"I've got a *new* band," Derek said. "We do bluegrass, Old Time Country. Lots of the Carter Family, Hank Williams."

"That cowboy shit?" The big biker let out a whoop and made the yodelling noises of a cartoon cowboy in love. "You can't peel to country music." He did the first steps of a mincing, strutting dance while lethargically picking open the buttons of his vest—a burlesque variation on the linebacker-in-a-tutu routine. "*My truck burned down. My barn blew up. My girl blew the preacher.*" He ended with a falsetto exclamation that demonstrated, more than any show of force, his familiarity with sudden, brutal violence—the pool cue to the skull, the eye gouged with a thumb, the testicle-crushing kick.

"I'm talking about your *real* band," the leader said. "Folks love the oldies."

*Oldies*. That had to hurt.

"I'd have to call up the boys," Derek said, realizing it was not a request. "They'll bitch 'til they're blue in the face but they'll be there. It'll be like old times."

Formal negotiations concluded, the leader nodded and flashed a hammy smile his men must pray to see on bad nights. "The clubs are packed in the summer and hunting season," he said. "Pussy, dope—tourists love it. Winter's dead. That's when we got to get the locals in."

"We brought in some peelers from Russia," the Muscle said. "Nikita Bityacockoff!"

"*Fresh.* Eighteen." His boss shrugged. "That's what their passports say."

Derek forced the corners of his mouth to rise. "Everybody's gotta hustle these days," he said, taking out his Zippo lighter, which the big biker intercepted.

"Psych!"

Derek lacked the hardware to bust the biker's balls in return. The big man did Derek the honour of *not* pulling out the vial of coke from his pocket, allowing Derek to hand it over.

"Derek—that's a German name, eh?" the biker said as he lit a smoke. He spoke a German word that sounded like "shit pig" and did a toot from the vial. He said the German word again. The leader liked the game. Derek answered in German.

"*What?*"

"You spoke in German," Derek said. "I answered you."

"I'm not fucking German." The biker stared at Jimmy the old hippie. "Your boss thinks I'm a fucking Kraut. Do I look like a Kraut?"

Jimmy was happy to lend the giant his outrage.

"Do Germans ride fucking Harleys?" the biker said, inches from Derek's face. "Would a fucking Kraut be out here working at four in the morning?"

"No way," Derek said. Forty years of sitcom watching couldn't rescue him from the biker's lame routine.

"Exactly. He'd be in bed with his fatty frau."

He stepped back and laughed. Derek did some of the coke. If he didn't get this situation under control the bikers would end negotiations by cutting out the middleman and hiring the vet to run the grow-op. These were not good men—they were not "cool." They prowled the edges of cities and towns and former Soviet-bloc nations siphoning up the lost girls and the desperate men and putting their bodies to work.

It was time to go. Joseph backed away from the tree, staying in the column of shadow. He waved away a cobweb that brushed his face, sending it swinging out into the light, where it transformed into a bright silver thread before vanishing back into the darkness. The web came to rest in his hair, and it stuck to his finger when he tried to pull it free.

The pain was so sudden, so sharp, that an image of a spider biting his fingertip flashed in his mind. He tried to flick the spider off but it bit down to the bone. How could half an inch of fingertip emit so much agonizing sensation—an entire leg shouldn't have so many nerve endings. He held up his left hand to the light. A fish hook was stuck clean through the tip of his middle finger. So much pain, as if his body were saying "fish hook" a thousand times a second. He could taste the metal, like the hook was stuck in his tongue.

The men were staring in his direction.

"You said no one knew about this place," the big biker said.

"It's a raccoon," Derek said. "No one would dare come here."

Alex clamped his hand on Joseph's wrist.

"Don't move," he whispered. "Not a sound."

Joseph's arm was shaking. The fishing line was taut, pulling the punctured flesh with it. He bit his lip to stifle a cry. Alex held his wrist with a crushing grip.

"Just wait it out," Alex said. "They can't see us. Give them a few seconds and they'll forget they heard anything."

"I can't," Joseph said. The pain ran like liquid ice through his finger, eating its way up his arm. He needed release, through screaming, through running, through pounding the tree. His silent tears did not oil free the hook. "I can't. Just cut me free. My knife."

Alex set the rifle against the tree, took the knife from Joseph's pocket, and leaned closer to get a better look at the fishing line, careful not to pull on Joseph's finger. The wind picked up, rustling the branches, and Alex pulled the line down, loosening the tension but not relieving the agony.

"It's a steel line," he said. "I can't cut it with this."

The line slipped through Alex's fingers, jerking his finger up, the sensation like a nest of hornets trying to sting their way out of his flesh. Joseph must have moaned because Derek pulled out a huge black pistol—two steel bars welded together, the kind of gun movie thugs fire with the barrel tilted on its side.

The big biker pushed down Derek's erect arm. "Whoa there, Mr. Pink!"

*Mr. Pink*: did everyone watch the same fucking movies?

"Someone's out there," Derek said.

The leader stepped toward the trees, his eyes searching the darkness beyond the headlights. Everything extraneous had been pared down and sharpened to serve the man's will, even his capacity for pleasure—Joseph could imagine the coke granules going exactly where the leader ordered them to. His expression changed as he moved away from the other men, revealing a longing in his eyes, maybe a wish to be overpowered or awed by a superior force. He seemed to know that Joseph was strung up on a hook and wanted to see him do something extraordinary or at least unexpected in his predicament. If Joseph failed, the biker's wet black eyes would be the last thing he'd see before he died.

"It's not the cops," the leader said. "They'd have started the light show by now."

"I'm going to pull it out," Alex whispered. He raised a stick up to Joseph's mouth. "Bite on this."

Joseph clamped his molars down on the stick, not tasting wood or anything else. The biker was fifteen feet away, tops. He was rubbing his hands together, the muscles in his forearms contracting like steel cables.

"It's going to hurt," Alex said. He'd coiled the line around one hand and held Joseph's arm with the other.

"I know."

"No, you don't."

"Do it."

Alex pulled hard. The pain seemed to drag Joseph's bones out through his fingertip, but he was not free. His finger throbbed with the force of a horse's heart.

"Get behind the tree," Alex said as he lifted the rifle and aimed it at Derek and the bikers.

Someone was going to die here.

"Think we caught us a big fish," Derek called out, finally getting a laugh from the bikers.

The leader shrugged, bored of the game, and turned around and pointed at Derek. "Fucking deal with this!"

Derek's face was ghastly, the sunburned skin encased in sweat, his panicked lips muttering nonsense, the pistol shaking slightly in his hand. He pushed his body toward the trees, holding up his gun like it was a magic lantern, perhaps sensing that he was in someone's rifle sight.

"Don't do it," Joseph said. "We'll never get out of here alive."

Alex lowered the rifle and put his hand on Joseph's shoulder. It felt good. "Just run," he said. "The line will either snap or pull the hook free. When you get out of this grove, turn left. We'll meet up at the road."

"Alex."

"You can do it." He squeezed Joseph's shoulder and ran into the night.

It was Joseph's turn to run. *Fuck no—anything but that.* He had a better plan: swing his arm like he was throwing a ball. He planted his feet and took a deep breath. *One, two, three, throw!* The branch yanked his hand back. He nearly passed out. He swung his left arm again and let out a howl. Derek was ten feet away now. Time for Alex's plan. Joseph's finger would either follow or stay behind on the hook. He ran and the skin ripped like a ream of thick wet paper, and he let out a high, outraged scream as his legs gave out beneath him. The pain was abstract—he wanted to argue with it—and liquid heat spilled across his hand.

"You better fucking run, cocksucker!"

The first bullet pulverized a thatch of bark a few feet from Joseph's head and the second hit somewhere closer. He got to his feet and ran, trying not to panic. Derek would be blind for the first minute after he entered the woods.

"Let it go, Derek," Joseph mumbled. "You'll never catch up." He pressed his thumb against the wound and reached into his left pocket to get the knife. Only the case was there. He checked his other pocket. Nothing. Alex still had the knife.

Derek was at the edge of the trees, scanning the area with a flashlight. Of course he had a flashlight—everyone was so fucking *prepared* out here. Derek picked up something from the ground.

"What is it?" the leader shouted.

Joseph knew the answer a half-second before Derek answered.

"The fucking yuppie dropped his iPhone!"

He heard branches snapping deeper in the grove, followed by a muffled grunt of pain.

"Joseph!" Alex called his name in a loud stage whisper. He was close. "I'm hurt! Over here!"

Alex's plan fell into place: Lead Joseph to the grow-op. Pretend to get injured. Put a bullet in Joseph's chest when he comes to help. Let Derek deal with the fallout. Fucking brilliant. Except Alex didn't know about the iPhone.

Joseph saw something move near the base of a tree: it was Alex's head, arms, and chest. The rest of his body seemed to be neatly tucked under him like a cat's legs. Joseph moved closer.

"I've wrecked my knee," Alex said. "*Shit!*" He tested his leg and winced, making the hissing sound of an athlete who can't walk off the pain. "It's a fucking booby trap."

The hole was about as deep as you could dig without a bulldozer. There was no way Alex planned this. The rifle lay next to the pit. Joseph picked it up, but there was no need to aim it at Alex.

"You have to get out of there," Joseph said.

"I don't think I can put weight on my knee."

"Try! We don't have a lot of time."

"No." Alex leaned against the lip of the hole, a tree root providing a natural slouching post. "If I try to run they'll catch me in the open. Just go. I'll hide here until they're gone."

"That's not going to work. Derek has Mike's iPhone."

Alex looked like he'd been punched in the stomach.

Joseph wanted to scream. The phone was out of batteries, but it wouldn't take long for Derek to figure out that it belonged to Mike, information he'd pass on to the bikers.

"They'll trace it back to you, Alex. Mike will tell them."

Which meant the bikers would be at the farm by lunchtime, prepared to kill Alex and anyone else who got in their way. Even if Franny was safe now, she wouldn't be out of danger for long.

Derek was moving into the woods, his flashlight sweeping the trees, but Joseph's mind remained focused, aware of an overriding fear without submitting to its power. He'd never felt anything like it.

"I'll draw him away from you," Joseph said. "Then I'll get that phone back."

"How?"

"I don't know. But first you have to tell me—are the girls safe?"

Alex tried to bury his head in his hands, and when that didn't work he shrank into the hole.

"I don't care what happened," Joseph said. "Just tell me if they're safe."

Alex raised himself up. He looked ashamed, but also relieved. "They're safe. There was a note. A bush party. They went to a fucking bush party." He shook his head. "I didn't want anyone to get hurt."

*Maybe not at first.*

There was no time to argue the point. Franny was safe, but for how long? He handed the rifle to Alex. "You're helpless here."

Alex gave him back the knife. They each tried to exchange a meaningful expression but Alex broke the tension by smiling.

"Use the knife," he said. "Hurt him so he can't get up."

Joseph ran across the burned field as quickly as his injured ankle would take him, occasionally letting out a yelp to let Derek know where he was heading. He found a path back into the forest, waiting for the flashlight beam to start jumping around the trees near him before he started running again.

"I'll find you, asshole!" Derek shouted.

Joseph drew him deeper into the woods, faint lines and shadows guiding him between the big trees, the darkness making every running step a dare completed, a jump into a river from a high rock. Derek pursued him, shouting "Cocksucker!" and "You're dead!" They both knew the drill: Derek, the armed hunter; Joseph, the defenceless prey.

Joseph tried to pick up speed, his legs falling into a rhythm his lungs couldn't keep pace with. He was swallowing bagfuls of air and the bags were shrinking; his ankle threatened to tip him like an overloaded trailer, spilling its human cargo onto the ground. He hadn't pushed his body to full speed in years, and his finger hurt so badly it might have been trying to tear itself free of his body. What was the point of so much pain? He knew his finger was injured—he didn't need second-to-second updates.

He stopped to make sure he hadn't gotten too far ahead of Derek. His only play was to ambush Derek, then knock him out with a rock or a log and take the phone. Joseph had a knife; Derek had a gun, fresher legs, no wounds, and the feral-dog energy of the bluffer forced to prove his worth. But Joseph had surprise on his side, and the distraction of the coming storm. It would have to be enough.

"I can do this," he said out loud. His voice sounded unfamiliar, but he found the strangeness comforting, as if he had a friend in the woods with him.

He ran for a few more minutes, then stopped to take the weight off his injured ankle. Having exhausted the pain receptors in his muscles and tendons, the throbbing ache had moved deep into the ankle joint. Then he heard it, the first burst of birdsong, a chirping trill that seemed to displace the darkness, releasing a little of the night's grip. He'd pulled enough all-nighters to know that dawn was at least an hour away.

He couldn't keep up this pace. Derek probably couldn't either, but he was dug too deep with his new partners to let Joseph get away. The iPhone wasn't enough—Derek had to either bring back a scalp to the other cowboys or hand over his dope farm. His flashlight beam was barrelling in Joseph's direction like a locomotive's light. Derek was coming to kill him. Another asshole with a gun. History was full of them, stealing fathers from their children, husbands from wives, sons from parents. He thought of Franny in ten years, another easy target for weak men, searching for someone to replace the father who'd bounced in and out of her life before bouncing out for good, the father who should have cooed over every gold sticker and ribbon she won and laughed at every joke that caught her fancy. He couldn't lay that burden on her.

The long-awaited rain began to fall, cooling his face. He saw the flashlight heading toward him, then heard Derek letting out a string of curses. He was still following, going along with Joseph's plan. *Good*. What other advantage did Joseph have? There was his anonymity. Derek must have a shortlist of suspects he thought he was chasing through the woods—a kid looking for an easy score, some local pothead come to check out the rumours, a rival grower, variations on the standard-issue coward who stumbles onto something bigger than he can handle. By fleeing, Joseph had numbered himself among the harmless, another man-boy hoping for rescue, seconds away from breaking down and begging his pursuer for mercy.

He searched the ground and found a jagged, heavy piece of quartz. It would do the trick. One smash and Derek would be unconscious. The flashlight beam bobbed in the dark, jumping from tree to tree like a wild cat hunting its frightened prey. Joseph was doing exactly what Derek expected: running away as fast as he could. But Joseph was *not* that guy, not this time. No more running away. What had he been doing his whole life but avoiding conflict, quietly backing out of promises and bedrooms, hoping no one heard him leave?

He held up the rock, already wet with blood from his finger. One blow to the head. It sounded easy enough, but

Derek was a fast-moving, armed target and Joseph had to execute the knockout blow with a wounded left hand and a right arm he could barely raise above his head. He'd never get a good swing in.

"Think!" he said out loud.

The plan came to him, as clear as a set of instructions in an appliance box. He calmly stepped off the path and behind a tree. Derek expected whoever he was chasing to keep running, and men like Derek never second-guess themselves. He would run right past the tree, oblivious to Joseph's presence.

Derek acted according to type, flying down the path and into the darkness. Joseph moved to Phase Two, dropping the large rock. He calmly applied mud to his face and strung pine branches through his belt loops. Then he stepped back onto the path and pocketed a few palm-sized rocks.

"Keep going, Derek. No one here but us trees."

He started walking, speaking quietly but refusing to lower his voice to a whisper. "I know who you're chasing, Derek," he said, warming to the game. "Some poor coward praying that you'll fall down a very deep hole. But *this* guy, he's right behind you and he's not afraid of you." If there were any justice Derek *would* fall into a hole or impale himself on a branch. "But I'm not waiting for an accident."

Joseph was getting carried away. Enough with the voices. The rain was turning the sandy ground to paste. He stepped lightly, sneaking closer to Derek, who stood silently, his flashlight beam cutting a tunnel through the rain.

This was it.

Joseph moved a little closer and crouched in the low grass beside the path, settling gently onto his tender ankle. He needed Derek to stay stupid a little longer. He dropped lower in case of a sudden backswing of the flashlight, and when the light passed he stood back up and put one of the rocks into his left hand. His finger was still throbbing from the fish hook, but the rest of his arm was strong enough. Derek was less than thirty feet away. If he saw Joseph at this range, the game was over. Joseph raised his lame right arm as a counterweight and leaned back, his left hand dipping below his hip, the posture borrowed from movies where GIs cleared out Japanese pillboxes with a grenade toss. He started to calculate the rock's trajectory, realized he had no idea how to do so, and aimed the rock to pass over Derek's head.

The rock skimmed through the branches, a gust of wind masking its route until it came down with a thud in the dark. Derek was after it like a dog let off its leash. Joseph sprinted after him, giddy with power and the adrenaline of being in command.

"I heard you, cocksucker!"

"Go on," Joseph whispered. "Keep shouting, dickhead."

The path curved left, but he could see Derek through the trees, swinging the flashlight everywhere. Joseph was gaining on him too quickly. He took the next few steps lightly, fear creeping up his legs. There were too many trees between him and Derek to risk throwing another rock. He had to get closer. He walked slowly, stretching out his steps, a bird stalking a mud flat, before ducking behind a tree. Derek's back was turned, his lowered flashlight sealing his pant leg in a narrow cone of light, like a display case in a dark shop window.

"Hey man, why don't you just come out?" Derek spoke as if he knew Joseph was close by. He made a lazy scan of the trees. "I *saw* the blood. The hook must have hurt." He listened and pointed the flashlight randomly. "I've got the fucking phone. If you come out now, I'll be a little less pissed off."

*Keep talking, asshole.*

Joseph transferred another rock to his left hand, assumed the position, and sent it over Derek's head—a near-perfect throw that got Derek running before the rock hit the ground, Joseph chasing after him. *I'm really doing this, tracking another man. He'll have no idea what hit him when I smash him from behind.*

Derek didn't chase the rock as far the second time. He was getting wise without knowing what he was wising up to. Joseph hid behind a tree and took out another rock from his pocket, watching Derek snort from the coke vial.

"All right, smart guy, let's cut a deal! I'll put the gun down."

Joseph had to keep his head here. Derek was not the cool guy back at the farm joking about the apocalypse.

"You can see me put down the gun. I know you're watching me, man."

Joseph stepped onto the path and threw the rock, his body suspended in the brief silence before it cracked off a tree trunk. Derek whipped the flashlight beam toward the sound of impact. Joseph took out the knife.

It was time.

He ran down the path toward Derek. Twenty more steps. Fifteen.

The world exploded with a loud flash. Derek stood inside a life-size snow globe, pistol raised, every falling raindrop and wet leaf illuminated by the white flash of the gunshot. He was firing into the forest. Everything was blacker than it was before, and Joseph ran, knife descending, into the suddenly vacated space where his quarry had been standing.

"I heard you!" Derek screamed from inside the woods. "You fucking pussy! Come out and be a man!"

The insult seemed to punch Joseph in the solar plexus, obliterating his thoughts. There was no more Joseph, just a cascade of anger charging through the trees, bearing down on that useless fucking asshole Derek. He moved the knife to his right hand and threw his last rock without stopping, not caring where it landed so long as Derek stayed distracted. Lightning lit up the forest. They were descending into a ravine, Derek racing down to where the rock had landed. The bank was getting steeper, too steep to charge. Joseph cut to the right, holding to the higher ground until he found his moment to strike—and he would, silently, with force, with rage. He took his place next to a tree with a clear sight line on Derek, who was stood in the gully, gun raised—puzzling, puzzling. Where was his target? How did he get away?

Derek turned off the flashlight. The forest was still dark but the sky seemed to show faintly through the branches. Beneath the sound of falling rain, the forest throbbed like blood, flowing over Joseph's eardrums, the collective rush of sap throbbing up through the trees, from roots to trunk to branches. The storm was close. The elements were on

Joseph's side. Another lightning flash showed Derek's silhouette moving closer.

"Hey, buddy!" Derek wasn't shouting now. Somehow he knew Joseph was close. "You've been fucking with me." He laughed. It might have been genuine. "That's cool, man."

He lit a cigarette, knowing Joseph didn't have a gun to sight on such a clear target.

"Who are you, man? You ain't a cop, and you're no gangbanger."

He took another snort of coke.

"You were probably snooping around, thought you'd sample Nature's bounty." He made a loud noise like a beeper on a game show: "*Baaamp!* Wrong.

"Just a taste, a little baggy for your personal stash. *Baamp!* Wrong."

How long had Derek been waiting to use this routine? All he needed was the 1970s soundtrack, and some badass funk to add "Negro" authenticity.

"Maybe you should come over to my place when I'm not home and fuck my wife."

The pause, for performance's sake.

"No one's using that pussy, right? A little taste won't hurt. *Baaaaaaaaaaaamp!* There's no victimless crimes!"

Derek was pissing, a beer-fuelled geyser that dared Joseph to make his move, but he sensed that the ground was too slippery for a direct charge. How had the tables turned so quickly? He felt exhausted, pulled closer to the earth by the retreating adrenaline rush.

"You learn a few things when you're out on the road," Derek said.

And he was about to share them.

"Like how to stand around doing nothing for long periods of time."

Joseph got it: Derek was going to outlast him. Joseph disagreed. He could crouch by this tree for hours. He had a genetic gift for crouching, it seemed—secondary muscles evolved from generations of ancestors hiding in the forest, waiting for the Saxons, Mongols, Vikings, and Romans, with their period-appropriate tag lines and locally scented beer piss, to burn down the village and move on.

"Look buddy, we can both stand here 'til we shit ourselves or the sun comes up. Or we can talk about this, man to man. *You* can be a fucking man!"

Joseph's superior intellect could not stop Derek's clichéd words from stabbing him in the soft places physically powerful men probe for sport. It was true: Joseph could not face his opponent in open combat. Why didn't Derek just die? What organic force protected him while thousands of decent, hard-working men and women expired before their time?

The ember of Derek's cigarette pointed briefly at the sky before it was hurled out of sight. "You had your chance, cocksucker!"

Derek's instincts were drawing him up the incline, his flashlight moving in methodical, 180-degree sweeps. When the beam passed Joseph's tree, he switched the knife back to his left hand and reached the next tree up the hill in four crouching steps. The flashlight froze in place. Derek stopped to listen, searching for a flash of eyes, the glint of a belt buckle. He moved up the hill, closing a little more distance between them before he slipped and cursed, giving Joseph time to scuttle to a small copse of trees higher up the ravine. A lightning flash revealed patches of squat pine trees farther up that would provide the shelter he needed, and beyond that a high mound that might be a haunted castle but was more likely a hill, a geographical extremity he could use to his advantage. Between him and the pine trees was a stretch of earth spiked with a few birches no thicker than a value-size Coke bottle. Hopefully they'd provide some cover if Derek started shooting.

Joseph ran, his foot smashing into a root on the second step, sending him sprawling into the leafy mud, the knife flying from his hand. He dug through the dirt and leaves, twigs digging at the throbbing hole in his finger. Derek was shouting insults again. Lightning revealed the knife a few feet away. Joseph picked it up and scrambled on his hands and feet up the hill, his movements too noisy, every crushed twig as loud as a finger bone snapping. There were ways to move silently through the woods, but no one had taught them to Joseph. Luckily, no one had taught them to Derek either. He trudged through the undergrowth as though Joseph were a partridge he could flush out into the air.

Joseph dodged the birches and reached the pines, throwing himself behind the first tree. He lay there fighting the panic, then slithered under the branches to look down into the ravine. Water collected behind the dams of his curled legs. The rain was picking up and it was colder, as if the drops were falling from an earlier season. Derek came into view near the hiding place Joseph had just abandoned, his gun ready to fire at the first available target, the flashlight weaving and then dropping like a dowsing rod over subterranean water.

"I know you, and I'm going to find you," he called out. The peal of thunder that followed was so synchronized with Derek's threat that it might have been staged by his limited imagination.

"Fucking iPhone! Fucking hipster! Used to see you fuckers at our shows."

Joseph *had* been to two Hardwar shows, the first with a group of pitcher-buying computer geeks Jane had met at a pub, the second on a date with a woman whose ruler-straight black bangs impressed themselves on his memory.

"You were the guy watching the chicks dancing at the front. A little too cool to dive in there, telling yourself you'd do a better job if it was you up on stage, putting down my band to your *ironic* friends."

Jesus, he could have been sitting on Joseph's shoulder both nights.

"You know what you didn't know? Me and the boys, and the girls who loved to dance, we were laughing at *you*!"

Lightning flashed, turning the forest into a giant photo booth, Derek the guy with enough quarters to last all night. The thunder came a couple of seconds later. The storm was almost on top of them. Joseph rose into a crouch, his ankle crying out under his weight. When another flash came and went he ran to a bigger tree. One more tree and he'd be out of the flashlight's range. The lightning came again and he ran until the rug of leaves was pulled out from under his feet, the impact forcing a squeak from his lungs and landing him on a branch that split with a loud crack.

"I heard you!"

Joseph crawled on all fours across the rock and moss until he reached a patch of topsoil. Another flash exposed a rock the size of a car, its sides smeared with lichen and crystal scabs. He hid behind it. Derek hadn't seen him, but in the darkness Joseph got a glimpse of the bobbing flashlight beam racing up behind him like a hound. Maybe he could still cut a deal. Derek would get what he wanted: the thrill of standing over a male body in the begging posture, another memento for his mental trophy room.

"The next one's going right up your fucking ass!"

He was shooting at Joseph. The impacts sounded like a spoon smacking against mashed potatoes. The next one would be closer and the next would find its target. Joseph ran, trying to avoid every crevice and slick rock face, his hands helping when the ground rose too quickly. Even when he made it to a copse of trees he didn't dare stop. The thunder held off long enough for him to hear Derek slip and fall and swear, his loud voice stripped of swagger.

"You're going to pay for that," he screamed.

Joseph had almost made it to what he guessed was flat ground a little further up the hill when his foot slipped into a hole, twisting his leg as he fell. Something popped in his knee, loosening the big hinges that secured the joint for a second before sliding back into place. The pain hit him like a slap from a giant hand. The knee supported his weight, but his bones felt like they'd slide apart if he pivoted too quickly. He was going to survive this. He was soaked and cold and his entire body hurt, but the pain was not of him, it was *around* him.

He half-limped until he reached the top of the hill with about a fifty-pace lead on Derek. He stood behind the biggest tree he could find and waited. The trunk was still dry, the bark against his soaked skin a reminder of the warm, dry life waiting for him if he got home alive. Derek would reach the top of the hill in a few seconds. This was it. Moral indignation was not going to grant Joseph the strength of ten men, and he could replay every fist and kung fu fight he'd ever watched onscreen and be no closer to defeating Derek. Joseph was not a small man, a fact easily forgotten while seated at his desk for ten hours a day, his active body parts narrowed to two eyes and ten fingers. Why had he never learned to defend himself? All the martial arts courses in the city—had he enrolled in one? Had he learned to build a house or sail a boat or read a compass or start a fire without matches? No—he'd watched movies, half-read a thousand books, talked in bars and restaurants, fucked.

Derek came over the hilltop, drenched like a wet dog, stripped of taunts and speeches. He wanted to end this, to kill Joseph and leave Franny without a father. Joseph clenched the knife and wiped his eyes on a damp swath of shirt. Derek was less than twenty feet away. When he turned to his left and pointed the flashlight, Joseph stepped away from the tree, set his back and shoulders to the task, and ran straight at his opponent, gaining speed with each step, feeling every raindrop that touched his face, a feeling of protective tenderness toward Derek unexpectedly rising in his chest. Derek turned just before impact and raised his arm, deflecting the knife and grazing Joseph's left shoulder with his elbow as their bodies came together with a slap,

Joseph's head slamming into Derek's chest. The men stayed upright as they careened toward the slope, arms entwined, legs kicking for purchase, like a four-legged beast trying to run in two directions at the same time. Joseph pushed against the bigger man, the posture familiar from childhood fights against his older brothers. Derek got his knee up, filling Joseph's mouth with the taste of pennies and warm milk. The knife was gone from his hand. He snapped his head up, catching Derek on the chin, and then they were weightless, holding on to each other, their bloody mouths almost kissing as they went tumbling down the hill, accelerating with each rotation of their locked bodies.

Joseph awaited the final impact. He saw Franny's face, really *seeing* it this time—her shy but curious eyes, how she used to pinch her lips together when she drew beautiful dresses for the ladies of the court and armour for the knights. He wished he'd paid more attention to the stories she wrote in the margins.

*This is Sir Joseph, liege to the King and Queen.*

His bottom front teeth broke.

The sound of impact, of breath exploded from lungs.

A thunderclap, this time inside his head.

He couldn't see. His head hurt. A new gap in his bottom teeth. Raw, tender gums. The taste of copper.

"I know you, man!" It was Derek, far away. No, not far away. Standing right over him. "What the fuck are you doing?"

Bright light stung Joseph's eyes. This was going to be bad. When they shine lights in your eyes, you're in trouble.

"I fucking know you!"

"I can't see," Joseph said, pushing the words through the space between his teeth. He spat out blood and a piece of tooth, feeling shy about his newly exposed gums.

Derek lowered the flashlight. Joseph raised himself up onto his elbows.

"You can just keep hugging that ground, bro," Derek said. He still had the gun.

"Your partners didn't see me."

"I gotta take care of this, man. This isn't the fucking schoolyard."

Always the speeches.

"They didn't see me," Joseph said. "They couldn't have."

"They'll want proof that I'm a player."

"I'm Alex's friend."

"I know who you are. What you're doing here is my business. *You're* my business." Derek stepped closer. "I didn't think you'd pull something like this. I knew you were slick the second I saw you, but *dude*."

Derek's need to deliver the send-off speech was buying Joseph a little time to craft an appeal to the reasonable, misunderstood gentleman behind the villain's mask.

*Dr. Blood, you can't be mad enough to go through with this . . .*

"I was lost."

"Late-night hike?"

"Alex thought—"

"Alex?" The name added weight to one side of the scales squeaking up and down in Derek's head. "Where is he?"

This was it: Joseph could tell the truth and implicate Alex, handing him over to the bikers while trying to strike a bargain for his and Franny's safety. Or he could tell Derek he'd lost Alex hours ago, ensuring Alex's well-being a little while longer.

"We got separated," he said. *So this is what it feels like to be virtuous.* Not that different, really, but better. His mind felt less crowded. "I took the wrong fork in the path hours ago. I saw the light at your . . . camp . . . and came looking for help."

Derek blew out a gust of air. "You saw those dudes back there. You know what this is about."

"They didn't see me."

"Stop saying that!"

The gunshots, coke, and villain's catcalls hadn't completely turned Derek—he might have swallowed the idea of murder, but he clearly hadn't digested it yet.

"Take them my teeth," Joseph said. "Tell them you beat me so hard that I'll never get within a hundred miles of this place. It's true. You're not a killer. It's different when you *have* to kill. Like back there, when you thought I was a threat. You could live with that. You could walk back into your life, sit down to breakfast with your wife and daughter."

Derek's face was slack, his expression inward, but he was listening.

"If you shoot me here lying in the mud you'll be crossing a line. You'd be deliberately taking another man's life and orphaning his daughter. Nothing would ever change that. You could save a busload of kids from going over a cliff, but you'd still be the guy who shot a defenceless father. You'd be on the other side of humanity."

"Maybe I want to be on the other side. There's not a lot to recommend this one."

"Do you want to risk that?"

"Maybe I'm already on the other side."

"You're not. I've seen you with your daughter."

Derek was laughing again, hamming it up. "This is *great*, man. You got a gun pointed at your head and you're, like, talking to me, *really* talking, and I'm standing here listening. It'll be like I always imagined: you'll say something beautiful, something poignant, and it'll be like, *bang*, I shoot you."

Derek's life highlights had been lived on a stage in front

of hundreds of adoring people and in front of a camera—who could blame him for wanting to make his first murder as cinematic as possible?

"It's just business," he said. "A guy changes his supplier, another guy loses his job and his kids don't get a visit from Santa."

"You have a daughter. I met her. She wants to be famous, like her old man."

Derek shrugged. "*No man lives unless he is famous*—Edgar Allan Poe."

Joseph saw him lean forward and lower the gun. He shone the flashlight in Joseph's face again.

"Holy shit!" Derek said. "You're Dylan Shaw! I told you I'd recognize you by the end of the weekend."

Dylan Shaw? Host of *This Week in the Arts*? The guy weighed at least 225 pounds.

"Guilty as charged," Joseph said.

"You spotlighting any new bands in the fall?"

"I'm always looking for pitches. You've got me at a disadvantage."

"Got your full attention do I?" The joshing frontman was back.

"I hear you guys are doing bluegrass. No gimmicks."

"Right," he said, smiling. "And Old Time Country. None of that Nashville shit."

And then he sang in that wavering, lonesome-road voice:

"*How came this blood on your shirt sleeve?*
*O dear love, tell me.*
*It is the blood of the old grey horse*
*That plowed that field for meee . . .*"

He was good. He could have been singing inside a boxcar crossing the lonely plains.

"Drop the gun!"

A dim flashlight flicked on in the trees behind Derek.

"I said drop it! Now!"

Derek squared his shoulders and ran a hand through his thick wet hair, the command pulling him back into the Bad Guy role.

"Derek, don't," Joseph said. "It must be the cops."

"It's not the cops." Derek lifted his arms without dropping the pistol and nodded as if to say, *You think our talk was cinematic—watch this.* He turned to face the flashlight. "All right, cowboy! I'll drop the gun if you do. If you even have a fucking gun."

"Drop the gun or I'll put a bullet in you!" It was Alex. His voice had changed in the last half-hour. The change scared Joseph.

"Come on man!" Derek called back. "Don't shit me."

"Drop it, or I'll drop you."

Joseph fumbled in the mud and found a good-sized rock. If he could get up and hit Derek on the head he might stop the terrible thing that was about to happen.

Derek stepped to the right, brought his arms together, and fired three white blasts at the flashlight, which didn't waver. Derek's head cocked like a dog's as he wondered how the man holding the flashlight could still be standing. He fired again, but this time his shot was answered by a burst of light that exploded a few feet to the left of the flashlight. Derek was lifted into the air as though he'd been pulled backward by a giant spring. His kicking feet came to rest beside Joseph.

The bullet had punched a fist-sized hole, pooled with black-red blood, in Derek's chest. It made a bubbling noise, audible over the rain. Derek's beetling eyes were confused, darting in their sockets as if trying to escape the narrow confines. Then they locked on a point somewhere in the murky sky, peering intently through the falling rain. The life left his eyes, replaced by an expression that was as beautiful and meaningless as patterns of breath crystallized on a window in winter.

Alex stood above them, clutching the rifle to his chest. He shook his head, disowning the lifeless body as he delivered his epitaph: "What an *asshole*."

# FATHERS

They buried Derek at the bottom of the ravine, scooping out earth and clay with their hands until they hit rock; then, without speaking, they laid the body in the hole and covered the grave with rocks and a rotting birch trunk, as if disposing of an enemy's body was an innate skill. Death had radically redistributed Derek's body weight—his limbs were as light as Styrofoam while his torso felt stuffed with ball bearings—but otherwise he could have been any aging party boy sleeping off a wild night, oblivious to the cruel joke his buddies were playing on him.

Joseph and Alex were now walking along a raised bed of packed gravel—all that remained, Alex said, of an old rail line that once connected the national park to the local towns. Its rails and ties were long torn up, the sparkling coal pebbles dotting the gravel the only reminder of its former use, but the rail bed elevated them above the marshy ground, making Joseph feel, for a few blurry moments, like he was riding a locomotive, barrelling through a rent in the wilderness to reach town in time for breakfast. The rain had finally tapered off, the mist rising from the ground promising another hot day. Joseph's knee was stiff and numb, supported by sticks and cloth strips torn from Alex's jacket, and his ankle was locked into place by the swelling. Only his torn fingertip, wrapped in a cloth bandage caked in mud from Derek's grave, still registered pain.

The rail bed was easing into a wide turn when Alex stopped. "See that?"

Joseph had to squint away the mist to see the mound, its vine-draped edges too uniformly straight to have been formed by nature. Alex limped toward it, his injured knee also done up in a makeshift splint, and stepped into the undergrowth, before turning to wait for Joseph to catch up.

"This was a storehouse," Alex said, his mood lightening as he pulled aside a curtain of grapevines to reveal an empty doorway set in a wall at least thirty feet wide and fifteen tall. "Come on."

Not much remained of the building. Most of the roof was gone and sections of the support walls had caved in or had been picked apart, the bricks and pipes and boards stacked in orderly piles against the one complete wall, suggesting a hallowed tradition of vandalism passed down through the generations. They passed into a small, partially intact office where a metal desk was encased in scattered file folders and papers hardened into papier mâché waves, the rain-swollen walls sprouting sprays of black mould that flowed and reformed in the faint, wavering light. Alex ignored the office, trudging purposefully to the building's buckled front doors.

*What now?* Joseph thought, but he followed Alex, emerging into a canyon of birdsong and vegetation, the sounds and damp, organic smell so thick they trapped the air in place. It was a ghost town—these places actually existed. Everywhere was life—birds, insects, trees, bushes, wildflowers—hemmed in by parallel rows of ruined buildings, which seemed to emerge from the misty forest like elephants congregating by a creek bed. They walked down the main street, stepping between the saplings and lustreless weeds that pierced the asphalt as if driven from below by a hammer. Through empty shop windows Joseph could see the ruined labours of each building's final tenants: a barbershop chair bent completely backward on its base; a dry riverbed of rusty water spreading from the doorway of a gutted hardware store; a catastrophe of shelving inside what must have been the general store. A few of the buildings were tagged with fading graffiti, but there were no signs of the nihilistic hedonism that had obliterated the logging camp.

Alex was smiling, refusing to hide or mute his obvious love for this place. "I hike out here every chance I get," he said.

Joseph could picture Alex exploring the ghost town, his imagination reconstructing the stores and warehouses and the humble community that supported them. Maybe it was the closest he got these days to articulating a utopia—a self-sustaining community that rewarded participation, hard work, and sacrifice. Life lived on a human scale, following the rhythms of work and the seasons; a life of sustainable pleasures and acceptable hypocrisies, surrounded by neighbours you could rely on without having to necessarily like.

It sounded pretty good to Joseph.

Then again, it was easy to love a ruin.

He watched Alex limp toward the town's church, taken aback again by such blatant enthusiasm. Vines clambered up the walls and spilled into the church's broken front windows, but the steeple was intact, its highest point now a perch for a hawk scanning the ghost town for its breakfast. Alex propped the rifle stock on his shoulder and disappeared into the shadows beyond the gaping doorway, leaving no doubt that he expected Joseph to follow.

Joseph paused at a stone well that stood beside the church stairs, its mouth half-covered with rotting boards. He couldn't see to the bottom, and when he bent over to get a better view, he imagined jumping into the well to hide from Alex. But that was ridiculous. The girls were safe, the phone retrieved, and, according to Alex, they were only a couple of miles from the farm. He took the stairs one at a time and entered the church.

Alex stood in the centre aisle near the altar, bathed in one of the nebulous shafts of light leaking through the roof. He looked different, lighter somehow, but Joseph couldn't pin the change on anything tangible. Alex turned to face the side of the church, pulling back his head and shoulders, as though he were about to welcome a visiting dignitary. The wall was covered in a stylized spray-painting of a passenger train of the steam era, the graffiti artist's work incorporating the church's boarded windows, the furthest of which became the train conductor's cabin, the controls manned by a skeleton in a top hat and monocle. The other windows showed skeleton passengers in eerie silhouette, their smiling skulls attired in bowlers and extravagantly feathered hats. *The Midnight Train Rides Again* was written in Teutonic script in the steam billowing from the engine's funnel, and though the painting was at least a decade old, no one had defaced it or added their own take on steampunk Victorianism, a minor miracle in these revisionist times. The artist had done something to the train's outlines to give it a quasi–3-D appearance, as if the whole picture could be peeled off to reveal an older image underneath.

"It's beautiful," Joseph said. "Imagine the *work*. Carting out all that paint to the middle of nowhere."

Alex beamed a quiet pride that made Joseph suspect him as the actual artist. But Alex couldn't draw, and he'd never make such an obvious play for a compliment.

Franny would love the painting. She was always taking pictures of the graffiti sites in his neighbourhood, studying the esoteric cartoon murals and competing tags on her laptop. What was it she said about the giant, multicoloured tag behind his apartment?

*It looks like a maze, with a cracked heart at the centre.*

*Franny*—her image rushed to him in converging waves of love and panic. She was safe. He knew that now. But was he?

Alex was watching him, his expression now guarded. What were they *really* doing here? He tried to follow a line of speculation but it petered out in his hands.

Alex had left the rifle leaning against a broken pew in the back row. Joseph reached it in three steps. He lifted the rifle, his finger flaring with pain as he pumped a shell into the chamber and held the barrel high enough to blow a hole in Alex's chest.

The men stared at each other across the floor of rotting planks and ferns, Joseph straining against Alex's superior will—and losing.

"I wish I could beat you in a fight," Joseph said.

"Would it matter now?"

"It would to me."

"And then what? You'd be a man?"

Just like the old days: Alex always one answer and two questions ahead of him. "We're not talking about me," Joseph said. "I've got the gun!"

Alex didn't hide his grudging respect. "What are you going to do with it?"

"I don't know. This has to end." He'd shoot Alex if he kept pretending to play dumb.

"It *has* ended," Alex said, without condescension in his voice. "You think I would have left the gun there if it hadn't?"

A shudder went through Joseph. Even after all they'd been through together, he still couldn't tell if Alex was lying.

"How can I know that?"

Alex shrugged. "You can't. Not on paper. I thought we were past all that."

"That's not good enough for me!" He was already losing the conversation's thread. The gun was gaining weight by the second in his hands. "When did you decide not to kill me?"

"The night we met."

"You don't mean that. Tonight—you were planning to kill me. You had a *plan*!"

Alex let the word hang in the air, as if pausing for the church's invisible congregation to ponder its meaning. "A plan?" He started to laugh. "Let me guess: puritanical Alex gets revenge on Jane and her wild friends? You were *never* that wild."

Joseph felt himself getting lighter, as if his clothing were being stripped off one piece at a time. He must be in shock—Alex too, their bodies numbed by clinical disassociation while their minds went on wild flights through the church rafters.

"What was *your* plan, Joseph?"

"I didn't have one. I never have a plan."

"Bullshit!" Alex's voice chased a pair of doves through a hole in the roof. "You've always operated with a plan and you've always gotten exactly what you wanted. You're just too much of a coward to admit it." He leaned against the altar. The stained-glass window behind him showed a robed man who must be Jesus—the figure's head was missing—leading sheep down a steep mountainside. "You got what you asked for. Now you want me to explain *why* you did what you did."

"I must be such a disappointment after all that time you put into bettering me."

"Don't flatter yourself."

"You took care of one failed reclamation project tonight. You didn't have to *kill* him." Jesus—they'd made a girl fatherless. Never mind that her dad was an idiot, he was *her* idiot.

"Maybe I should have let him shoot you," Alex said.

"I was cutting a deal with him, in language he understood."

"Is that what you think—you were playing *him*? You'd cut a deal and call it even?" Alex shook his head. "You have no idea who you were dealing with. You'd have been paying him back for the rest of your life—and mine. Every time he needed a job done, we'd be dragged back into his bullshit outlaw life until we ended up dead or in jail. He's already got a dozen people in town under his thumb." Alex stepped away from the altar. He'd wrestled the conversation from Joseph. The rifle was next.

"Derek would have destroyed this community if I'd let him."

*This community?* For a few seconds he thought Alex was talking about the ghost town. Joseph couldn't draw a full breath. The church felt smaller, darker, as though his and Alex's combined weight had sunk the building deeper into the ground.

"Where's the note from the girls?"

Alex snorted, as if he couldn't believe Joseph still hadn't figured it out. "It was stuck to the fridge door with a magnet. I slid it under the fridge. It's just lying there, waiting to be found." He blinked a few times, clearing his eyes for the impassive stare he directed at Joseph.

"It was *you*, wasn't it?" Joseph shouted. "*You* saw us in the clearing. That's why you wanted to kill me!"

A terrifying rage flared up in Alex's face, and his upper body seemed to expand its contours, like the haunches of a cornered animal warning off a more powerful opponent. "Jane can never know that! Not a word, about *any* of this!"

So that's what Alex wanted: a pact of silence. He wanted his old life back, and only Joseph could give it to him.

"Why didn't you kill me when you had the chance?"

Alex lowered his eyes to study the rotting floorboards. When Joseph didn't retract the question or lower the gun, Alex turned his attention to the mural. "I wanted to. I almost did."

Joseph felt the rifle veer in his shaking hands—he'd blow apart a rickety pew if he fired it now. The mural had brightened in the morning light. Five skeletal picnickers dressed up for a jaunt to the countryside.

"You kept doing something to save yourself," Alex said. "Those boys in the shack—I wish I'd seen the look on their faces." His voice was warm, even protective, as if he was retelling a favourite anecdote.

"But you shot Derek."

"He brought it on himself."

Which meant, at least in Alex's eyes, that Joseph hadn't. *I don't deserve to die*, he thought. Not much of a life manifesto, but not a bad start. He released the stale breath he'd been holding in.

"We hid Derek's body well," he said. "They'll never find him."

Alex nodded. "You're right."

Joseph could barely support the gun's weight anymore. He let the rifle scrape along the floor as he walked out of the church, the sound of limping footsteps trailing him into the overgrown yard. He pulled a board free from the well and, as Alex took his place beside him, he held the rifle over the gap, ignoring the throbbing in his finger. The rifle still felt good in his hands, but he let it fall into the shadows, only lowering his arms when he heard a plopping splash.

"We both fell down a ravine," Joseph said. "You dropped the rifle and couldn't find it in the dark. I'd already lost my flashlight by that point." He dropped his flashlight into the well and nodded at Alex's.

"Mine broke in the fall." Alex smashed the flashlight against the stone rim.

"You have the iPhone. Throw it in."

Alex did.

"The fall knocked out my teeth," Joseph said, "messed up my arm and leg. You twisted your knee. It was slippery as hell."

"What about your finger?"

"I'll come up with a good cover story. I have a lot of experience at that."

Was that a hint of a smile on Alex's lips?

"The cops won't dispute our story," Joseph said. "Neither will anyone else. We were trying to find our missing daughters, for God's sake." Never mind if it was all a misunderstanding: Franny would know what her father had done for her. "What about the bikers?"

"They're good capitalists," Alex said. "They want a quick profit with minimal effort. If there's too many hassles, they'll move on." The confidence had returned to his voice. The grow-op and meth shack had temporarily escaped his wrath, but they would not survive the summer. What was one more fire in the woods?

Later, after they'd left the rail bed to take the last path back to the farm, Joseph asked Alex what it felt like to kill a man.

"I don't know," he said. The bags beneath his watery eyes were the size of a baby's bottom lip. "Ask me again in a year."

"I will. I mean it."

"Me too."

The time to process Joseph's portion of the blame would come later, in the anxious nights and mornings, when Derek's dead face appeared to him like a hologram on a ten-dollar bill held up to the light. Now was the time for the last push through the forest, through wet vegetation, along muddy paths, the men supporting each other's weight through the worst of it.

"The story you told me about that crazy C.O. of yours," Joseph said. "You stole that from a movie."

Alex smiled. "It's called *Dog Soldiers*. You dragged me to see it. You were always a sucker for melodrama."

"At least it didn't have fucking subtitles."

Their laughter outraged a few robins hunting worms on the path. It felt good to be laughing. The trees around them slowly grew brighter, and then it was as if a curtain was lifted to reveal the pasture behind the farm. Their eyes strained in the light. Alex looked terrible. Joseph must look worse.

It didn't matter. They staggered on, their limping steps comical as they half-raced for the back fence. Joseph heard the cock crow to greet the morning, a first for him and a beacon for his wild hopes as the farm came into sight through the light mist. Alex reached the fence first and leaned against the damp white boards. They could see the back porch, where Franny and Rebecca, wrapped in blankets, slept in lounge chairs with the surviving dog curled up between them.

Joseph felt the lump in his throat rise and then evaporate into tears when it reached his eyes. Franny had waited for him.

They watched their daughters sleep, and the scene, so without precedent in Joseph's life, seemed strangely familiar, as if he'd imagined it many years ago: the tearful homecoming after a long odyssey through a dark wilderness; danger and tests of courage at every turn in the winding path. He must have worked over the details, honing them to satisfy his need for drama, even planning the soundtrack: an old Irish ballad; one of those tear-jerkers from Jane's doo-wop albums; "Under Pressure," by Bowie and Queen.

Joseph was romanticizing again. He'd let himself off the hook one last time.

## ACKNOWLEDGMENTS

This novel was a long time coming, with many people helping along the way. Thanks to my circle of readers for their advice and encouragement: Doug Dolan, Julie deCarufel, Darren Alexander, Ross McKie, Annie Bradley, Samantha Haywood, Nicholas Dinka, and the late Derek Weiler. Special thanks to Robert Wiersema, who read several incarnations of the novel and helped spark its conception. Thanks to the Ontario Arts Council's Writers' Reserve program for a timely grant. To my agent, Chris Bucci: all the work, meetings, and guidance are much appreciated. My editor, Anita Chong, worked tirelessly on *Harmless*—it is a far better novel because of her insight and creativity. Finally, all my love to my children, Petra and Charlie, to BNN, and to my amazing wife, Laura, to whom this novel is dedicated.

## A NOTE ABOUT THE TYPE

*Harmless* has been set in Sabon, an "old style" serif originally designed by Jan Tschichold in the 1960s.

The roman is based on types by Claude Garamond (c.1480–1561), primarily from a specimen printed by the German printer Konrad Berner. (Berner had married the widow of fellow printer Jacques Sabon, hence the face's name.)